RUIN ME

SAVAGE BOSSES

MELVERNA MCFARLANE

MCFARLANE PUBLISHING, LLC

AUTHOR'S NOTE

May you all find a man as dedicated as Kent Luxe.
Love, Melverna

SENSITIVE TOPICS

In Ruin Me, you will find the following topics.
Kidnapping
Violence
Murder
Sexual Assault (off the page)
Spanking

Please keep your mental health in mind if you find these topics distressing or triggering.

KEEP UP WITH MELVERNA MCFARLANE

Join Melverna McFarlane's newsletter to get updates, bonus scenes, and more. Once you've finished Ruin Me, click here for your bonus scene.

Damitrice thank you for telling me about your fur baby Tyger. I'm honored you allowed him to be part of this story.

BLURB

Years ago, I ruined her for every man that came after me. Now, she's returned, older and bent on ruining me.

Madison was too young the first time she confessed her love to me. Hell, she's my daughter's age. I may have been too harsh when I let her down, but I swear, it was for her own good.

It's been years since our last encounter and she's grown now. Gorgeous and intent on revenge. But I'm her boss and I call the shots. This time I'll ruin her plans and claim her, once and for all.

CHAPTER 1

$\mathcal{M}$adison

Mmm.

A tortured moan ripped past my compressed lips. As sensations buffeted my body, liquid seeped from my opening to paint my desire along my thick thighs. My breath hitched as I touched another sensitive nerve, imagining it was *him.*

His powerful jaw that kept so much unsaid. His piercing blue eyes that immobilized me more effectively than his arms. And those fucking arms... Why'd they have to look so powerful? So thick, all his shirts stuck possessively to his muscles, making love to every bi and tricep? He could probably throw my big body in the air without getting winded before using me like a rag doll.

Fuck!

Another groan escaped as more wetness coated my fingers.

Despite everything I'd done to eradicate him from my memory, he was always there. Monopolizing my thoughts, feeding my desires... Controlling my pleasure. And I hated him for it.

I pushed two fingers into my pussy while circling my clit, wishing they were his and despising myself for my weakness. Would he reach deeper inside me? Would he be cruel and keep me on the edge, never giving me the last push into euphoria? Or would he be gentle, coaxing me to come on his hand?

A shudder rolled through my body. Nearly there. I was so close. If I could only reach out and touch the oncoming wave, it would rip me apart and sew me back together into a beautiful tapestry of fulfillment. I doubled my efforts, squeaking through my arousal and rushing to the end goal, because I wasn't supposed to be here right now.

I should have been out of the door ages ago and on my way to my new job. Instead, I was in my bedroom, barely dressed and trying to take the edge off a craving I had eight years to kick but failed. Now, the only thought dominating my mind was to come. One big orgasm that would make what I was about to face more bearable.

Frustrated tears pooled beneath my lids at my false hope. When was the last time I had a big orgasm? At this point, I'd take any relief, no matter how small.

The need to touch myself hadn't slammed into me out of the blue. I'd fought it off for as long as I could until I risked walking into my new position with ruined panties and a lethal dose of inappropriate horniness.

I had to take care of myself before I exposed myself to the masses and faced an arrest for public indecency. Images of my face and sex offender and other labels flashed in my head.

That's why I was currently plunging in and out of my wet pussy while circling my engorged clitoris with my thumb like a nymphomaniac coming off a long fast.

Mmm.

I moaned as my walls spasmed around the digits, and I tried like hell not to scream the name I'd forbidden myself to say aloud whenever I was alone. Into the silence, my sex squelched as heat rose from my skin and my heavy breaths painted the air.

So close. Why couldn't I come?

The familiar face I ran from for so long rose in front of me again. Despite all my resolutions to the contrary, the man mocked my good intentions. I never meant to masturbate to his image, but my subconscious refused to let him go. Despite my best efforts, I couldn't forget his devastating good looks or ignore the many fantasies I had of him doing the filthiest things to me.

It was so like the ornery bastard to disturb any sense of equilibrium I'd gained since accepting this job from hell.

If only I'd ignored Ife's call.

But I hadn't.

I could never. She's been my partner in crime since we were six years old. She knew everything about me. Well, except one thing. This thing.

Another shudder racked my body as my obsession's dream substitute continued to dominate my pleasure. As he tortured me by focusing on that sensitive part of my clit. Then left me in suspense to flutter his fingers around the nerve, keeping me in needy suspension. His name rose to my lips, but I bit it back before it could shatter the fantasy—a fantasy I shouldn't be having.

Ife would murder me if she knew I had the hots for her father. I wasn't supposed to be this bad off after so many years away from where we grew up. Maybe if I'd told her about my feelings, she would never have browbeaten me into taking this job.

It wasn't like I needed a job from the great Kent Luxe. Damn... his name alone caused my nipples to draw tighter; the buds called for firm stimulation. I plucked at them, shuddering as sensations zipped through my body.

Still, I refused to lend a voice to his name. It was the only thing holding back the surge I needed. One guaranteed to leave me weak and unable to walk, let alone think. And that was dangerous since my entire career required me to think fast, be flexible, and pivot as the situation required. I made a good name for myself and my consulting company where I managed crises every day. I was so in demand that Olivia Pope and the woman, Judy Smith who she was based on, would have to take notes.

But being an expert exposed me to doing favors for my best friend, and she was quick to use the BFF card that landed me in my current predicament; minutes away from facing the only man that inspired this level of immeasurable lust.

It had to be lust and only lust. I *needed* this feeling to be rooted in the physical because I hated him. He broke my heart, and I couldn't justify keeping those feelings alive after all these years.

Too bad my body never got the memo.

The huge tsunami I'd hoped and begged for with tortured moans I silenced. I stretched to receive a lager-than-life event only to have a small crest lap at my body. I nearly wept as my muscles tensed from the unsatisfactory orgasm. My shoulders, neck, and back screamed at me for teasing them with a euphoria that never manifested as they locked up in protest.

Why did I think today would be any different? I cleaned myself up, fighting back the frustrated tears that would destroy my mascara and eyeliner. After a hasty glance in the mirror to refresh my hair and lip stain, I squared my shoulders and walked out the door.

A shitty start to my first day working for my best friend's dad. If calling at the last minute to cancel the arrangement wouldn't reflect badly on my professionalism, I would do it in an instant.

But Ife's pleading voice rang in my ear. Her father and his company needed my help. Although guilt and shame led me to agree to her request, I would face Kent Luxe and revamp his and his company's image at all costs.

Because the one thing I couldn't do was admit my most shameful secret to Ife, the reason I'd moved away from Douglas with no intention of returning. Despite violating the first rule of our friendship contract—No secret shall exist between us—she didn't need to know that I was one hundred percent prepared to wreck her home life for a chance to be with her dad. I doubt she would forgive me even if I was a teenager at the time.

Not when her father's company was the center of a murder scandal that dominated international news.

CHAPTER 2

ent

"What the fuck is going on?" My chief operating officer, Mal-chin, slid a tablet across my desk after stomping into my office.

I glanced at the screen. The headline, *Another Unidentified Body Found At Billionaire Mogul, Kent Luxe's Headquarters,* glared at me. I tempered the urge to smash the device that turned my hectic day into another waking nightmare on top of the many emergencies I had to handle.

"The fuck if I know. This is the sixth body in two months. I'll have to call Hal and my personal attorney because there's no way the cops won't show up on my doorstep."

Hal was the general counsel for my company, Luxe Locations. He handled all legal issues, including anything that might paint my organization as a criminal entity. He was a fucking genius, able to sanitize our connection with the local arm of the DeLuca crime family. And I needed to call on him again to handle what was coming my way.

No sooner had I gotten off the phone with my attorney, Quarren, did Douglas PD appear on the floor. The glass walls facing the office floor allowed me to watch as the two men marched toward me. Detective Glass led the way. Annoyance and suspicion dragged their mouths into unpleasant frowns that mirrored my own.

As they stepped into my office, I activated the special feature that convinced me a glass bowl office was worth sacrificing my privacy for. The invisible walls frosted over into an opaque landscape, barring onlookers from seeing inside, but not the other way around.

"Detectives," I greeted them, stiff and unwelcoming.

Glass's partner, a young man who seemed incompatible with the more experienced, stubbled cop, reintroduced himself. "I'm Detective Salinas. We have a few—"

"I know the drill. This is your fifth visit here, after all." I turned to Mal-chin and nodded toward the door.

He shook his head. "Don't mind me. I'm an independent bystander making sure the police don't overstep their authority." He dragged a heavy chair meant for wooing new business partners beside my desk and angled it to best watch me and the detectives. "By the way, the name's Mal-chin Kang. Please, continue as if I'm not here," he finished with a mime of locking his mouth and throwing away the key.

Independent bystander, my ass. With a sneer, I gave him the middle finger. I shouldn't have. Mal-chin grinned and winked at me. If he were anybody else, he would be on the streets living the Trading Places life. His sense of humor rankled on the best days. I wished I could chop it up to him being the youngest CFO in Douglas, but the brilliant asshole was too successful at his job. He didn't have to work for me, and he knew it.

"Now, Mr. Luxe, where were you two nights ago?" The older detective took the lead.

"He was probably fucking some model, actress, or social climber looking to live the good life," Mal answered for me.

"Aren't bystanders supposed to remain silent?" I gritted.

Glass and Salinas shared a glance. "Is what Mr. Kang said true? You have an alibi?"

"I'll wait for my lawyers to arrive before I respond to your inquiry.

You know how it is." I smiled at them because this wasn't my first visit, nor did I expect it to be my last. "While you wait, may I offer you some refreshment?"

They both requested coffee. I relayed their desires to my assistant. A few minutes later, he entered the office with Hal and Quarren dogging his heels. I sat through the men reacquainting themselves and waited for my assistant to leave.

"Now where were we?" Detective Glass asked, pulling out a notepad and pen.

"Confirming Mr. Luxe's alibi for two nights ago," Detective Salinas responded, following suit. "The body of Jane Engleman was found abandoned on the property line this morning. Her time of death occurred between ten and midnight Saturday night."

The woman's name sounded vaguely familiar, but I wasn't sure. While married, and for years after my wife died, I hadn't expressed interest in other women. That all changed about five years ago, but the women I saw fulfilled one purpose: to scratch an itch.

With few exceptions, I never saw them more than once. The memorable ones earned a second night of fucking to convince me otherwise. To this day, my longest streak was two dates. The women I saw rarely sparked any interest outside the bedroom, and I never pretended they had a chance at something longer than one night.

Salinas pointed a pen at Mal. "Mr. Kang offered a possibility that could clear you of suspicion. Was he right?"

I conferred with both attorneys, who nodded their approval for me to respond. "No, he's wrong, a state he's not used to being in." I glared at Mal from the corner of my eye. "My social calendar has seen a lot of cancelations recently, which is why I worked late last night."

"Did anyone see you leave?" Glass tapped his pen against his note-book, not attempting to record my account.

"No, not that they would. When I pull long hours, I usually stay in the penthouse apartment on the top floor. The only access is through my office." I pointed at a discreet panel hiding the elevator keypad.

The elevator had four stops, the parking garage where I kept a half dozen cars at my disposal, my office, and the two penthouse levels above. The top was for my use and the second was for important visitors from any of the international markets where Luxe Locations did business. From looking at the wall, no one would recognize the seamless blend of mahogany wood paneling and mirrors as a ploy to hide the secret access.

"Did you have a history with the victim?" This time, Glass pressed his pen against the pad.

"I'm not sure. I'll have to ask my assistant if this woman, Jane Engleman, ever met with me."

Salinas rubbed his neck, an aggrieved grimace hinting at an unwelcome exchange. "Mr. Luxe, you're not giving us anything to work with. We want to clear you, but with each new body, you're looking more like a suspect. It's bad enough that the bodies keep showing up on your properties. When we add your intimate relationships with each woman to the mix… Well, at some point you have to agree, these aren't mere coincidences."

"I don't do relationships, intimate or otherwise." I stared down the detectives, not for one second concerned about the tension growing in the room.

Quarren cleared his throat and stepped forward. "Although we agree these incidents aren't from happenstance, that's all we agree on. My client is another victim of these crimes. He's done nothing wrong. Yet the person maliciously murdering women with a loose connection to him continues to damage his reputation and that of his company. And that's assuming the latest victim is someone my client knows."

"We're just trying to do our jobs. Someone is making the streets of Douglas unsafe and all the signs point to Mr. Luxe being at the center."

"Really? My client is at the center of your investigation? With what proof? That he knew the women? Please be for real. Unless you want me to call up the new Chief of police and ask him to explain why you're harassing my client with this flimsy accusation."

Hal, Mal, and I watched the exchange in silence. My input was unnecessary and nothing the police officers said had anything to do with the company, but unease skittered along my nape.

Glass stood and snapped his notepad shut. "There's no need for that. Before we approach Mr. Luxe again, we'll be sure to present you with evidence."

"If another body doesn't show up first," Salinas added as he glared at me and my team.

When they left, Hal and Quarren took the evacuated seats.

Hal glanced at his watch and sighed. "It's too early for a drink, but I swear every time that detective comes around, your bar calls to me."

Mal rested his leg over his knee. "Didn't you hire a crisis manager who's supposed to handle things like this?"

"I did," I said as I folded my arms and pressed against my chair.

"Then where is she?"

"She's late," I bit out, furious about my current predicament.

"How did you find her?" Quarren asked.

"Ife made me hire her."

The men broke into gales of laughter at my expense.

"Of course, only your daughter has that kind of control. But since she's a pity hire, you can fire her with cause. Late on the first day." Hal shook his head.

I pierced him with a scowl. "Would you fire the person who rehabilitated that prince's image? The one from Ras Al Najib."

"You mean Emir Javed ibn Al-Kamran? The Arab prince accused of genocide?" Quarren straightens in his chair.

"I remember that." Mal retrieved his tablet and typed something into it before turning it to face the rest of us. "I knew I heard something about that being a hoax. The genocide thing was a campaign orchestrated by internet trolls to discredit him from the line of succession by one of his uncles."

"Still, if Ife's friend can sanitize his image, she'll have our man in line for sainthood in no time." As exaggerated as Hal's observation was, I had to agree.

My company was losing investors in the most lucrative markets. With ten high rises in various stages of construction, I needed to stop the hemorrhaging. Unfortunately, I didn't like who my savior in the wings was. I loved my daughter and respected her insight, but I would never forget how Madison disrespected my wife and my marriage. Having to trust my life's work to her felt like having my skin punctured by invisible splinters. No pore was safe from the aggravating presence.

"Do you think she'll find you a famous rockstar like she did with the Arab prince?" Quarren asked.

I shrugged. "I doubt any woman she finds would work. And few women have the all-around appeal of the lead singer for Liquid Obsession. Not that I would be interested, anyway."

Mal leaned forward in his chair to scrutinize me. "Speaking of your interest, or lack of, how is it you didn't have an alibi? And don't give me that bullshit about cancelations. There's a long list of women biting at the chance to be photographed beside you in the society pages."

"Mal has a point," Hal mused. "You haven't been with a new woman in... damn near eight months."

"Has it really been that long?" Mal began mumbling and counting down with his fingers. "I can't believe it, you're right. You've shown up single for every fundraiser and office function in the past eight months."

"Are you ill?" Quarran stood and approached me.

I blocked his hand from touching my head with a glare. "Fuck off. I don't pay you to be intrusive."

"Maybe it's the type of women you've been going out with. Ever since Oyinlola, your type has gone in the opposite direction. The number of blondes you kept on your arm had me concerned you were trying to expand the Aryan race." Quarran shuddered. "Thank God they never last more than two dates. I had Children of the Corn invading my dreams because of you."

To calm myself, I clenched my fist and imagined crushing Quarran's face in it. "Isn't it about time for you all to leave?" I deactivated the privacy setting on the glass walls to shut down the conversation. "I have work to do."

"Well, damn! Who is she?"

Mal's outburst caused us to face the office floor. The head of our human resources department led a tall, full-figured woman from desk to desk. From the welcoming smiles of my employees, the newcomer was making a positive impression. I pressed my lips together to prevent a harrumph of disapproval from escaping.

Although I couldn't see her face, I knew who she was. And based on the suit she wore, nothing changed my opinion about her. She dressed to seduce, but she was wrong if she thought her wiles would succeed with me.

"I hope she isn't an employee because she's a sexual harassment suit waiting to happen," Hal said. "And I'll be the first one to put the company at risk."

"Get in line. A sistah like that will be all over what I have to offer, without the conflict, since I don't work here." Quarren straightens his tie.

"Like you stand a chance. I'm the only one out of the four of us that's closest to her in age. The rest of you are old enough to be her father." Mal patted his hair as if a stray strand would rebel against the product he used to tame his locks.

"Still… I wouldn't mind her calling me Daddy." The seriousness in Hal's voice drove me to end their back and forth.

"She's off-limits," I pronounced.

"You're shitting me," all three men said in concert.

"Wait! She isn't even your type. And all jokes aside, you shouldn't be in the public eye flaunting your new flavor of the week right now." Hal turned a concerned frown on me. "We've lost the trust of our investors in the Asian markets. No need to give them more reason to doubt Luxe Locations."

"You've got the wrong idea. She's Ife's best friend, Madison, not someone I'm staking a claim on. And neither can the rest of you."

"You're pulling one over on us. Just admit it," Mal said.

"I'm not and I won't stand in Ife's way when she murders you for your dirty thoughts, either." Of course, as I made my pronouncement, Madison turned to face us.

We all groaned though I kept mine silent.

The eight years since I last saw her were more than good to her.

Even her vitiligo complemented her beauty. Her skin, a beautiful patchwork of dark brown and light areas lacking pigmentation, enhanced her slanted brown eyes and full lips. As a teenager, she had the foundation to surpass most women who met society's beauty standards. As an adult, she had no competition. Seeing her now posed a serious problem for me.

The reason I hadn't dated for eight months wasn't by choice. My body rejected every available woman. Until now.

Blood rushed to my cock, reminding me in the most fucked up way possible that I was a man with a healthy sexual appetite, and my new craving was off-limits.

CHAPTER 3

 adison

Carol, the HR manager, led me around various departments to introduce me to some employees. Although I was a third-party consultant, she treated me like a new hire. I accepted her conduct because anything that delayed meeting Kent Luxe was a gift. The extra time aided my silent affirmations and self-confidence.

And I needed the boost, however small, because embarrassment warmed my body despite the time it took to drive from my parents' house. Apparently, I hadn't outgrown the shame that followed a self-pleasuring session. Not when my teenage obsessions Adam Levine, Bruno Mars, and ASAP Rocky stared down at me from their prominent positions on my walls.

"Before we meet the big boss, you'll want to make friends with Omar." Carol stopped before the desk of a handsome Black man. "Omar, meet Madison Montgomery. She's the new hire Ife brought on board."

There went the other reason I didn't correct her. Under her tone was some major butt-hurt energy that she wasn't part of the hiring decision. I made a note to myself not to piss off the HR lady any more than necessary.

I held my hand out to Omar, who stood with a dazzling smile that complimented his tanned complexion.

Appreciation warmed his eyes as he sized me up. "Friends? If I have my way—"

Carol cleared her throat.

"—we'll be the best of friends." Omar shook my hand.

As attractive as Omar was, I wasn't here to find a man. I wanted to do my job and bounce without more connections tethering me to the CEO of Luxe Locations. It was moments like these that I appreciated HR. Their sole purpose was to protect the company and Carol just saved Luxe Locations from a possible sexual harassment issue.

"I look forward to working with you and collaborating our efforts to weather the current storm," I said.

At that moment, the door to the office I'd avoided peeking into opened. Three men, dressed in tailored suits that fit their impressive physiques to perfection, exited the corner office dominating the floor. I silently exhaled. My time was up and I was about to meet the man who could make my life a living nightmare.

Ife, the next time I see you, you better have a year's worth of bribes. Maybe two.

"You can go in. He's been expecting you for a while." Omar squeezed my shoulder. "By the way, the morning was off to a rough start, so be careful where you step."

His warning made me rethink my initial reaction. He might be a good friend to have.

"That's my cue to leave. If you have any questions, don't hesitate to ask," Carol said before turning her back, duties discharged.

The glass walls hid nothing from view. Kent sat at his desk, an overlord overseeing his domain. I squared my shoulders and entered the lion's den, doing my best to ignore the thunderous beating of my heart or the intense desire rushing through my system.

Almost all my affirmations pfft into a cloud of ephemeral smoke as I walked in with more confidence than I felt.

"Close the door behind you," Kent snapped.

Shake it off.

I wasn't some low-level employee being taken to the floor for losing the company money, but neither was I prepared to unleash my temper on the man.

He's Ife's dad.

The reminder failed, yet served its purpose. Kent being Ife's dad never stopped my fantasies as a teen, and seeing him in the flesh after eight years didn't help matters. Thankfully, the reason I stood before him helped to cool me down. Somewhat. Enough to have an intelligent conversation with him.

"Do you think your relationship with my daughter allows you to show up to work late?"

Breathe Maddy.

"I was on time."

Despite this morning's session to clear my mind, I made it on time for my meeting with Carol. Had I intended to arrive earlier as was my habit? Yes, however I was too professional to allow a nutting session to undermine my reputation. Especially in a hostile environment.

He checked his watch. "It's after nine. You were supposed to report here at 8:30."

"Was Carol aware of this?"

"Why would Carol know? She's a lower-level employee. Deke handles my hires himself."

"Then someone missed the memo. Carol's been in charge of my schedule since I arrived, and I certainly wasn't informed about a one-on-one." I pulled out my phone to search my calendar and email. "Nope, no meeting requests came through, but if you would like to focus on what is an obvious miscommunication, by all means, let's. You pay me by the hour, and my fee is a hefty one." I folded my arms and arched my brow at him in challenge.

Rhythmic ticking along his jaw showed I'd hit a nerve. Kent pushed a button on a device on his desk and the crystal clear glass walls turned into opaque whiteness. He stood, buttoned his suit jacket, and strode toward me. His swagger was everything a multi-billionaire had, effortlessly sexy, power with each step, and so much big dick energy he sucked all the oxygen out of the room.

Don't think about his dick, Maddy!

When he stopped, he was so close his scent wrapped around me; money and sin. "Let's get some things straight before we do this thing." He pointed between us. "You're only here because of Ife. Given the choice, I would have chosen an intern showing up for work on their first day over you."

I swallowed my response at being upbraided for no reason. "Understood."

He stared at me, scrutinizing me while I tried to uphold a neutral facade. "Alright then, while you work for me, you'll abide by my rules."

"That's fair."

His nostrils flared, as if my accommodating response was equal to waving a red flag in front of an enraged bull. "When we're together, all that should be on your mind is work. Don't think you can seduce me or expect that one day I'll see you and become so overwhelmed by need for you I'll forget everything you did and fuck you. Because I can't stress enough that you'll *never* be my type."

I stood in humiliated silence and fought back tears as he rejected me for something I did as a teenager. "What are the other rules?"

"Just those. I'm not a forgiving person and will not tolerate any attempts on your part to sway me." He pointedly stared at me, his gaze traveling the length of my suit.

Although it wasn't his intention, I was sure, his eyes stripped me bare. I fought the urge to cover myself for fear of validating his worst impression of me.

"And make sure you wear something more appropriate tomorrow. Follow me." He strode past me while I remained rooted to the floor.

It was Omar clearing his throat with an understanding smile on his face that got me to move. Since Kent walked so quickly he was no longer in sight, Omar led me to a conference room in the middle of the floor. Similar to Kent's office, frosted glass enclosed the space.

I entered with no idea what awaited me beyond the doors. Inside, a long mahogany table gleamed with polish. A projector screen with Luxe Locations' logo dominated the furthest wall. A pile of binders and boxes sat on the corner of the table.

"Although you know Ife, I'm sure you aren't aware of Luxe Locations' extensive history here in Douglas and internationally. In those files, you'll have information on pertinent staff and the history of every building under our management."

"I'll read them over to see if there's any information I haven't gathered from my research." I flipped through the files to keep my hands busy or else I wouldn't be able to face Ife after I choked her father to death.

"You've researched me?"

"I don't know what kind of amateur you think I am, but I assure you I didn't come here with no knowledge about you or your company. And to be clear, my research on you was because you are the company."

"Hmph," he grunted. Without acknowledging my prep work, he said, "In instances like mine, I should probably step back and avoid publicity. If you look at the personnel files in the folder, we can start by finding a new face to represent my interests."

"I don't mean to burst your bubble, Mr. Luxe, but that's not the first order of business. While I understand you're accustomed to leading, I have ground rules of my own."

His lips firmed in disapproval. "What are they?" he bit out.

"Don't micromanage me. You may be my client, but if you undermine my strategy, I will fire you. Consider this your only warning. I don't mind differences of opinion but state them respectfully and we can discuss the matter before coming to a solution. If you have a problem with my problem-solving, I'll end our contract and go about my day."

"You have a lot of escape clauses."

And you have a lot of audacity.

I responded in kind to his previously demeaning attitude by looking him up and down. I hoped he couldn't hear the blood pumping in my veins, see the desire I'd been fighting in my stare, or smell my body's reaction to being alone with him. "These are standard rules for all my clients. And I'd like to clear something up because you seem to be under a misconception. My presence here is as a favor for Ife. She refused my offer to refer you to someone else or hand your account to a junior member of my company. I'm not here because I need your business or because I have a personal agenda."

"Are you telling me you want to be here as much as I want you here?" he scoffed.

We entered a staring contest in which I refused to budge or respond to his question.

"If things are as you say, can we get started on those prospects?" he grumbled, breaking our standoff.

"We have something more urgent to discuss." I sat, opened my leather satchel, and retrieved my laptop and a file.

Once the laptop booted, I opened the manila folder. A photo of a crime scene sat on top.

"Where did you get this?" Kent asked as he pushed the first picture aside.

More photos lay beneath. He spread them out until he uncovered the police reports.

"I have a guy."

This time, when he stared at me, a glimpse of admiration escaped. If I were petty, I would roll my eyes. I didn't need his approval.

"I've seen these reports already, so what makes them so urgent?"

"Your connection to the victims. While my people investigate their lives, I need to understand the extent of your histories together. Right now, your alibis are shaky at best. A good prosecutor could take you down on circumstantial evidence. Only your wealth and privilege are protecting you, but the longer we take to control the narrative, the more likely they'll be to come after you."

"Which is why we need a new face to represent the company. Ife refuses to do it because she hasn't earned that kind of responsibility and she has her own dreams to chase."

"Which leaves you, Mr. Luxe. No one else can represent Luxe Locations when your name is on all the properties."

"Call me Kent. None of my employees call me Mr. Luxe."

I rested my spine against the chair and considered him in silence. "I don't think I will. As I'm not your employee, I wouldn't want to confuse what this is." I pointed between us the same way he had earlier.

Okay, maybe there was a tiny corner inside me where Petty Becky lived, and she chose now to raise her ratchet head. His earlier preemptive strike when he rejected me chafed and lit a fire inside me.

But I was a professional. One who would lather him in top-tier professionalism until I made him and his brand so squeaky clean Mr. Clean would come begging for a brand endorsement.

Violence was never the answer.

"Now, Mr. Luxe, the fastest way to jumpstart your new image is to start a new relationship. Something that speaks of stability so that Kent Luxe, the man, will be untouchable from the rumors about Kent Luxe, the billionaire bosshole."

"Where do you get off calling me a bosshole?"

"Not me, your employees." I pulled up the Boss Be Damned website and did an advanced search for the hashtag MBITA and de-luxe_digs in the chat rooms. "Part of my research into your image required that I get your employees' unfiltered opinion about work here in general and you in particular."

"I don't understand. What am I looking at?" He pulled my laptop closer to peer at the comments.

"This is a place where people vent about their bosses. It's supposed to be anonymous, but if you read enough comments, you can infer a company's name. For example, I'm sure you'll agree that these comments about de-luxe_digs are referring to Luxe Locations."

"And MBITA? What does that mean?"

"My boss is the asshole. I'll refrain from adding my opinion to the consensus," I said, without hiding the small uptick on my lips.

Kent swore under his breath as he read the comments painting him as unreasonable, full of his self-worth and ego, and out of touch with his employees' needs. He shoved the laptop toward me in disgust. "So, I need a woman to help soften my image? You used the same tactic for another celebrity client."

"Because it works."

"This better not be an excuse to date me. I've already made myself clear where you're concerned."

"In your dreams. I only date men my age. I'm not into feeding the elderly or wiping their asses. No, we're going to find you a girl-next-door type that will get people rooting for you instead of raising their pitchforks and demanding to eat the rich."

The lie tasted bitter on my tongue. I'd tried dating men my age. I dated other older men. None compared to the Kent I'd built up in my head since childhood. It wasn't his money, though he was richer than some countries' entire gross domestic product. It was the way he looked at me during the brief conversations that meant the world to me. I thought he saw me as an equal, someone he respected and valued; not some kid he had to appease for his daughter's happiness.

"Do I make the final choice for this woman?"

"As long as your preference aligns with mine." I fan out the photos of the victims my team collected, not the crime scene images, but candid shots they posted on their social media accounts. "Based on these women, you've developed a type since your wife passed." I caught the next line and smothered it because while I didn't mind insulting him, I refused to use Ife's mom to do it.

"There is a charity ball in three days, so we'll start reviewing applicants for your date tomorrow. If you provide me with a list of traits you're looking for in a companion, I'll consider your needs during the initial vetting process."

Kent tapped the table. A frown pulled his lips down.

My hand itched to slap him for the crime of being so attractive while disapproving of me.

"We've talked about my image enough. What are your plans regarding the investigation?"

CHAPTER 4

ent

Madison Montgomery was trying to mind fuck me, and I was falling for it. Her digs bore under my skin, but I couldn't fault her professional recommendation. Her tactics worked, consistently surpassing expectations. Who was I to challenge her methods?

A knock on the door drew my attention from the militant gleam in Madison's dark brown eyes. Their depths drew me in on more than one occasion during our meeting, bewitched where they should have repulsed.

Omar opened the door, and I reluctantly turned to face him. "Your 10:30 appointment is here."

I nodded and stood, ready to leave, until I caught the smile Omar sent Madison's way, although it was her reaction that froze me in place. Her face relaxed and although she wasn't flirting with Omar, her warm reception rankled.

"Omar, set up a space in my office for Madison," I said when I stood in front of the door.

"But I thought you wanted her as far aw—"

"That won't work any longer. Make sure she has a desk, computer, and office phone by the end of the day." I left them feeling their unvoiced questions slamming into my back.

Even if I had an answer, I wouldn't give them one. I curled my fingers into a fist, squeezing my hand since I couldn't punch my frustration out. All during my meeting, I kept picturing Madison, smiling at the employees, accepting their compliments, and charming my staff in ways I hadn't.

The urge to kick myself grew every time I saw some comments on that website she showed me. I should have memorized usernames, one in particular. What had she called herself? Now that I was her client, did she plan to comment in the chats?

"I'm sorry to say," the words spoken by a prospective investor I'd been wooing for three months finally penetrated my self-absorption. "As long as this cloud hangs over your head, we can't move forward with our talks."

"I hear what you're saying, but you should trust that this case will be closed by the time we're ready to announce our alliance. My and the company's names will be cleared. And if we continue now, we'll finish due diligence once that happens and can make a public announcement."

"Kent, our board is sensitive to your plight, but we have our image to worry about. We've recently survived a scandal of our own and we're not ready to expose ourselves to another so soon. I'm not saying we're completely closing the door on working together. We'll be more open once you come back to us when you're on the other side of this. Until then, we don't have a deal." He stood to shake my hand.

With more calm than I felt, I returned the gesture and bid him farewell. Alone in the conference room, I breathed in and out to refocus my anger. It was pointless to expect it to disappear. For the past eight years, fury has been my constant companion. Since losing my Lola, I haven't known peace.

Nothing worked. Not when I exacted my vengeance on the piece of shit that drove her to run the red light. Not the doctors who delayed treatment until they realized who her husband was. And not the dreams. No, they made everything worse. After all this time, they still did.

Lola's voice grew fainter as the years passed, but the circumstances of her death still haunted me. She still haunted me. That she wasn't with me today amplified my rage for the smallest provocation.

"Kent," Omar's voice reminded me where I was. "I have maintenance and IT here to set up Madison's desk."

Madison... another woman who incited my anger was about to work feet across from me and I was at fault. Why had I insisted on her being in my space when I'd initially told Omar to place her twenty floors below?

"Send them in."

As the people filed in, one person was missing.

"Where's Madison?" I barked at Omar.

"Mal took her for an early lunch to commemorate her first day." The easygoing attitude fell away once Omar clocked the storm brewing around me. "He took her to Kori's Food Truck." Omar fiddled with his phone. "You're in luck. She's in front of City Hall. Ever since Douglas' First Lady named them in The Douglas Times' article, Kori appears there regularly."

I nodded and stormed past Omar. Sloane De Luca may have put Kori on the map, but Mal was trying to seduce Madison with her food, and like hell would I let him succeed. I didn't bother questioning why the thought of Mal making moves on her bothered me. I'd just lost a valuable investor, and she needed to answer for that.

When I arrived at City Hall, finding Mal and Madison wasn't hard. A beautiful, dark-skinned woman and a handsome Asian man weren't typical in Colorado.

As I drew closer, their proximity recharged the irritation I'd held onto since Madison's arrival. Those two needed a few more feet of separation for me to calm the rage building inside me. Although calling what I felt rage rested on my shoulders like an ill-fitting suit, there was no other plausible emotion I could name.

Instead of wasting time to figure out my situation, I rushed to interrupt Mal and Madison's intimate lunch.

"Now you know I'm going to tell everyone that we're the new M&M. Just look at how good we look together." Mal stretched his hand forward and snapped a quick selfie shot. But that wasn't what stopped me cold.

Madison's laughter as she tilted her head back and let the sun sprinkle its rays against her skin held me transfixed. My gut clenched, and I tried to swallow, but doing so was a challenge. I wasn't blind. I could recognize a beautiful woman while feeling nothing for her. That had been my state for the last few months, so why now?

The gentle smile slipped from her lips as she caught sight of me. I immediately missed the way it softened her face.

"What are you doing here?" She asked me.

Meanwhile, Mal rested his arm on the back of Madison's chair with a smirk I wanted to wipe from his face; preferably with my fists.

I glared at my CFO while relaying the recent development. "We've lost CL Holdings."

"Shit." He sat upright, and I suppressed my glee as he retracted his arm from behind Madison's shoulder. "If they got cold feet, our expansion plans are going to suffer."

"Which is why I'm cutting lunch short. Madison, you're with me." I turned around to head to my car, expecting her to be on my tail.

When I opened the passenger door and she didn't pass me to get inside, I realized she intended to defy me. I slammed the door of my limited-edition Maybach and searched to find where she went.

She stood at the rear of the food truck talking to a Black woman wearing an apron while a massive line at the window grew. As I was about to storm over to Madison and explain why provoking me wasn't a good strategy, they exchanged a takeout container for some cash. Madison took her sweet time coming to me, but no complaint reached my lips. I was too busy being put under the spell her hips wove.

Working with her was bound to create problems if all she had to do was breathe to distract me from more serious concerns.

"Let's go." She opened the passenger door and settled in, leaving me feeling like she took something from me.

The sentiment ran circles in my mind until I pulled into one of the many spaces in the garage dedicated to my car collection.

"You know, when you first showed up at Kori's with this car, I thought you did it to make a statement, but I was wrong. This is the real statement, isn't it?" Madison asked as she let herself out of the car.

I bottled the response to tell her she needed to sit her ass down until I opened the door. She wasn't my woman, and I wasn't trying to make her mine.

"What statement do you think I'm making?" I followed her to the elevator and scanned the fob to call it.

"That you aren't the same man I fe—used to know. Message received."

I should have left things at that, but even after getting on the elevator, her response niggled at me. Her words festered into a wound I couldn't ignore.

When the silence grew and got the better of me, the words, "How am I different?" burst from my lips at the same time the elevator opened.

She exited the lift. With a shrug, she said, "Everyone in the neighborhood knew you were one of the wealthiest men on the planet. Yet you lived in the same modest suburban home you bought when you had Ife and drove the same Lexus my whole life. Now, you have more cars than days of the week, and you live in a penthouse. Anyway, here. I figured you didn't have time to eat." She handed me the container from earlier.

"You bought me lunch?" I stared at the container in my hand, unable to understand why she thought to make the gesture.

Except for Ife, women bought me things as an investment. They always had a hidden motive behind their generosity.

"Don't worry, it'll be on your bill. I didn't buy it to put the moves on you." Madison walked further into the office. "Looks like they set everything up. We should get to work, but first." She headed toward my desk and depressed the intercom linking my phone to Omar's. "Omar, can you bring my briefcase in for me?"

"Anything for my future wife," he said.

I compressed my lips, unsure what would escape if I mentioned their interaction.

"We'd have the shortest marriage in the Guinness Book of World Records," she said.

Damn right they would.

I shook the thought from my mind. I didn't have any business interfering with her and Omar.

But I should. To protect him from getting hurt.

Omar had been with me too long for me to let Madison waltz in and snatch him away. Thank God I came to my senses and shut the fuck up before I made a tense situation worse.

Once she had everything she needed, we sat around a small table with her files laid out before us.

I silently vowed to stay on topic. "To maintain this year's growth strategy, we need to handle this murder investigation. What is your plan?" I dug into the jerk chicken japchae.

Kori's food never disappointed.

"I'm a miracle worker, but solving murders isn't my job. What we have to do is find you an alibi."

"They already know I don't have one for the most recent murder."

"Do you seriously think whoever is killing these women is done? Until the police figure out who the perpetrator is, you need to have someone with you at all times. Meanwhile, my team back home will do what they can to help the Douglas PD find the culprit."

"And who do you expect to monitor me 24/7?"

"Ah, Kent..." Omar opened the door with a shell-shocked expression.

"Oh, you made it!" Madison jumped from her seat to greet the blonde woman standing beside Omar's stiff body.

The new woman put all the women since Oyinlola to shame. She was the most sought-after supermodel—perfect by anyone's standards —but I couldn't take my eyes off the woman beside her.

"Elsie, I'd like to introduce you to Mr. Luxe. If you two hit it off, I'll start reserving your media tour and make sure you have something to wear at the charity event in three days."

Madison did it again, flummoxed me with no effort. Between her grating insistence on referring to me as Mr. Luxe and the atomic bomb she dropped in my lap, I was going to explode.

"Excuse us," I said to Elsie before grabbing Madison's arm and dragging her onto the elevator.

Despite her struggle to free herself, I kept my hold firm until we reached the vacant apartment below mine; no way was I letting her into my living space. As the doors opened, I flung her inside.

"Explain how the fuck Elsie, the biggest international supermodel, is the girl next door!" I bore down on Madison, who had the goddamn audacity to stand her ground.

"You don't get more wholesome than our home-grown mid-western girl. Elsie is from a small farming community right here in Colorado and she knows how to appeal to the audience we need while drawing the publicity we want."

"Get rid of her."

"I don't think so," she smugly replied.

I advanced on her. Even as her eyes widened with the realization that I would walk through her if she didn't back up. Even as she made the first step backward, ceding me the ground I demanded. Even as she pressed her back against the wall.

With our breaths mixing as we glared into each other's eyes, I said, "I told you I get final say and she's out."

A smirk crossed her lips. "And I told you that you don't. What? Are you mad because I've got your number? Elsie is gorgeous and tall and can adapt her look from innocence personified to a sensual knockout. And she's got the media savvy to match."

Madison pushed against my chest, and I snapped. Yes, I was furious that she over delivered on her claim because, just like the last eight months, I felt nothing for Elsie. The only person causing blood to flow to my cock stood in front of me, crowing a victory that didn't exist and forcing me to remember why I'm supposed to hate her.

All that meant nothing as I mindlessly slammed my mouth down on hers and sank my fingers into her soft, cottony hair, and pressed my hard cock into her softness. I took advantage of the gasp that escaped her by plunging my tongue into the small opening. Then I drank. The rage I'd bottled up flowed into that kiss. I wrenched moan after delicious moan from her, licked and bit without finesse. But it wasn't enough.

I returned to plumb her depths, only to return thirstier than before. On the verge of drowning in her, a swift shove to my abdomen disconnected me from finding something I'd been barred from since I lost my wife.

Lola.

The thought, followed by Madison's angry slap to my cheek, didn't lessen the need flowing through my body.

"What the hell is wrong with you?" she panted.

Her breasts heaved with every breath she took. Her nipples poked out in a plea to be touched, and fuck if I didn't want to do more than touch. But I shouldn't because this was Madison causing the havoc inside me.

"You're baiting me. I don't know how you knew I wouldn't reac— No, you fucked around and now I'm showing you my response. Tell me, when you picked Elsie, did you ask yourself who was the complete opposite of you? If so, you blew it out of the park. And when I fuck her, you'll never know what you're missing, what you'll never get because you pushed me too far this time."

CHAPTER 5

 adison

I slammed through the front door of my parents' home, still reliving Kent's umpteenth slap to my confidence. That he dared to prove his point by giving me the hottest kiss I'd ever received rankled more because I knew Elsie would gladly sleep with him.

My body had yet to cool off from the inferno he started. Yet another reason for me to hate Kent fucking Luxe.

"Maddy, is that you?" my mother's voice reminded me I didn't have the luxury to vent my frustrations. Since I was staying with them until I finished my contract with Kent, I couldn't act the way I did living by myself.

"Yes, Mommy." I made my way to the kitchen, where she was wiping the table.

"Do you work this late in D.C.?"

"Sometimes later. Let's just say there's always someone doing dirty that needs my finesse."

"Tsk. While you take care of everybody, who's taking care of you?"

"All those life skills you and Daddy gave me." I smiled at my mother as she punched three minutes into the microwave.

Nikita Montgomery had boundless energy. She was a senior partner at Dietz, Simpson, and Montgomery, Douglas' premier law firm, and she was a hands-on mother. She never missed my competitions or dinner at home; even if it meant returning to the office late at night to work on a case. She set the plate of meatloaf, mashed potatoes, and mustard greens before me. It was pointless to tell her I'd had something at the office; she wouldn't consider a protein drink proper food.

I forked a mouthful and groaned at what I'd been missing as the flavors hit my tastebuds. "Where's Daddy?" I finally got around to asking when I was more than halfway done.

"You know that man is downstairs playing God with that miniature town he's been building since you were in middle school. You should go down and talk to him. He won't say anything, but he's been sulking since you returned because he hasn't had enough one-on-one time with you."

We shared a smile. Dennis Montgomery hid his softer-than-a-plush-toy interior beneath a gruff exterior when it came to me. He took me moving away for college and deciding to stay away the hardest.

I rose and washed my plate. "I'll go see him now." With a kiss to my mom's cheek, I headed to the basement.

"When you return, I'll have a glass of wine waiting for you. I want to know what had you slamming through my house like a bull elephant in musth."

Her reminder brought back my rage from earlier, but I cleared the emotion from my face and nodded.

Downstairs, I watched in silence as my father detailed the shingles of a roof for one of the three-dimensional houses he designed. My father was a master carpenter. Dignitaries and celebrities alike sought after his talent, keeping him busy.

Being exposed to his clients helped me when I began my career while I attained my accelerated law degree at Penn. After my disastrous confession to Kent, I'd busied myself with every distraction under the sun, pouring my broken heart into my studies and later into Madison Consulting.

"I know I'm pretty, but my good looks don't stop you from greeting your daddy properly."

I smiled at his unsubtle demand for my affection and ran over to hug him from behind. "Did you miss me?"

"Hmph, what's to miss? I haven't seen you in so long I almost forgot I had a daughter." He laid his work down and patted my forearm before turning and breaking my embrace. "Ah, yes, you look familiar now. Almost like looking in the mirror, you so pretty."

"Daddy!"

"What? Instead of denying who gave you that good DNA, give me a proper hug." He pulled me into his arms and wrapped me in his warmth. "Now, how's my baby girl doing?" He released me to cup my face and study my response.

I shrugged, not wanting to burden him with the stresses from my day. "You know how it is. Working for friends is never easy."

"Ah, yes. How is Kent doing? Ever since Oyinlola passed, he hasn't been the same. His old place sits empty, and he rarely comes around anymore."

"Ife never mentioned that."

"That's because he stays there whenever she visits, which is a lot more often than some daughters I know."

Guilt niggled at me because Kent and the odd chance of seeing him were the reasons I stayed away. If I'd known he spent most of his time in his penthouse, I would have visited more often.

"You've added a lot to the city since the last time I saw it." I changed the subject, unwilling to dwell on my reasons for avoiding my hometown.

He glared at me. "Because it's grown since you moved away, and I need to update this place with the changes. I can't afford for Ulysses Murphy to upstage me." He shifted an entire section of buildings off the original board onto a second cityscape.

31

A notecard beside the second board labeled the new the city's name with a date range to reflect the historical time period.

"Ever since Douglas' First Lady created the Best Little Douglas competition during the annual Spring festival, that old man has been riding my coattails. Except for last year." Daddy glowered at the altered miniature downtown landscape he was redesigning. "Murphy's focus on the train routes throughout the city put me in second place for the first time."

"But Daddy, isn't the competition only three years old?"

He switched his vexation to me. "And I was going for a three-peat. He broke my winning streak! And I bet it's because I didn't update downtown with the fancy new Luxe buildings and the new shopping and eating districts that have popped up over the years."

I nodded with a fierce frown transforming my face into the formidable version of myself I employed when handling a particularly troublesome crisis. "This means war. Tell me what you need."

"About time my actual daughter showed up. What I need is a showstopper that will outshine this Mr. Murphy and his moving trains."

I spent another hour with my father, helping him with his never-ending project like I did as a high schooler. By the time I returned upstairs, I was willing to let the stunt Kent pulled go.

"I know you aren't thinking about ducking me when this glass has been waiting for you." My mother stopped me as I planted one foot on the stairs to my room.

"Why would I avoid the most cutthroat litigator in Colorado?" I said, reversing course and dropping onto the couch beside her. "I bet you sent me to Dad just so I would be calm enough for you to rile me up again."

"Guilty as charged. Now, spill. Something's bothering you and your father's calming presence isn't the cure, but your mama's advice sure is."

I laughed, although she'd never led me astray. After a long sip of the sweet red wine, I sat with my head against the cushion and looked at the ceiling. "I'm facing a situation where I know I should be the bigger person and let things go, but I also know that won't solve anything."

"And you can't give me details because it involves your client?"

I nodded.

"I'm not surprised Kent is on some bullshit. After the mess he pulled, he's lucky I didn't wail on his ass like I would have with someone else."

"Wait." I straighten in the chair. "Are you telling me he did something to piss you off and he's still got all his limbs? What happened?"

"It was when Oye died. He was alone. I felt sorry for him, the way he stopped talking to his friends and was barely keeping himself together. So I cooked him some meals. Then one day I came home to find a cooler at the front door. On top was a note with one word: Stop. That's it. Inside the cooler were all the meals I'd made for him, untouched. You know I haven't said a nice thing to or about that man since. And your daddy is quick to remind me he was grieving. Hmph!" Nikita drained her glass and refilled it.

"He never apologized?"

"The only person that man has ever said sorry to was Oyi. Maybe Ife, but no one else. I doubt you can get an apology out of him, but you would be the next likely candidate after Ife."

I stared into my glass. My mother had no idea that I was permanently moved to the last person on earth some years ago.

"But I'm going to tell you, until you get that apology, rake his ass over the hottest coals you can find and make your mama proud."

"What happened to 'he's grieving'?"

"That was eight years ago. Don't look at me like that. I've seen the women who have helped him get over his grief. Tear his ass up, Maddy."

"Not sure how to do that, if I'm being honest." I shook my head. The last thing I needed was for my mother to feed the angry flame inside me.

"One thing about Kent is he doesn't share his toys."

"Mommy, I'm not a toy."

"Of course you aren't." The weight of her strange stare burrowed beneath my skin.

The one thing I most wanted to do in this moment was avert my gaze, but my mom was a shark when she suspected me of withholding information. My only hope was not to blink first.

Mom exhaled, though suspicion ran strong beneath her glare. "You need to find what he's fixated on now and take it from him. Better if it's something you gave him in the first place. I'm getting a vicarious thrill just thinking about how you'll put him in his place."

"I'll think about it." I kissed her cheek and made my way upstairs.

In bed, I tossed, unable to shut my brain and body off. Time and darkness stoked all the conflicting emotions inside me, forcing me to relive our moment in the penthouse. The one when I felt his kiss to my core. The need inside me burned brightly until he stabbed me with his words. Yet despite my reasonable side telling me to back off and take the higher road, arousal made it impossible for me to sleep.

With a frustrated growl, I threw the covers off my body and retrieved the vibrator I hid inside a discreet throw pillow. I ended my day the way I began; with a small unsatisfactory orgasm and a body so tense my muscles locked into a painful vise. I was near tears from the futility of it all.

Maybe my horrible night was why I woke up the next morning, resolute. I was going to take my mom's advice and become the toy Kent Luxe didn't want to share.

As I dressed in a killer skirt suit that clung to my curves, leaving little to the imagination, I decided my best revenge was to make him fall for me, then leave him to wallow in humiliation. Before leaving my room, I added an accessory that I hoped I wouldn't need to use, but based on the prior day would have to rely on just to make it until I finished work.

I was resolute, but my body was no Iron Woman.

CHAPTER 6

ent

After asking Elsie to meet me this morning, I was at a loss for words. She arrived early, and I stalled for time by having her order breakfast from Omar, which didn't take as long as I'd hoped. I checked my watch and counted down the seconds until Madison walked through my doors to find us together.

Would she look at me the way she did yesterday after my cruel words? I squeezed my fist, hoping the pressure would help me focus. Madison's feelings didn't matter, they couldn't. Not when her image haunted me all night; from the tears that refused to fall from her soulful brown eyes to the forbidden lure she represented.

Elsie shifted in her chair and crossed her legs. Slim thighs and legs that drove most men wild with lust did nothing for me. Although I appreciated her form, appreciation was all I could muster. None of the madness that had fueled me yesterday or driven me to taste Madison was present, not even a flicker.

"Kent, I'm not sure why you needed to see me again. Madison laid out a comprehensive plan for our public outings. She's got me busier than my publicist, which thrills my stylist." Elsie smiled, probably at the thought of all the free designer clothes she'd get for her appearances.

With great timing, Madison entered the office.

For a second, my mind blanked as I took in her attire. She wore a skirt suit that would be modest on anyone else. On Madison, she might as well have put on a sign that dared every heterosexual man, lesbian, and bi-curious person to touch, lick, and fuck her until her carefully slicked bun became a sultry mess and her lips doubled in size.

"Morning, Mr. Luxe... Elsie." She strode toward her desk.

I sat rooted in my chair. It was the most control I could exert over myself because if I unclenched for a second, I'd forcefully drag her home to change her clothes; to something baggy and shapeless. Who was I kidding? Even a nun's habit on her would tempt a eunuch.

Instead of acknowledging Madison by word or gesture as Elsie did, I said, "To answer your question, I thought we should discuss how close we want this act to look to outsiders. Specifically, if you want to move into my penthouse with me."

From the corner of my eye, I spied Madison as she missed a step once I finished my offer. She took a deep breath and firmed her posture before setting her briefcase on the desk.

"There are three bedrooms, so you don't need to feel pressured into anything." Despite addressing Elsie, my gaze locked onto every move Madison made. "I work long hours, so unless we're attending an event, you won't see me most nights."

"You're moving in together?" Madison's lips pressed into a thin line, inspiring an urge inside me to free them for my personal abuse.

I was going to have to do something with this inexplicable need that arose inside me whenever I thought about Madison or was near her. Only one woman had ever driven me to obsession, and that had been after being around her for years. In less than forty-eight hours, Madison had lulled my senses, and I needed to wake the fuck up.

"Do you think we should?" Elsie asked.

Madison's throat worked overtime, as if suppressing the words she wanted to say. I sat in suspense, eager to hear her comeback.

"Like everything you do from now on, there are pros and cons to your actions. Living together will undoubtedly give Mr. Luxe positive press. They'd say, how can he be a suspect when Elsie believes in him enough to sleep with him every night? But should things fall apart, all that good press will turn violently against the both of you."

Disappointment filled me as Madison logically broke down what Elsie and I would face. Where was the jealous reaction, the desire to one-up Elsie? My words should have incited a stronger response. She wasn't behaving like a woman with an agenda, and I began to question if I'd misjudged her.

"Kent." Elsie rested her hand on my arm. "Based on everything Madison said, can we wait before deciding things now? First, let's see how the press responds."

A surprising sense of relief drained the tension from my body. Suddenly, the idea of Elsie living and walking around my home with her things cluttering my space lost its appeal. More disturbing was the sense of loss when a brief flash of Madison on my couch wearing my pajama top popped into my head.

"Sure," I said, more confused than when I began this charade. "Let me walk you out. I'll have Omar take you home, or, if you've the urge to buy something, he'll get you something nice."

When we neared Omar's desk, I handed him my black card and asked him to see to Elsie's needs. The brief absence allowed me to breathe and reorganize my thoughts and remove the tempting image of Madison in my home.

As I stalled, Carol strolled onto the floor. Seeing her brought a lot of my frustration to the forefront. She was responsible for my first of many blow ups at Madison yesterday. While I observed her, she glanced in my direction more times than was warranted. I couldn't deny that Carol was a beautiful woman, blonde, tall, and lithe. Eight months ago, she would've ticked every one of my boxes, but I would have refrained since she worked for me.

Her presence on my floor was unusual. Now that I had time to observe her, doubts about her involvement with Madison arose. I rarely question my managers' hiring decisions, but I couldn't ignore the suspicion about Carol's credentials riding my back. I crooked my finger, beckoning her over.

A flirtatious smile curled her lips, and she swished her hips as she approached. "Hi Kent. I'm glad you're here. I wanted to check on our new hire, but the desk I designated for her seems to have disappeared." When she stood before me, Carol's expression shifted to one of concern. "I'm worried she's not taking her role here seriously."

"Deke seems to have a lot of faith in your work. However, when it comes to Madison's role and performance, that's not something Deke can relegate to an HR manager. If she presents to be a problem, I'll have Deke handle it personally."

"Oh, of course." The corners of Carol's mouth tightened. "I won't overstep again."

"And one more thing, Carol." I infused cold steel into my voice. "My meeting requests supersede any curiosity you have. Don't let it happen again because Deke won't be able to cover for you next time."

"Yes, sir," she gritted.

Gone from her demeanor was the air of conspiratorial camaraderie and flirtation. *Good.* I had enough problems with my current PR crisis, criminal investigation, and the woman in my office. The brief respite from her presence did nothing to clear the fog of confusion from my head, but I had an international organization to run.

As soon as I reentered my office, my hackles rose. Madison stepped out of the bathroom. Her glossy eyes widened in shock before she averted her gaze. Her lips were fuller than before when I walked Elsie out; as if she'd been nibbling on them. Perhaps biting them to hold back sounds? Not that she would have had to. Thanks to soundproofing in my office and bathroom, sounds never escaped.

Suspicions whispered in my ear, but I discounted them. There was no way she would use my bathroom for *that*. I narrowed my eyes at her to pick up more clues.

Her body showed no signs of lassitude, so she hadn't released her tension. If anything, she was more tense than when I'd left her. Under my intense stare, she brought her hand up to cover her necklace.

The protective gesture rubbed me the wrong way. Was it a gift from another man? Was that why she slapped me yesterday? Because I'd trespassed on someone else's playing field? With a viciousness I reserved for my business rivals, I crushed my curiosity into dust. I had no business wondering or getting upset about who gave Madison gifts. Not when her presence was a constant reminder of how I'd failed Lola.

Madison straightened and a determined gleam entered her eyes. "We should prep for your appearance for the event in two days. I have a list of media and political people you need on your side."

She met me at my desk with a dossier. Jasmine, fleeting and arousing, wafted from her position standing beside me.

To stifle the urge to inhale deeply, I breathed through my mouth and curled my fingers into my palm until the sharp bite from my nails helped me to focus.

Madison's list comprised a few people in my circle, including Douglas's mayor, Valentino DeLuca. There were also a few surprising names of people I'd courted for years but never got my foot in the door with.

While schooling my features, I segmented the personalities. "I have ongoing dealings with this group and won't need to spend much time with them other than to show my face."

Madison reached for the pile, momentarily brushing the side of her soft breast against me.

My muscles locked in place, and I forgot to breathe through my mouth. Jasmine flitted up my nose to fill my lungs and paint sensuous scenes where I wrapped Madison's naked body around myself.

"Mayor DeLuca has connections to some of the hottest fashion houses coming out of Italy right now," she said, noting I'd singled out Valentino DeLuca's name from the rest of the list.

The reminder cleared the increasingly disturbing images of the two of us from my mind.

"Spend more time with him to give Elsie face time. After all, you both need to benefit from these events." Madison stacked the names to the side, and I couldn't stop myself from staring at her delicate ear or the soft luster of her skin as I trailed my gaze down her neck.

Maybe you should be the one on my arm.

Instead of allowing the rogue thought out, I grunted and shoved another set of names at Madison. "These people will be more challenging."

"What? Are you afraid that you can't win them over with your sunny disposition?"

I glanced at her face, wondering if my imagination was fucking with me. Had a note of flirtation entered her voice? The slight uptick of her lips could be the same sarcasm she'd been handing me from our reunion. But I... Hell, I didn't know if I wanted her to be unfeeling or not anymore, and I didn't like being confused. I was a decisive man in all my dealings, yet somehow Madison could shift the ground from under me.

"Let's just say I'll need more than my enviable status to get these men to give me the time. Once I'm in front of them, they won't be able to deny my charm or the benefits of doing business with me."

"That's where Elsie comes in. Have her approach Hayden first." Madison pulled the dossier on Hayden Mills, heir to one of the largest international media conglomerates. "He's never met a model he doesn't try to steal from someone else. I'll have her drop my name before—"

"What will your name do that my name won't?"

Madison chuckled while shaking her head. "That's between Hayden and me. What matters is we'll have given him two reasons to meet you."

Whatever was between Madison and Hayden wasn't my business, yet my gut churned from the possibilities. Even as we discussed the other names on the list, I surreptitiously watched Madison. To hell with her keeping her secrets. I was going to find out how close Hayden was to Madison, and if she knew what was good for her, they better be long-lost siblings separated at birth.

CHAPTER 7

$\mathcal{M}$ adison

The first time I confessed my love to Kent Luxe, I was sixteen. My pubescent heart didn't care that he was Ife's father or that he was married. I blurted out my feelings with no regard to where we were or who was around. Lucky for me, we were alone in the kitchen while Ife and Oyinlola were in the den.

What could I say? I was determined to be a home wrecker if it meant having my crush for myself.

No other man in my life really saw me until Kent. The boys in school saw me as exotic because of my vitiligo, wanting to see just how much of my body was unmelanated. They didn't care if I fought with my parents, the stress I was under to perform to Nikita Montgomery's standards, or my inability to cope with disappointment.

Kent did.

He wasn't patronizing, like some of the other kids' parents. He spoke to me as an equal, where everyone else treated me like a child. He showed me how to confront my shortcomings in a way that wasn't destructive. He was everything my teenage heart saw as a hero, and incredibly handsome on top of everything else.

Even after my first confession when he distanced himself, I couldn't stop my feelings for him. At eighteen, I planned an elaborate declaration, convincing Ife and her mother to go on a mother-daughter weekend trip and leaving Kent at home and alone.

I cringed now, thinking about how I snuck into his bedroom, determined to seduce him when I had zero clue what seducing a man meant. The wait was so nerve-wracking I almost ran to the bathroom several times to purge myself while waiting for his telltale footsteps to approach the bedroom door. Despite my agitated state, I didn't chicken out, though now I wondered how things would be different if I had.

Instead, I lay in his bed while nervous sweat dotted my back, armpits, and thighs. Nothing prepared me for the horror that over-took his features or the intense anger and scathing dismissal he gave me. It was a million times worse than his first rejection, leaving a wound that I thought I'd healed.

While away, I worked to rebuild the confidence he'd shredded in one sentence and a scathing laugh. When he called me a sexless child who could never tempt a man's appetites, let alone move his heart, I planned on never returning to Douglas. Yet being here now proved that a part of me wanted his approval. I still wanted him to see me as an equal, and as someone he desired.

I hated that for myself. He needed to pay for crushing me the way he did. I spent years in college putting myself back together while masking the mess I was. More years after graduating, I funneled my energies into my company. I barely spared time for a social life that didn't advance my professional goals.

Despite my achievements, one day with Kent brought back the pain and humiliation from the past and shook my confidence. How could I not embrace my mother's advice for revenge? Yet I'd almost lost my nerve yesterday when he offered to move Elsie into his pent-house. My plans for vengeance seemed unachievable, but then I remembered the passion in yesterday's kiss.

No sexless adolescent could inspire such heat. And I wanted to make him burn hot enough to fry his brain. It would serve him right since being in the same room with him drove me to use my necklace. The little vibrator looked like a sleek bullet pendant and would have probably done the job I needed had I not been so tense from Kent's presence.

The tiny orgasm did nothing to ease my taut muscles, nor did it eradicate my need to see Kent on his knees. This time, there would be no confession, no heart to offer him. And my efforts were paying off.

He couldn't disguise his flaring nostrils and stuttered breathing when I leaned toward him, or his clenching jaw when I brushed against him. I barely hid my body's reaction, which was primed now that I shared his office space.

To give myself a breather, I wrapped up our strategy session about tomorrow night's charity gala and headed to my desk.

"By the way, Madison, you failed to mention when you would make an appearance." As offhanded as he sounded, his tightly pressed lips told another story. He'd tried to withhold his curiosity about me from me.

Yes! He's fallen into my first trap.

I turned to him with a smirk, loving the idea of me burrowing into his mind like an underground mole village. "You're a big boy. With Elsie's help, you won't need me there."

"It isn't a question of need. I require you there."

"I don't see why—"

"As my consultant."

"Your consultant?"

"To ensure things run smoothly."

"But you're a pro. And with that famous Luxe charm you recently reminded me of, my presence would only dim your light." I winked at him and packed a few items in my briefcase. "By the way, I'll be out of the office for the rest of the afternoon."

"Doing what?" Kent rose halfway from his chair before settling into the seat, a frown marring his handsome features.

"Oh, you know, consultanty things. Earning my obscenely expensive rate." I rushed out of the office before my shaky legs gave from under me, praying I portrayed a confidence I didn't feel.

I drove around Douglas until I reached the library. After my intense morning with Kent, I needed a breather, but I still had to work on his and his company's images. I logged into the BBD site to monitor the chatter about Kent and Luxe Locations.

The internal company image needed a revamp as much as the external reputation. I scrolled through the recent discussion and drafted a few posts to plant under my username, Boss_Wrecker before I decided how to interject in the most recent bosshole discussion.

@OfficeVixen69: I don't know how everyone can ignore the murderer ⚔️💀 in the room, especially when he turns his temper on us.

@In_The_Know: @OfficeVixen69 tell me about it. I saw him unleash in person. I don't know how the board at #de-luxe_digs hasn't voted him out yet. He's ruining the company inside and out. I wonder if I'll have a job in a few months. You know I need that 💰.

@Nose2TheGrindstone: Did I miss something? I swear, every day he tops his worst. Like, how low can this man go? At this point, he's below whatever is under hell. And I don't know about y'all, but I'm with @OfficeVixen69. There's no way he isn't the culprit. I've dyed my hair black just to be safe.

@PeoplePleaser13: @Nose2TheGrindstone that's a good idea. Only blonde women keep turning up. Come to think of it, @In_The_-Know, didn't you say you were blonde, too?

@In_The_Know: @PeoplePleaser13 you aren't funny.

@Boss_Wrecker: Hey @everyone. I'm new here. What are we talking about?

@In_The_Know: Hey @Boss_Wrecker. We're talking about the man we always talk about. The top honcho whose stare can melt the melanin off you.

@Boss_Wrecker: He is intense, but I guess I'd be, too, if the company I bled to build was under attack. I mean, other than the rumors, has anyone from the office disappeared?

@PeoplePleaser13: @Boss_Wrecker has a point. He's never looked twice at an employee, but that could be his cover to make us vouch for him.

@Boss_Wrecker: Nah, you can't always judge a person by how they manage people. I bet outside the office he's a softie.

I glanced at the time, then at the chat once more. Without going overboard with my defense, I planted the seeds for other Luxe Locations employees to question @OfficeVixen69 and @Nose2TheGrindstone's assertions. At least two other users who've posted about deluxe_digs commented after I stopped chatting, showing their support of the company, if not of Kent.

In another chat, I lurked, unable to deny my curiosity about the site. Did my employees post about me? I was sure some of my team thought I overworked them, maybe even called me a bosshole behind my back. I made a note to search for clues when a chat with @Desk_Pet caught my eye.

Her situation with her boss sounded messy. I shook my head and squelched the urge to offer advice. People paid me a lot to handle their crises, and I wasn't the charitable type to give my services away for free.

The next day, I arrived in the office expecting to exchange more barbs with Kent. Like the day before, I dressed to highlight my body's curves, and his penetrating stare told me I'd succeeded. Maybe too well.

My skin itched from feeling his eyes on me. In response, I tried to bait him, but he refused to give me the satisfaction of replying. Instead, his calm demeanor left me feeling like a hormonal adolescent lashing out for no reason.

I endured for two hours before leaving the office. This time, I called my team to find out if they'd made any progress on the open murder investigation. There were few leads, and digging into the women's lives didn't turn up many clues. All the women linked to Kent were last seen with him more than eight months ago.

Was the reason he hadn't publicly dated anyone since been because of the murders? Did they have other connections we could use to deflect attention from Kent and his company?

The next time I glimpsed the time, it was late enough that Elsie and Kent would have left for their first event together. I tamped down the jealousy desperately fighting for a foothold on my emotions. I knew what I was doing when I linked those two together. Their complementary looks would leave people in awe.

I rubbed my chest bone. Deciding not to attend tonight had an added benefit; I wouldn't exhaust myself pretending Kent didn't affect me. I needed to live rent-free in his mind, not the other way around. After a long exhale and arm stretches, I headed home.

Nikita's cooking slapped my tastebuds the second I walked through the door. Eager, I helped set the table for our first family meal since I arrived. My butt hovered above the seat at the dining table when the doorbell rang. Both of my parents looked at each other before glancing in my direction.

"Are you expecting someone?" my dad asked.

"No, but I'll check if it's someone from my team. If they traveled here, there must be an emergency I'll have to deal with." I stared longingly at the smothered chicken, greens, and red beans and rice.

"Go on. We'll leave you a plate." My mom spooned a healthy serving of smothered chicken gravy over her beans and rice.

"Who is we?" My dad shoveled a mountain of the rice dish onto his plate. "Don't go volunteering me for altruist of the year when it's your famous chicken in front of me. Maddy can always call Grubhub."

"Daddy, you are cold."

"Don't you worry about me. All this good food will warm me right up."

I shook my head as I moved toward our mystery guest. Through the stained-glass front door, Omar's sheepish brown face stared at me.

"Omar, what are you doing here?" I asked, after letting him in.

He raised a garment bag he held in one hand and a shopping bag in the other. "Kent sent me. I… uh… have to escort you to the event tonight."

My mind raced. Kent couldn't have spent a full thirty minutes at the party before sending the well-prepared Omar over.

"When did you have time to shop for me?" I unzipped the bag to find a gorgeous emerald sequined gown inside.

"Technically, I didn't. This afternoon, Kent sent me to pick up everything. I don't even know what is in all the packages."

I wanted the dress, but I refused to let Omar see my desire, or else he'd report my reaction to Kent. One thing I wouldn't abide in the war I was waging was seeing a satisfied smirk on that man's face because he managed to one-up me. Hoping for an easy excuse, I checked the size.

"This is my size. How?" I asked, staring dumbfounded at the discreet tag.

"Beats me." Omar checked his digital watch. "So, do you mind putting these on so we can leave? Kent was rather insistent."

I glared at Omar. "What were his exact words?"

"Look, Madison, I'm just the messenger. You'll be doing me a solid by dolling up and coming with me. So can you, please?"

"Omar..."

He slumped his shoulders and evaded my glance by looking at the ground. "He said if you know what's good for you, you'll do as you're told, wear the damn dress and get your"—Omar cringed—"ass to the gala."

I patted Omar's shoulder. "Thanks for telling me. Don't worry, I won't bite your head off."

"That's a relief because I really like you. As a friend, promise." A smile returned to his face and relief replaced the stress lines around his eyes from moments ago. "So, how long do you think you'll need?"

"Not long at all." I shifted my hold to Omar's elbow and led him to the door. "Because I'm not going. And you can tell Mr. Luxe that someone else has already filled the role for my father, and I don't need a second one telling me what's good for me." I gently shut the door in Omar's face and returned to dinner with my parents, with a lightness to my step and a grin I tried to suppress.

CHAPTER 8

ent

Tonight's charity event supported Douglas' Children's Hospital. Although Douglas couldn't compete with metropolises like New York, Felicidad, or Los Angeles, the attendees more than made up for it. Celebrities, dignitaries, and ambassadors mingled with local business executives. The attendees made an eclectic mix that rivaled many White House dinners.

Women dressed in their best finery, their jewels glimmered in the overhead lights. Wives and girlfriends exploited their networks to introduce their men to new contacts. Soon, their men sidelined them for the more attractive business deals and budding partnerships.

I maneuvered Elsie through the crowd to show my face to my long-time acquaintances. The owner of Sussex Club, the exclusive gentlemen's club I'd joined as did other celebrities and famous members of various royal families, the Director of Douglas' Boards and Commissions in charge of approving many of my construction projects, and the CEO of my company's bank stopped me within the first five minutes of entering the main hall. After the expected small talk, I spotted the mayor and his wife, but before I could head toward them, Hal intercepted us.

"Kent, I didn't realize you were attending tonight. Weren't you on hiatus?" My company's general counsel stared at my date, a speculative gleam in his eyes.

"Hal, meet Elsie. Elsie, Hal is my company's legal representation."

Elsie held her hand out to him, and Hal kissed her knuckles.

"I've returned to my roots as a social butterfly. Do you like the new look?" I asked.

"Ah, your fixer put you up to tonight." He nodded while gazing around the room. "Where is she, by the way? Don't you need her around to make sure you stick to the script?"

His reminder rankled. I couldn't tell if my annoyance stemmed from Madison's defiance or a genuine need for her to be close at hand. After she left the office, her absence left me with an empty feeling I had yet to fill.

Elsie's soothing touch along my arm made me aware of my tightly clenched fists. I patted her hand and forced my body to relax.

"Hal, with a woman like Elsie on my arm, there's no need for a script." I twirl her around for effect.

She speared him with a dazzling smile. "Kent, you flatter me too much."

"He has a point." Hal's admiring gaze held a hint of envy.

If he knew Elsie failed to capture my interest, I wondered how he would react. "I won't keep you. We all need to show the public that Luxe Locations is still worthy of their support."

I led Elsie away to find Valentino, but Deke impeded our progress. Carol was on his arm in a showpiece gown that rivaled red-carpet award show attendees. As the head of my Human Resources department, I hoped he hadn't risked my company's reputation for the beautiful manager. In looking closer, I realized Carol's grip on Deke was a commandeering one. Perhaps she, and not Deke, was the mastermind behind their relationship.

An unsubtle nudge from her prompted Deke to blurt, "Kent, I've never been happier to see you than I am now. Carol convinced me I needed to attend tonight, although this really isn't my scene."

"What Deke means to say," Carol interjected with a forced smile. "Is with all the terrible publicity the company's received lately, we wanted to do our part to represent the company. And what better way to do it than while wearing pretty clothes? I'm Carol, by the way." She held her hand out to Elsie with the air of a regent expecting her subjects to bow to her. "You are?"

"Kent's date, Elsie. I hope you continue to do all that you can to help him and the company tonight." Elsie rested her hand against my chest. "Although we haven't known each other long, I know the rumors about him are false."

"Wow, Kent, you've won another woman over in so little time." Carol pulled her hand away without the expected response from Elsie. "It won't be too long before the police and press know what everyone else at Luxe Locations does; you wouldn't hurt a fly. Makes me wonder why you need Madison's services at all. If Mal knew her rate—"

"Are you implying that my CFO, the man in charge of our company's finances, isn't doing his job?" I frowned at Carol and dismissed her in the next second. "Deke, enjoy what you can of the night, but don't overextend yourself. I want a meeting first thing tomorrow morning." I glanced at Carol then at Deke as a silent message to him about who the subject of the meeting would be.

Carol had overstepped one time too many for my liking. This time, she served as another reminder of Madison's absence.

Stifled by the current situation, I pulled Elsie away. "Thank you for that."

"Not a problem. It's not like I was lying. You may be a little distant, but you've been open with me since our first meeting. I almost feel like this isn't work."

"Allow me to repay you. Madison mentioned you wanted to meet Valentino DeLuca. We have a lot of mutual interests, and an introduction from me will go a long way in attaining your aspirations."

"That'll be amazing, Kent. Working with Madison and now you

has really done wonders for my network." Elsie beamed up at me, giving me pause. I would have to address the cause later, since Valentino stood before us.

After a brief introduction, I joked, "Valentino, if you aren't careful, I'll have Sloane on my other arm asking me who Valentino DeLuca is."

He wrapped his arm possessively around Sloane's waist and skewered me with a fierce frown. "Kent, why would you want to ruin a friendship by touching my wife?"

Sloane patted Valentino's chest. "Ignore him, please. He's been out of town on a business trip and this is the first time he's seen me in days. He'll be a bit feral until tomorrow." She winked at me, then whispered something in her husband's ear.

Valentino pulled away to stare heatedly into her face. "You promise?"

At her nod, he lost the menacing aura around him and gently kissed her cheek before directing his famous charm at Elsie. Despite his absolute devotion to Sloane, one mild inquiry made the single and married women of Douglas instant fangirls of the mayor. Elsie was no exception.

While they discussed Italian fashion houses, I checked the entrance to the ballroom. Anticipating Madison's stubbornness, I'd sent Omar to pick her up, although it was still early in the evening. He hadn't returned, and faced with Hal then Carol's reminder about her absence I was left itching to see Madison.

It was more than making her submit to my demands, too. I'd picked out the outfit I wanted to see her wearing, knowing she would shine brighter than every jewel here. And I needed to see her to confirm my vivid imagination.

Instead of the beautiful patchwork of brown and peach skin wrapped in sequins that I expected to see, Omar's guilty face appeared.

No one stood beside him.

"Elsie, I need to step out for a moment." I motioned to Omar.

She nodded, although disappointment shadowed her eyes.

"Valentino, I'll talk to you later about a new project. Your brother

Sansone and cousin Enzo might want to get in on it. If we want things to run smoothly, we'll also need to get your Board Director in line."

"I'm all ears for anything to help further the family business."

I shook his hand and made my way to Omar, uncaring if anyone noted the haste in my step.

When I reached my assistant, the simmering anger I'd held at bay pulsed through my veins, causing me to breathe deeply to restrain it.

"Before you bite my head off, she refused to come and kicked me out of her house. And before you ask, she made me tell her verbatim what you said. Sorry, Kent. I tried."

"Tell me her exact response."

"Man, I like my job."

"I promise you'll be fine. What did she say?"

Omar cringed while relaying Madison's response.

I firmed my lips and nodded. "Where are the—"

"The clothes are in my car." Omar held out his keys, and I grabbed them.

"Stay here with Elsie. Tell her I'll return later and to enjoy herself in the meantime."

Without giving Omar time to respond, I left the venue, picturing Madison's delicate neck in my hands. Tonight, she'd learn she could only push me so far.

I arrived at her home with no memory of the drive and forewent the doorbell to bang on the front door. The garment bag and shopping bag dangled over my forearm.

Nikita swung the door open, fury illuminating her face and highlighting the resemblance between mother and daughter. "Who the hell do you think you are, treating my door like a festival drum?"

"I need to speak to your daughter." I tried to bypass her, but she stood in the middle of the entryway.

"Not without showing me proper respect in my home. I don't know where you put your manners, but you better become an archeologist and dig them up before you think about getting past me to my daughter."

I stepped back. "You're right, Nikita. I was disrespectful. If it wouldn't be too much of a bother, could you ask your daughter to come outside?"

She took in my appearance, which contrasted with her pink velour sweatpants with white piping along the seams. "Aren't you a little overdressed for a conversation?"

"Nikita, what I have to discuss affects her work. Do you really want to stand in her way?"

Nikita narrowed her eyes and stepped back into her house. "Wait here," she said before slamming the door.

In seconds, an angry Madison faced me wearing a matching set of sweatpants, except hers was white with pink piping. She reminded me of a little bunny, adorable and soft. She was at once different from the vixen in my office, but still the same. Not even the anger radiating from her could prevent the urge building inside me to wrap my arms around her and inhale her jasmine scent.

"What do you think you're doing here?" Her words were a bracing wake-up call from my disturbing thoughts.

"You forgot your presence is required somewhere else." I shoved the bags at her.

"Mr. Luxe—"

"Kent!"

—"I made myself perfectly clear to you and Omar. Now, never show up at my home without a written invitation from me."

I grabbed the door before she could slam it like her mother had. "Madison, I'm not in the mood for your tantrum. You have two choices: you can put on this gown, or I'll dress you myself. And that dragon lady you call a mother won't be able to stop me." When she opened her mouth as if to protest, I said, "Try me."

She slammed her lips together and grabbed the bags.

"You have ten minutes before I come to find you."

Her response was to slam the door. Like mother, like daughter. Now that I had seen her, the tension riding me all afternoon into the evening dissipated and I breathed my first free breath in hours.

Exactly at the ten-minute mark, the door swung open, and my heart stopped. Madison stepped out and the sconces bracketing the entrance glimmered off her body. My imagination paled compared to reality, and words stuck in my throat. Unable to free the compliment burning on my lips, I grunted.

"I truly can't believe you left the event to come get me," she grumbled as she stomped toward the car. "After all the work I put in to give you an opening to woo the people we needed to help you with your image, this is how you act?"

I opened the door for her, still speechless, and let her rant. What could I say? She was right, and I let my grievance with her overshadow the opportunity she made for me.

"I hope Hayden will still talk to you after this. Do you know how many people swarm him at events? And you had Elsie, the epitome of his weakness." She continued, half lamenting and half reprimanding until we pulled up to the function.

Instantly, her persona changed to one of an agreeable companion. When we stepped into the ballroom, the emcee announced it was time for the meal.

Madison grabbed my arm and hauled me toward a group milling by the open bar. For some reason, she had yet to realize that I hadn't said a word since leaving her house. "Look out for Elsie. If you can signal to her to meet us, I'm going to get you a seat at Hayden's table. Please, don't squander this chance."

Elsie was easy to find, though I had no intention of gaining her attention. She and Omar had their heads bent together, sharing an intimate moment. At least I wouldn't have to feel guilty for leaving her alone, now that I had Madison on my arm. Later tonight, I would take the time to reflect on the sense of rightness having her here gave me. But I'd neglected my purpose long enough.

"Hayden Mills, why is it at every event I find you causing trouble?" Madison pulled away, leaving a noticeable void beside me.

Hayden swung around to face her. "Madison Montgomery?" He dragged her into a hug that raised the hair along my nape. "Had I known you were here, I would have sniffed you out earlier."

"Funny story about that. You have my associate to thank for me being here. Hayden Mills, meet Mr. Kent Luxe."

"Mr.?" Hayden arched his brow, then placed a proprietary hand on her hip.

Between her insistence on formality and his hand where it didn't belong, I'd had enough. Channeling a little of Valentino's possessiveness, I hauled her to my side, ignoring the shocked gasp escaping from her mouth. With her beside me, I executed our plan to charm Hayden and gain the coveted invite to his table.

During dinner, his surreptitious glances at Madison told me she'd miscalculated. Although Elsie might have been his weakness, like me, he'd found a new one in Madison.

"How long will you be in Douglas?" he asked Madison during the brief lull in conversation.

"I'm here for work. If all goes well, I'll have the major pieces in place within a month. Then I'll head back to D.C."

"Great, let's make time for dinner. There's a new Greek restaurant I've been dying to try."

Madison laughed and playfully punched his shoulder. "You think you're slick. I don't have time for you to fly me to Greece for dinner when I'm on assignment."

While he openly flirted with her, I silently fumed. For the millionth time, I reminded myself I had no right to her. I was still harboring a great resentment toward her, although the justification seemed to dwindle with every hour I spent with her. She sparkled brighter than the crystals dangling from the chandeliers. As I stared and studied, I realized, her beauty was only partly responsible for holding everyone's attention.

Her intelligence and charm kept people returning to her orbit. No conversational topic left her stumped. Like in the office, whenever her team consulted her on a different project, her mind filtered everything with lightning speed. She gave clear, efficient, out-of-the-box solutions that made me want to create a more permanent position at Luxe Locations for her. She would be an asset to any company, and no matter what my personal feelings toward her were, as complicated as they continue to grow, she's a hell of a professional.

During the rest of the evening, Madison introduced me to eight more useful contacts. They would not only help rehabilitate Luxe Locations' reputation but made us available to new business opportunities. We were in the middle of securing funds and the proper permits for another Douglas project my new contacts could be instrumental in advancing.

At the end of the evening, when I dropped Madison at her parents' home, I had to accept that I was feeding my anger with what happened in the past. If I had any chance of resolving the conflict inside me, I'd have to confront what happened with Madison and Oyinlola.

CHAPTER 9

adison

Confusion swirled around me as I entered the office the next morning. He wasn't at his desk, which gave me time to think. My plan to ruin Kent felt off as if I'd experienced a setback, but I couldn't pinpoint where I'd gone wrong. Last night, one minute Kent showed signs I was getting to him, but the next he was distant.

Watching him mingle with everyone showed me a side of Kent that I couldn't help but admire. His passion for his company and employees wasn't an act and ran counter to the impression some users on the BBD website tried to portray. Once again, the man I admired as a teen appeared.

Coupled with the casual touches and almost possessive hold, he'd left me in a state that no amount of self-pleasuring eased. Why did he have to plague me so? Even now, surrounded by his belongings and his domineering scent, I was too weak to deny myself the chance that maybe this time, I'd get what I needed. While he was away, I had to take advantage of his absence to clear my head and prepare myself for this battle I was determined to wage against him.

I headed to his bathroom and released the discreet vibrator from my necklace. It was a godsend and a devil's bargain wrapped in an inconspicuous package. I tried to tend to myself quickly, knowing that Kent would soon arrive. My body had different ideas. Like every other instance where I tried to relieve my tension, thoughts of Kent worked my desire to feverish heights, but nothing pushed me over as hard as I needed to be pushed.

Today was no different. After a minor orgasm, I collapsed against the sink while a mini-breakdown took over. Why did he have so much power over me, and how was I ever supposed to wrest it from him? As frustration built inside me, I sobbed my hatred for the man who held me in invisible shackles.

I didn't know how long I sat there pouring my emotional burdens out through my tears, but I had to get a grip. When I caught my breath, I stared at the wrecked woman in the mirror, a grown up version of the teenaged girl who ran away from Douglas and her memories. I hated that girl and thought I had erased her from my current life, but reminders of her never disappeared. In the reflection of my glossy brown eyes, she stared back at me, wondering when she would be enough.

"No," I whispered while straightening my stance and glaring the girl into oblivion. "I'm nothing like you, anymore."

I washed away the signs of distress and reapplied my makeup with shaky hands until they no longer trembled and the girl in the mirror faded. One good thing came from this recent session in the bathroom. I'd firmed my resolve. Kent would not see me weak.

As I stepped out of the bathroom, the first thing I noticed was the frosted glass enclosing the office in privacy. Earlier when I walked into the bathroom, the walls were clear and everyone filing in to start their day could see me. A frisson of awareness skated along my back.

"How often do you use that fancy piece of jewelry at the office?" Kent's voice startled me. He sat behind his desk, a mask of mild curiosity hiding his thoughts from me. "Well?" His prodding made one thing clear.

I covered my necklace as shame washed over me. "How do you know about this?"

"I'm not used to sharing my bathroom." He stood and advanced on me. "Imagine my surprise when I opened the door to you moaning my name. Pleading for me, not that ineffective toy, to give you what you needed."

"That's not... Don't get the wrong idea." I squared my shoulders, recalling the anger I'd exited the bathroom with and allowing it to override my embarrassment.

"How could I? After all, you made it clear to me you don't desire me." He rubbed the cheek I'd slapped after he'd kissed me. "So what I witnessed must have been a fever dream."

Slowly, I backed away from his approach. He'd caught me, but I could salvage things. I had to. "Mr. Lux—"

"My name is Kent. I know you know it. Heard you moaning...no, begging me by name to give you what you so desperately needed. Now, say! My! Name!" he demanded, towering over me.

It was hard to resist submitting to his domineering presence, but I was no longer the type to bow under pressure, I reminded myself. I didn't run and hide to lick my wounds. Not after he rejected me. And if I stood any chance to make him hurt, if only for a fraction of the pain he'd inflicted on me, I had to stand strong. I had to erase the power he held over me. I had to hold firm against the raging desire buffeting me at both ends. His and mine. What a potent combination. Passion this strong toppled empires, but I wouldn't let it best me. Self-preservation demanded I fight with what little I had in my arsenal.

"Mr. Luxe—"

He wrapped his fingers around my neck and brought my face close enough to his that the golden flecks in his blue eyes distracted me from my precarious position. "Defiant little girls get punished, and you've more than earned what's coming to you."

I glared at him, trying to pull away, but he held firm. "I'm no little girl."

His lips twitched as he took me in from the top of my twist out to the bottom of my stilettos. "I suppose not, and your punishment will reflect that."

"I already told you I have a daddy, and I don't need another."

"Good thing I'm not looking to be your daddy, isn't it?" He hauled me over to his desk and bent me over the icy surface.

With a few hard yanks, he pulled my skirt above my hips and dragged my panties below my knees. I pushed up against the desk, but his heavy palm against my spine held me in place.

"Mr. Luxe—Ah!"

His hand met the flesh of my ass, the sound harsh and erotic in the confined space. Despite the noise, each contact, though firm, wasn't painful after the initial sting.

"First, you lied to me. Teased me. Defied me. Had me so fucked up in the head that I thought you hated our kiss." With each offense I'd perpetrated against him, he slapped my butt, warming the area. "You made me want you...crave you as I've never done for anyone. And you know the worst thing?" His blows turned to gentle caresses, soothing my inflamed skin and reigniting my desire.

"What else have I done to warrant this punishment?" I sobbed, not from his disciplining me, but because the tears pouring from my eyes were releasing a heavy burden that my earlier bout failed to do. The remembered pain and humiliation began to dim, and the weight that had bogged me down for years became lighter with my outpouring.

Kent inhaled, and I knew that amid my tears he could smell the perfume from my desire permeating the air. His voice broke as he confessed, "Worst of all, you've been living in agony, and I could have helped." Kent released the pressure on my back and fixed my clothes. Soon, soothing circles warmed my spine as I continued to cry.

When the last tear was wrung from my body, he helped me stand. "Will you follow me upstairs? I have something I need to say to you, and the office isn't the right place for it."

With all my resistance and fight gone, I nodded while avoiding eye contact. I wasn't strong enough to see pity in his eyes. I'd rather the anger and disdain he held for me.

He led me onto the elevator and to his penthouse. Inside, he sat me on the living room sofa. "Please look at me." He squeezed my hand, making me aware for the first time that he hadn't let go of me since we were in the office.

Tentatively, I raised my gaze to his. Warmth and regret greeted me. He pushed a lock of my hair behind my ear. "I owe you an apology... more than one, if I'm being honest. I hope after I reveal everything, you'll understand me a little and we can work past the anger, resentment, and hatred."

Speechless and too exhausted to fight him any longer, I nodded.

"Last night, I saw you in a different light and it made me shine one on myself. You see, I had numbed myself for years after Lola's death. As you've probably guessed, I used women who could never remind me of my wife to move on. I thought it worked until it didn't. Then you returned and brought up painful memories that I hadn't worked through."

"I don't understand. I was the only one that walked away hurt." I hugged myself, reliving his crushing response to my confession.

"Which is the first of many apologies I owe you. I was the adult back then and should have taken more care with you. I see now the role I played and regret my tactless responses then and now."

"But what does that incident between us have to do with your wife's death?"

"Nothing and everything." Kent stood and paced the living room as silence descended between us.

In the moments it took for him to gather his thoughts, I observed him and found details I had missed during our interaction downstairs. Dark circles underlined his eyes, a testament to his time reflecting on our situation. Lines bracketed his mouth, and his hair wasn't in its pristine, gelled do.

"What I have to tell you, not many people know, including Ife." Kent returned to sit across from me. "Lola's death was preventable."

"How? I thought her injuries from the car accident were too severe."

"After you two left for your graduation trip around Asia, Oyinlola went to meet a man. I'd been so busy burying myself in a new project to expand my location into the Chinese market, I neglected my wife. I assumed she knew things were only temporary because I'd never stopped loving or being in love with her. She never complained about my long hours, and by the time she confessed what had happened leading up to her accident, it was too late."

"She cheated on you?"

"For years I wished she had. Then maybe she wouldn't have been driving." At my look of confusion, Kent continued. "The man who gained her attention was my business rival, Duncan Trent. Rumors surrounded him, just like they're circling me right now. The difference is the stories about him were true, but Lola knew nothing about him. He used his charm to lure her to a hotel, but by then she'd changed her mind."

"I know I don't have the high ground here, but I always knew Oyinlola was loyal and would never hurt you. One of the reasons I fell deeper in love with you was because of her. Your wife embodied everything I wanted to be, and she had your devotion. I know I tried to take that from her—"

"You were a kid. I've stopped blaming you for your actions back then. You should, too."

"So what happened when Oyinlola changed her mind? And how do you know what went down if she died soon after?"

"Lola's sense of honesty prevailed. She showed up at Duncan's room to tell him she'd changed her mind. Sorry, I need a drink to finish the rest of this. I didn't realize it would be so hard since I haven't spoken about it to anyone." Kent disappeared and returned with a glass filled to the brim with some kind of brown liquor. In his other hand, he carried two bottles of what I assumed was the same alcohol in the glass.

I took the two from his hands. "Probably be best to pace yourself if you want to get through everything tonight," I said.

Kent raised his eyes to mine. Within their depths, I saw a lost man wandering through painful memories. "Where was I? Oh, yeah. Lola told Duncan she couldn't go through with an affair, but he trapped her in that room." He emptied his glass and poured another healthy portion from the bottle I'd taken.

"When he finished... violating her, he allowed her to leave. She was hurt, traumatized, and abused. She shouldn't have been behind the wheel, but she was because I'd failed her. I was supposed to protect her. I'd promised to show her my love for her every day, but I broke that promise."

"Oh, Kent."

"You asked how I knew? Because Lola would never keep a secret that big from me." As tears silently dripped down his face, Kent closed his eyes. "Maybe if I hadn't shown up at the hospital after her surgery, she would have had time to calm down. But she woke up to find me beside her, and I think that broke her. She confessed everything to me. While begging for my forgiveness and as the monitors went haywire, she cried so hard that she ruptured her incisions. Can you imagine? While begging me, the most unworthy husband alive for forgiveness, she bled out before the doctors could answer the alarm. And I watched helplessly as I lost my wife."

"Why are you telling me this? Do you want me to feel bad? Because I do. I never meant her any harm, and she didn't deserve what happened."

"No, she didn't, but don't misunderstand. I'm not telling you this to guilt you." Kent rubbed his chest as the brackets around his mouth deepened. "I needed you to know what happened. Because until you showed up, I hadn't felt anything deep enough to move me, and I hated it was you of all people, to make me feel again. I honestly don't know what this means long-term, but I'm tired of fighting myself when you're right here. And now that I've glimpsed the hell you've been living in, I don't think I can stay away from you even if I wanted to."

"This is a lot to take in," I said. "And I don't think after everything else, I should make decisions right now."

"I understand, and I won't rush you..."

"I sense a but."

"It's just that... I'd really like to hold you."

His response surprised me and filled me with warmth. All this time I'd been tempting his lust, but instead of pushing for it, he demanded a different level of intimacy.

"I'll be honest. Having you in my arms is partly selfish. I need to know that you'll be okay after what I did downstairs, but above that, I'm hoping we can soothe each other's pain. We've been carrying it around for eight years. Aren't you exhausted?"

I hugged myself as I thought about his request. "Where did you want to hold me?"

"We could lie on the couch or in the bedroom. Wherever you're comfortable."

Now that my emotions have leveled out, I scanned the room. This was my first time in Kent's penthouse, but I couldn't be comfortable here. This was the place he brought his one-night stands. Meaningless hookups that had no future.

"Can we go somewhere else? Your house if it isn't too painful… or a hotel. Maybe the other penthouse," I rushed to add when his eyes widened in shock.

"I haven't brought a woman home since Lola."

"The downstairs penthouse, then." I nodded, a little disappointed, although I understood.

CHAPTER 10

ent

I led Madison to the elevator. Though a sense of relief stayed with me, the disappointment I'd glimpsed in her eyes when I mentioned my house was a boulder-sized weight on my shoulders.

Instead of clicking the button to go to the second penthouse, I selected the garage. She turned questioning eyes on me, but I didn't have the words needed to explain my actions. I let her wonder in silence if I was taking her to a hotel, but doing so felt too impersonal after what we'd experienced.

We traveled in silence to my house, but when Madison stood at the threshold, she paused.

"Why?" she asked.

I looked at the home I'd shared with Oyinlola, the place Ife still found comfort in. There were so many bittersweet moments under this roof that I forced myself to face whenever Ife visited. But one thing had changed. The pain I avoided was no longer a raging menace, and it was thanks to Madison. Suddenly, the words that escaped me crystallized.

"I can't expect you to explore these feelings we have for each other if I can't show you I'm ready to move on from Lola. And I want the chance to rewrite *our* history in this house and give you something positive to remove the sting from what I did the last time you were here."

"You've been agonizing over this before I made my request, haven't you?"

I shrugged, not proud of my behavior but wanting with everything inside me to overcome my shortcomings and gain something more with Madison.

She stepped through the house. Not much had changed over the years. A cleaning service came in every week to maintain the space, but all the furniture and photos were in their usual spots. As Madison trailed her fingers over wooden surfaces and photo collages, I watched from inside the door.

My instincts were right. Seeing her here didn't cause a violent revolt inside me.

"About what happened in your office..."

My body stiffened at her words. I hadn't planned the punishment I doled out, neither could I say how I felt about it. Despite restraining the power of my blows, I'd done something out of character, and Madison had every right to call the police on me.

"I didn't know how much I needed that kind of release. If ever things build up for me like that again, would you... I can't believe I'm asking for this." She shook her head while avoiding eye contact with me.

"You want me to punish you in the event you act up?"

"I guess that's what I'm saying."

I strode to her and took her shoulders in my hands until she found the courage to look at me. "I'll try to give you what you need, but only if you promise to tell me to stop when you've had enough. The damage I could have done today... I don't want to think about how bad it could have been. That's another reason I need the day with you." I pulled her toward the couch and lay our bodies on the soft cushions.

Madison willingly came into my arms and I breathed my first free breath in days as her body sank into mine. "Thank you for bringing me here."

I kissed the hair on top of her head, reveling in the soft curls. "Thank you for giving me a second chance."

For hours we didn't move except to talk. I satisfied my curiosity about her meteoric rise as the owner of such a successful crisis management company. In listening to her impassioned speech about her company and employees, Hayden Mills' question popped into my head. Now that I wanted to be ready for her, I couldn't imagine her leaving in a month.

"You've come a long way at a young age. Do you have plans to expand your operation?"

"I hadn't thought about it. People come to me, but I've had a few clients recently that have required extensive travel. Having satellite offices in strategic cities might be my next option."

Her vague response left an emptiness inside me, but now wasn't the time to rush into anything. We had to get to know each other, though I was certain I would only grow to admire Madison more than I did.

When her stomach grumbled, I ordered food, as the house hadn't been stocked in months. Even as we ate, I couldn't stomach too much distance between us and sat beside her, our legs pressed against each other.

As we packed away the containers, my phone rang. Omar's name on the screen prompted me to respond. Although I was taking the day off, I didn't have the luxury to ignore Omar's calls. He knew to disturb me for emergencies only when I played hooky.

"Kent?" he asked before I said a word. His frantic voice and the sirens in the background put me on alert.

Madison paused. A concerning frown pulled at her lips.

I motioned her over. "What's wrong?"

"It's Elsie. God!" The typically even-tempered Omar had disappeared. His distraught response alarmed me.

"What happened to Elsie?" I put the call on speakerphone.

Madison gripped my arm and sat down heavily beside me.

"Someone attacked her. We're on the way to Douglas General in an ambulance right now, but I think you should meet us there."

Voices calling out dosages and statuses sounded in the background as EMTs worked on Elsie.

"Madison and I'll be there soon. Did you call the police?"

"Not yet." Omar's shuddered breath shook me.

"Don't worry, I'll take care of it." Madison pulled out her phone to place the call.

"Omar, hang in there."

The ride to the hospital was fraught with worry and tension. Although I tried not to think about it, I wondered if the person murdering my past dates was at fault. The police had heard nothing new and had found no new bodies. Was Elsie a victim of the person targeting me?

We pulled into the parking area and rushed to the emergency room. Omar spotted us before we spotted him. He appeared aged and haggard compared to when I saw him yesterday.

"She's still in surgery but should be in intensive care soon. They won't tell me much else because I'm not family," he said.

"Tell us what happened. I'll need to contact Elsie's parents, her agency, her—"

"Madison, take a breath." I glanced around the crowded waiting room. "Let's find a quiet place to talk."

"The cafeteria's pretty empty. Follow me." Omar sped through the halls until we reached the dining area.

From the sparsely populated tables, we'd missed the lunch rush. After choosing a table away from everyone else, Omar spoke.

"Elsie and I were supposed to go on a lunch date. She told me to pick her up in her building's garage. When I pulled up, I saw a man standing over someone on the ground. All I could see were her crumpled legs."

"Did you get a good look at him?" I asked.

Omar shook his head. "I wish. I don't even know if I did the right thing by not going after him, but Elsie wasn't responding. There was so much blood around her head and she wasn't conscious." He slammed his fist against the table.

Madison cupped his hand. "Listen, we have to believe she'll pull through."

Omar sobbed. "Even if she does, she may never be the same. The asshole cut her face!"

Madison and I shared a glance, knowing what damage to Elsie's face could do to her career.

"There's no use staying here since we won't hear when she'll be up for visitors."

Omar silently agreed, and we headed toward the ICU's waiting room. When we entered, Detectives Glass and Salinas were arguing with a nurse to let them in to see Elsie. Glass noticed me first.

"Mr. Luxe, may I ask what brings you here?"

"I'm acquainted with Elsie and am concerned about her condition."

"How'd you hear about the attack?" Salinas came up behind me, suspicion in his voice. "The 911 call came from a Madison Montgomery."

"That's me. We were together when Omar called to tell us what happened." Madison maneuvered between me and the detective, as if shielding me from his ill intent.

"Looks like you have an alibi for when the attack took place," Glass said. "While we wait for the patient to wake up, I'd like to speak to this Omar person you mentioned."

"I'm right here." Omar stood to face the officers. "I don't know much, but I'll tell you what I saw."

"Don't you work for Mr. Luxe?" Salinas asked. The implication that he considered Omar's connection with me, a suspect in previous murders, was clear in his tone.

"I do."

"Why were you at the scene of the attack?"

Omar relayed the same information he'd told Madison and me

earlier, though under more grilling and a heavy air of suspicion. While Omar answered the same set of questions, albeit phrased differently, a doctor entered the waiting room looking for Omar.

Detective Glass pushed Omar aside to say, "Is the patient awake?"

"Yes, but she can only see one person at a time." The doctor turned to the detectives. "I respect your profession, but that rule also applies to you. One of you has to stay out here."

The police officers whispered to each other before Glass nodded and left the room. Meanwhile, Omar engaged the doctor with questions.

Salinas and I stared each other down until Madison pulled at my arm. "Now's not the time for pissing off the cops. I think something about the attack must have a connection with the other cases they've linked to you."

I turned away from the aggravating officer to give Madison my attention. "I think so, too. Otherwise, the police wouldn't have sent homicide detectives to investigate."

"But what I don't understand is the cut on Elsie's face. None of the other victims were marked that way, and it feels personal. Like something a disgruntled ex-boyfriend would do."

We walked over to a secluded area to share our thoughts.

"Although Elsie is famous and I'm sure we share some social circles, I doubt I've had dealings with an ex of hers. Or that he would take issue with the other women I've dated."

"Maybe he read the news and tried to mimic the other crimes?" Madison bit her lip as she pondered. "If you're involved, the only people who knew about you and Elsie were attendees at the Children's Hospital fundraiser. I'll get a list and cross reference the people there with people you have in common."

I folded my arms, imagining the daunting task. "That sounds like a lot to take on."

"You're right, but I have a team to help. And the sooner we clear you, the sooner your company will recover from the negative press."

Omar joined us, his face less worn after hearing Elsie would pull through. Madison and I shared our impressions, which caused him to frown.

"I hate to break it to you, but Elsie hasn't had a boyfriend since high school. All the men linked to her were arrangements like the one she has with Kent. I doubt a guy that far back is coming around now, especially from where she grew up. He's probably working his family's farm and has no idea what Elsie's done with her life."

At that moment, Glass barged into the room and made his way toward Omar. Salinas rushed to join his partner.

"Omar, are you certain the person you saw was a man?" Glass demanded.

"Yes, I'm sure."

"Did you notice any women in the area? Maybe before you entered the garage?"

Omar frowned as he concentrated, but shook his head. "No, I wasn't paying close attention."

"Why are you asking about a woman?" Madison asked.

"Because before she was hit in the head, Elsie heard a woman's voice say, 'Kent belongs to me, bitch.'"

"So, how does the man factor in all this?" I looked at everyone but could find no answers in their responding stares.

CHAPTER 11

ent

My apartment was too quiet. Even the heater ran on silent as if tiptoeing around me like everyone else since the news of Elsie's attack. Throughout the company, I was on the receiving end of suspicious glances. Again.

My innocence in question. Again.

And I had to walk around pretending the shit didn't affect me. I wasn't made of steel. Women had lost their lives, and this recent attack on Elsie hit harder.

Because it touched Madison. Although her relationship with Elsie on the outside seemed professional, the warmth and personal touch she used while handling Elsie's career spoke to a deeper connection. So, it was no surprise to me when Madison started skipping meals and working late to do what the police hadn't done since the first body appeared.

I wanted to admire her for her dedication, but I the dark circles under her eyes and those unappetizing protein drinks she used as meal replacements pissed me off. I didn't demand my employees to work long hours, and I didn't expect them from her.

I rolled onto my back, frustrated by my sleeplessness and the worry keeping my rest at bay. The clock on my nightstand read 2:33 AM.

Fed up and too tense to relax, I flung the sheets from my body and put on a robe. With my mind too wired, and a sneaking suspicion I hoped to debunk, I took the elevator to my office.

The doors slid open to a darkened office. I sighed in relief until I glanced in the corner where Madison spent most of her day. An eerie blue glow sparked my curiosity. As I approached, an eerie outline from the light took shape, causing my tense muscles to tighten even more.

I turned on the light but Madison's concentration never shifted from her screen. On her desk, two empty protein drinks lay on their sides next to her empty coffee cup and crumpled snack bar wrappers. Surrounding her bent body, discarded trash, papers, and photos covered the available surface on her desk.

"Have you moved since I left?"

"Eek!" She screamed and jumped in her chair. She swiveled her chair and clutched her hand to her chest while glaring at me. "You scared me."

"Answer me."

Her eyes widened and she lurched from her chair, sending it spinning toward the wall. She sprinted past me. "Oh, shit."

The wind from her speed blew my robe open. Momentarily speechless, I watched as she slammed the bathroom door. While waiting for her to come out, I got a closer look at her desk.

Madison was building family histories and connections of the victims for people to investigate that the police haven't questioned. A Post-it note caught my eye. A man's name, address, and time for later today stared at me.

She couldn't be thinking of meeting a stranger on her own. Not after what the police said about Elsie's attacker. I closed my eyes and repeated all the reasons she wouldn't endanger herself. I needed the time to calm myself or the minute she returned I would unleash my temper on her.

"Sorry about that. Whew, I was holding that in for… I don't even know how long." Madison laughs, her voice full of relief.

Before she sat again, I grabbed her elbow to stop her. "You didn't answer me."

The tension in her body wasn't typical. Feeling her arm flexing under my hold reminded me of another time I took her in hand when she refused to admit she was hurting. Her body was so tightly held, the wrong move could have snapped her. Only by a miracle did I stumble upon a solution she needed. But this situation was different. Wasn't it?

She shrugged my hand off. "Don't worry about it." She retrieved her chair, sat, and flipped through a few papers, already engrossed in whatever I walked in on earlier. "I think I've found someone who can—"

"Madison!" I take a deep breath. "What you're doing is unhealthy. You need rest."

She paused with her hand over a document. "I've told you before, I don't need another daddy."

"Madison…" I gritted, trying to keep myself calm. "When was the last time you slept? And I mean for more than two hours at a time."

She swiveled her chair to frown at me. "Mr. Luxe—"

"That's it." I pulled her from her seat while she resisted. "I've tried to be understanding. Watched you compromise your health. That shit stops now." I dragged her toward the elevator, but she managed to free herself and walk away from me.

"You're being ridiculous for no good reason. The sooner I find who attacked Elsie, the sooner I clear yo—"

I swung her into my arms.

"Kent put me down!"

Recognizing her stubbornness for what it was, I put her in the same position I'd put her in the day things changed between us: bending over my desk. "Woman, I admire your ambition, your work ethic, and your dedication, but I will not see you sacrificing your health for it." I shoved her pants and underwear down her legs.

Madison stopped wriggling when I caressed her ass. "Kent?" A note of anticipation rang in her voice. No more defiance. No more putting distance between us by not using my goddamn name.

I slap her fleshy rear. "That's right. Call me Kent. If you call me Mr. Luxe again, I'll prolong your punishment."

"Ow!"

I rubbed the area I'd hit. "Want me to stop?" I hovered my hand over her butt as I waited.

Seconds ticked on and I began to question if she'd meant what she said the last time I bent her over my desk.

"Keep going." The words seemed pulled from deep within her as if in the silence she'd fought a battle with her pride before succumbing to her need for my discipline.

I spanked her again. And again.

She squirmed and whimpered.

"Nobody's here, little bunny. You can scream if you need to let it out."

I landed another smack to her other cheek.

This time, she let herself loose.

"Please!" she cried, her sobs coming faster with each blow.

Between hits, I rubbed the area turning a darker shade of brown and trying not to get distracted by the intoxicating scent rising from between her thighs or the way her ass bounced from the impact. As hard as I was with the need to undo my pants and shove myself inside her, two reasons stopped me.

As turned on as she'd gotten, this wasn't about sex. Madison needed to understand I would never sit by and watch while she neglected her needs and her health. If I was going to be her man, then I would *be* her man. Be the person to ensure she lived a long, happy life, fulfilling life.

"Kent..." she sobbed while wiggling her delectable ass. "I'm sorry."

"What are you sorry for? Don't say the words if you don't know what got you over my desk in the first place."

Her ass was warm to the touch. I glanced around my desk and grabbed the glass paperweight to rub the chilled surface on her warmed skin.

"Mmm. I'm sorry for worrying you."

"Is that all?"

Her body stilled. With a sigh, I rested the paperweight beside her and began a new barrage onto her vulnerable ass.

"Okay, okay! I'm sorry for not eating right or sleeping. I'll do better, I swear."

Her admission lifted a weight off my shoulders, and I blanketed her with my body, my chin rested on her shoulder.

"Thank you, little bunny. Now let's get you to bed." I pushed off her and knelt to pull up her pants and underwear.

Her glistening skin and intoxicating fragrance stalled me.

My mouth watered, tempered by a thirst I needed to control. Yet the hand reaching out to her silken thighs acted on its own. The finger swiping through the stream slowly trickling down thick warm flesh did so against my better judgment. And my traitorous mouth opening to receive the offering was a betraying asshole.

I groaned as her flavor touched my tongue. Sweetness exploded and every reason I had not to make this sexual taunted me. I shook my head free of her temptation, though I wasn't completely success-ful. Before I made a hypocrite of myself, I pulled up her clothes.

When I allowed her up from the desk, her eyes were glossy from tears she shed, her lips plump from holding in her screams, and a healthy flush warmed her face.

Madison was an innocent, sultry goddess and she didn't know what it took for me to hold back and not wring more noises from her lips while swallowing her pleasure.

"It's too late for you to go home. Stay in the penthouse." I held my hand out to her.

She glanced at my appendage, then my very obvious hard on with a question in her eyes, but she didn't voice it and I didn't want to speculate. Desire rode high in her gaze, and it wasn't for another punishment.

I showed her to the bedroom. "Wait here and I'll get you something to change into."

I made the trip upstairs and back in seconds to hand her my favorite T-shirts. It was old and faded but soft to the touch and very loose on me.

"Thanks." She took the shirt. "Don't leave."

"I'll be here," I assured her with a gentle smile.

She nodded, then headed to the bathroom to change.

When she reemerged, I nearly swallowed my tongue. My favorite shirt became my favorite again for an entirely different reason. The material clung to her body, accentuating every dip of her thick, curvy frame. Her belly, so soft and round while the shirt dipped into her belly button taunted me, telling me, "Look at what I can touch that you can't."

Her hips stretched the material, transforming a loose piece of clothing into a lethal body con dress she had no business wearing.

"Okay, get some sleep and I'll see you in the morning." I swung around to leave.

"You aren't staying the night? With me?" Her vulnerable question stopped me mid-step.

"Little bunny, I don't think it's a good idea."

"Oh... Okay. See you in the morning."

I made it to the elevator with her forlorn voice ringing in my ear before I stopped and banged my head against the wall. I spun around and marched into her bedroom, throwing my robe in the corner.

She was already under the covers and reaching for the light switch. When she saw me, her eyes widened. "I thought—"

"Me too." I pull back the comforter and lie down. "Turn off the light."

Once she followed my command, I stopped resisting and dragged her body into mine, soaking in the pleasurable torment of having Madison in my arms.

"I could take care of that for you." She slipped her hand down my abs on a journey that would ensure she got no sleep.

I grabbed her hand and kissed her palm. "Another time. He needs to learn discipline and doesn't deserve a reward tonight."

Madison burst into a surprised chuckle before settling deeper into my embrace. "Thank you for tonight."

I kissed her forehead and waited for her to fall asleep, which happened faster than I expected, proving she was running on fumes. As I held her, my earlier sleeplessness didn't return. My body sank deeper into the mattress as relaxation removed the tension from my body.

I kissed Madison's forehead again. My second reason for not wanting to make tonight about sex was I wanted our first time to be about us, not because I turned something she needed to get out of her system about satisfying my lust. Otherwise, the way I felt about Madison, once we crossed that boundary, we would never leave the bed.

CHAPTER 12

*M*adison

"That's the place." I pointed toward a house that had seen better days.

"You're sure?" Kent slowed the car to a crawl.

We were in a lower middle-class neighborhood. Modest homes with better upkeep lined the streets. Most of the neighbors took pride in their houses with recent paint or siding and landscaping featuring neat lawns. Nothing I saw warranted Kent's caution.

"It's the address Mr. Edelman gave me."

"Remind me, why are we the ones asking him instead of forwarding his information to the police?" He parked by the curb in front of the address I'd jotted down.

I glared at Kent. My ass was still tender after this morning's punishment, but that wasn't why I gave him the sink eye. "If you think I'm going to entrust your future to those inept detectives, you don't know me. They don't like you because you're an entitled asshole—"

"Come again?"

"Kent, I have deep feelings for you but I'm not blind. You were an asshole to me, your employees have talked about it on the BBD site, and you were almost insufferable to the detectives at the hospital. Now, I'm not saying your behavior isn't always warranted, but don't think I don't see you for who you are, flaws and all."

Kent stared at me from the corner of his eye. "Are my flaws a deal breaker?"

"For years I wished they were. Wished and begged for my heart to come to terms with the darkness inside you." I rested my head against the headrest and watched the empty street before us. "But then I'd remember how you were with Ife and Oyinlola, and me before I revealed my feelings for you. If I haven't been able to rip you out of my heart by now, I don't think I ever will."

Kent took my hand and pressed his lips against my palm. "Thank you for not trying to change me, but if I go to that dark place, know it will be to protect you, not hurt you." He kissed my palm again and closed his eyes.

I brushed his hair behind his ear and cradled his cheek in my free hand, savoring the way his beard tickled my palm. "I—"

A loud knock on my window scared me into pulling away. I shrieked and held my hand against my rapidly beating heart.

"Are you the woman I spoke to last night?" Fred Edelman, the man I found with a connection to four of the dead women, said with an impatient frown. "I got a call from my cafe manager about an emergency. So I'll have to cancel on you."

I rolled down the window and offered Fred an understanding smile. "I understand. Your time is not your own when you run a business as popular as yours."

"Thanks." He glanced toward his house, his frown morphing into a contemplative one. "If you want, you can follow me and ask your questions there. At least then I won't feel bad about wasting your time."

"Not a problem. We'll follow you." Kent reached across me and out my window to shake Fred's hand. "I'm Kent."

"Yeah, Fred. See you in a bit," Fred distractedly said and quickly shook Kent's hand before hurrying to the waiting car in his open garage.

We followed him for the forty-minute drive to an up-and-coming restaurant district in downtown Douglas. When we arrived at the cafe, Brewfully Yours, Fred sat us at an outdoor table and had his servers wait on us. The service was as good if not better than I'd read about.

"How'd you find this guy? His name never came up as a potential witness in any of the police reports you compiled or from what my people could find." Kent took a sip of his cappuccino and his body relaxed into his chair.

"That good?"

"Try it." He handed me his cup.

I licked my lips, less interested in the coffee. I turned the cup until the drop he'd left behind on the rim aligned with my mouth and sipped with my eyes closed. "Mmm."

"Madison, behave. We're in public and if you don't want me explaining to passersby why I have my cock in your mouth, save those sounds for when we're alone." Kent growled, his eyes glowed with lust as his vision narrowed on my lips.

I smirked, not afraid of his warning. I've had too many nights of wanting to know how he felt in my mouth to be intimidated by a bunch of strangers.

"Sorry, it took so long." Fred slumped into a chair beside me. "I might have five minutes before they need me again." He glanced between Kent and me, but returned to Kent time and again. "What questions do you have?"

I pulled a picture of the first murdered woman from her Instagram profile. She was with her friends, dressed in activewear after attending her gym. In the background, Fred stood talking to people at the table beside hers. From my research, I learned Fred made a habit of getting to know his customers.

"Fred, do you know this woman?"

He took the picture and studied it. "Yes, but I thought I saw on the news she died." He peeked at Kent, his face closing up.

"She did. I hope you can help us with some other clues. Her death is still unsolved and there have been others since," I said, bringing his attention back to me.

I retrieved the other photos I collected from the other murder victims. All from Instagram. All in various clothes from brunch chic to executive on a break. All with various friends.

"Shouldn't you be asking him?" Fred nodded at Kent.

"I have, but he hadn't seen any of the women the months leading up to their murders. So I looked at things they had in common and found your shop."

Fred narrowed his eyes at me. "Are you suggesting I had something to do with their deaths?"

"Not at all. I'm hoping you remembered something from when they were here that could help with the investigation. The police are stalled, and a friend of mine almost became another victim to whoever's targeting the women he's"—I nodded toward Kent—"been seen with."

"I don't know how much help I can be."

His manager came to the table and whispered in his ear.

"Sorry, I have to handle this. Leave the pictures and I'll try to jog my memory."

I handed him the photos and watched him head toward the back of the cafe.

"I don't know, but it's worth a shot if it means clearing your name." I reached over the tabletop to hold his hand.

He squeezed my hand then laced our fingers together. "Well, what's next?"

"I want to stick around a while longer. From how busy he is, he'll likely forget about us."

"Fine by me. I've been eyeing a pastry I wanted to try." Kent raised his arm and ordered a white chocolate raspberry shortcake.

When it arrived, he pulled my chair next to him, cut into the pastry, and raised it to my lips. I opened my mouth without thought and hummed as the perfectly balanced dessert hit my tastebuds.

"Madison approved, I see. Now, let's discover if it's Kent approved."

Instead of cutting another portion, Kent gripped my nape and angled my face toward his. The blue of his eyes glowed with a feral light as he homed in on my lips.

"Open for me Madison. Let me taste how good the dessert is."

I did his bidding. Of course I did. Ever since Kent and I cleared up our issues, Kent treated me as too delicate to overwhelm with his need. His kisses were too few for my liking, and he cut short whenever I initiated, always teasing me with what could happen.

Dammit, I wanted what could happen and I wanted this kiss now. As soon as his lips touched mine, I was a goner. I always was. This time, I didn't have to fight myself. Didn't have to pretend I wasn't kissing the man who no other could come close to replacing. And that was before I knew his taste.

I wrapped my arms around his neck, uncaring of any random person with an issue about public displays of affection. I was greedy for Kent. Would always be. And there wasn't a person who could stop me from giving him all I am whenever he asked.

His thumb rubbed circles on my cheek. The innocent flutter against my skin while he devastated my mouth with his plundering tongue, set off new fireworks in my blood.

"Kent," I moaned, needing more.

He tugged on my arms until I reluctantly freed him. When we parted, his stare was wilder than before, but he reigned himself in whereas I had trouble recovering from our embrace.

"Definitely Kent approved." He pulled away and was about to feed me another mouthful when Fred reappeared.

"Good, you're still here. I felt bad leaving the way I did, but it looks like everything is under control now." He eyed the nonexistent distance between Kent and me. "Do you still want me to answer questions?" He placed the photos I'd given him earlier on the tabletop.

"Yes," I slurred, then shook my head to refocus on the matter. "Can you think back to any time these women were here if there was another person who looked suspicious? Maybe someone who showed them more interest. Came when they came and left when they left? Man or woman?"

"That's hard. I have a good memory, but not that good. You're asking me to recall something from over a half a year ago." He rubbed the stubble on his chin as he tried to remember anything to help us.

I reshuffled the photographs, trying to identify familiar faces.

Kent, who'd been quiet until now, leaned forward to inspect the pictures as well. He pulled one from the group.

"Do you recognize someone?" I asked.

"Not sure." He stared at a corner in the image before shaking his head. "I can't be positive."

"But there's a person who reminds you of somebody?" I pushed because we had nothing.

Kent returned the photo before snagging Fred's attention. "Is Paulina Finch a regular?"

"Paulina?" Fred broke into a smile. "She's a guest of honor whenever she comes around. She did me a huge favor and sped up my permits and licenses before I opened. I didn't know what the hell I was doing and was looking at delaying my opening and losing a ton of money. We call her Brewfully Yours' fairy godmother. She's always been flattered by the moniker and stops by two to three times a week."

"Is she significant somehow?" I retrieved the discarded photo.

Behind the now deceased woman, the photographer captured a partial profile of a woman seated with a blonde. Unfortunately, the other woman was facing away from the camera and only her hair and the back of her shirt was captured. I made a note to myself to forward the image to my team to enhance the corner. Even if I couldn't identify the second lady, maybe a clearer picture would provide another lead, however of a long shot it might be.

"I can't think how. She's the Director of Boards and Commissions. Unless these women were trying to open a business, they wouldn't have a reason to know her. And given this place's popularity, if the woman in the photo is her, she's there by coincidence."

Fred handed me the rest of the pictures. "Listen, I wish I could think of something, but I can't. Every interaction I recall having with them was normal and nothing from those days pop out as being memorable."

"Thanks anyway. I knew it was a long shot." I packed the pictures away and retrieved my business card. "But if something comes up, please call me. Clearing Kent's name is important, but not as important as giving these women's families the answers they need."

We departed from the cafe in contemplative silence, hand in hand.

"This morning when I found you in the office, I thought you were working so hard because Elsie had been hurt. I didn't realize I was the one driving you to these lengths."

I pulled out of his hold and waited until he turned to look at me. "I like and respect Elsie, but..." I took a deep breath. "As horrible as this will make me sound, it's your safety that drives me. I can't help but fear that whoever is targeting these women will turn their violence on you because you haven't given them something they wanted. And I couldn't live knowing I hadn't done enough to help stop them before they went too far."

"And I don't want you painting a target on your back because we're together now."

"But no one knows about us."

"Yet, and not because I want to hide you from the world."

I swallowed because he was right. I was the one hiding what we were becoming, although I had a lapse with the kiss we shared. I looked from left to right, wondering if anyone was watching us. If I'd exposed our secret because I was desperate for a kiss.

I cleared my throat. "How about a compromise?"

CHAPTER 13

ent

While Madison met with Luxe Locations' in-house public relations, I stared out of my office window, contemplating the state of my affairs. Speculation dogged me everywhere I went, dampening the little joy I'd eked out of life since Lola's passing.

I lived for Ife and my company since her death, almost certain I'd never feel adrenaline pumping through my veins again. Then Madison appeared and my heart raced with excitement. I was rusty at the relationship thing, but rediscovering what it's like to be someone's man again, to think about someone else's needs and provide them... I wanted that. Dreamt of us together for everyone to see.

To think, at the mere suggestion of more than one date from any of the women I've slept with in the past year caused me to ghost them. I'd been running from anything deeper for so long, but with Madison, I had no choice. She was my match in so many ways. She was perfect in a different way than Lola. What I felt for Madison didn't diminish the love I had for my late wife but neither were the growing feelings for Madison any less potent. They were stronger.

And with all the shit thrusting me in the headlines, painting me as a monster, I didn't want Madison's reputation destroyed because of me.

The irony. She only returned to Douglas to rehab my status in society, however she now needed to focus on not being too closely associated with me. And my real worry was her safety. Madison was gifted at re-engineering people's reputations. She could revamp hers whenever she wanted, but she shouldn't have to.

In my mind, whoever was targeting the women I dated months ago was the real danger, and I needed to protect Madison. But how do I convince her without scaring her?

We were still new. Maybe it was my age, but I didn't want to waste time. One benefit of conceding the fight against myself was without the ego and pride blinding me, I had every reason to knock down any barriers to claiming her.

But was she ready?

Despite admitting she hasn't stopped loving me from when she was younger, that was the love of a misguided child. She's a woman now. Did she understand the difference?

Not to mention, yesterday's reminder after our public kiss made her more skittish about publicizing our relationship. I clenched my teeth, hating the secrecy.

"Hey, Kent?" Omar's voice penetrated my contemplative bubble, reminding me I had a business to run. "Just a reminder. You should head out for your monthly lunch with Ms. Finch."

I turn from the scenery I barely noticed to nod at my assistant. "I'll head over now. Call me if Madison heads out before I return."

I headed to Mio Cuore, a DeLuca restaurant where discretion was as important as the famous people who ate there. Although this was a standing meeting, I needed other answers after yesterday's meeting with Fred.

As I approached the entrance, Detectives Glass and Salinas exited.

They hesitated before nodding in greeting toward me. I returned the gesture, but felt their stare even as I disappeared inside the restaurant. For a fleeting moment, I wondered if they were at the restaurant as part of an investigation or for lunch. I couldn't imagine them being able to afford more than an appetizer on a detective's salary, but as long as they weren't hassling me, I wouldn't bother wasting more time on them.

Paulina arrived before me and sat at the table already sipping a glass of wine. A year or two separated our ages but whether genetics or plastic surgery, she appeared to be in her mid thirties rather than a woman entering her fifties. She wore her midnight black hair in a bob, not a single gray strand in sight. Her skin was smooth and her appearance was as slick as any lifetime politician who wielded their power to remain in power.

We exchanged pleasantries while I waited for the server to take my order.

When she turned her head, I compared her profile to the blurry image from the photo I saw yesterday. It was only a partial and I couldn't be sure about the hairstyle. Women changed their colors, cuts, and styles frequently. I never kept up when my wife or daughter came home with a new hairdo, how would I remember when a woman I only interacted with for work wore the same style from months ago or if she'd changed it? With no obvious answer to condemn or clear her of my doubts, I kept my frustration from my face.

Once we were alone, she stared at me over her glass. "You're holding up a lot better than I expected given the headlines."

Already on alert, I peered at her more closely. Maybe I was being too sensitive. Her question referencing the murders surrounding me was a reasonable question, but with the potential danger to Madison, I needed to silence my doubts.

"I'm no stranger to pressure." I snapped my napkin open and laid it on my waist.

Okay, Paulina could have been at the cafe by coincidence. What remained was I had no proof she knew any of the murdered women.

And if she did, what would be her motive for murder? And on top of the multiple killings, why would she frame me?

Paulina and I had a long history of acquaintanceship before we ever started working together. We never became friends despite attending the same high school and undergraduate university. She didn't work in a competing field so we weren't business rivals. She wasn't a jilted lover I'd slept with and left like I'd done since Lola's death. And I'd never threatened her career. Our business had the usual tension endemic to bureaucracy. I won some, lost some. Overall, I had more wins than losses.

So what would be her reason for targeting me and women loosely associated with me?

I gritted my teeth, concluding I'd overreached. The lack of progress in the investigation had me either grasping at straws or had my mind playing tricks on me yesterday. Yes, I wanted this situation to end. The sooner my name was cleared, the sooner Madison's safety would be assured. Regardless, without Paulina commenting something less benign than how I'm not buckling under pressure, I was in the same situation as Madison. Searching for the real person who was after me. At the end of the day, I had to mark Paulina off my list. We had an understanding. She wouldn't hold up my projects for illegitimate or petty reasons, and all I had to do was help her stay in her position. None of those things would inspire a bloodthirsty desire to frame me for multiple murders.

She smiled at my response. "With an answer like that, you should consider entering politics."

"And make my entire day dealing with politicians?" I chuckled and shook my head. "No thanks. I prefer the business world."

"The only difference between our worlds is who you answer to. I answer to the public and you answer to shareholders." She arched her brow as she popped an olive into her mouth.

"Ahh, but I create the bureaucracy within my organization whereas you have to work within one created for you. Not to mention, your tenure is always at risk. I own the majority shares in my company. I and I alone control my tenure."

Silence settled between us as the server placed our the antipasti course in front of us. Another reason Paulina chose Mio Cuore was it served food like traditional Italian restaurants found in rural villages in Italy. Course after course of delectable food to encourage long conversations.

"So you don't intend to step down from your position while the heat is on you?" Paulina asked as she cut into the burrata cheese in her caprese salad.

"Why so interested in the inner workings of my company today, Paulina?"

She shrugged. "Understanding that the leadership in a company won't change while said company has a dozen projects waiting for permits and licensing from my department is understandable. We have a foundation built on trust. Someone new coming in? Not so much."

"Makes sense. However, rest assured, I have no plans to step down. But since you brought up my projects, my two largest ones are being delayed by your department."

"I'll look into it."

"Please do. I provide you with a lot of support to ensure you can continue to approve my business proposals."

"Speaking of..."

For the next two hours, Paulina and I discussed my various properties and the bureaucratic tape even she couldn't intervene on for my benefit. I left disappointed Paulina wasn't involved. She would have solved so many issues for me. How easy would my life be if I could focus on my budding relationship with Madison and not have to worry about someone in the shadows waiting to kill someone else while destroying my life?

CHAPTER 14

$\mathcal{M}$adison

Two weeks passed without word about Elsie's attacker or updates on the multiple murders shrouding Kent's reputation. My contacts in the police and my team hadn't discovered the connection the detectives on the case found that caused them to suspect Kent for Elsie's attack. Other than their one date at the charity gala, there was nothing for the police to paint Kent as the perpetrator.

Although the mystery worried me, Kent made sure it didn't consume me. Another punishment session set me straight, although I wouldn't mind finding ways to be under his hand again. I understood I was stubborn. I was the daughter of *the* Nikita Montgomery after all. Willfulness and pride was woven into my DNA. But under Kent's punishing blows to my ass, I let it all go. He freed me to be vulnerable, to weep when I needed to, with the knowledge he would be there to protect me as I rebuilt myself. Would it be as amazing without the pent-up emotions?

I surveyed my wardrobe as I contemplated the shift in our relationship. Another good thing that came from the fallout and he revealed the reason behind his antagonism toward me, Kent made strides to correct the harm he'd done. I wasn't a teenager any longer, but the wounds were deep. I also wasn't blind to my feelings. There was less infatuation when I looked at him and more awareness of him only a woman could appreciate. And he started looking at me the same way.

One sweet date at a time, Kent began to heal the wounds he'd inflicted. I still had work to do on myself, but I was open to him in ways I had never been before.

We'd gone on four dates already, and tonight would be our fifth. Despite my appreciation for how slowly Kent was taking our romance, I wanted more. My libido was in trouble and my body showed signs of returning to the days when small orgasms caused more pain than relief. And although I wanted to test my theory about the spankings, I wanted penetration more. I wanted to ride him like a professional taming a wild Stallion.

I picked out the sluttiest dress in my closet, banking on weakening Kent's defenses. I tousled my stretched hair, leaving it down and slightly messy. With my smokey-eye makeup and glossy lips, I looked like a woman who had either been fucked or was about to get fucked. There was no way I was returning home tonight.

To ensure my plan worked, I packed an overnight bag because Madison Montgomery did not do walks of shame. With my look finished, I ran downstairs, hoping to avoid my parents. My mother, standing guard in front of the door, told me I hadn't been subtle during my preparations.

She eyed me up and down. "I know you're grown, but I'm asking, anyway. Do you have protection? Because I'm too young to be a grandmother, and that dress is daring a man to knock you up."

"Mom!" I tried to push her gently aside, but she didn't budge until I whispered, "Yes, I have protection, and I'm on birth control. Now, please let me leave before I die of embarrassment."

"I hope, whoever the man is, that he's good enough for my girl."

"He's trying," I said without telling her who he was.

Right now, I wanted to keep my relationship with Kent a secret. When I told him, he agreed, but I sensed his disappointment. I didn't completely trust what was growing between us yet. At the same time, I wanted to explore everything there was to discover with Kent.

She let me leave with a hug and whispered, "If his performance is less than satisfactory, we'll have waffles and ice cream floats tomorrow."

I shook my head as I drove to Kent's second penthouse, a compromise we'd agreed on since I was uncomfortable in the top-floor apartment and his old house was off-limits while we hid our relationship.

Kent met me in his private garage. As soon as I exited the car, a scowl took over his face. "Hell, no. Go back home and change."

Doubts filled me, eroding the confidence I'd built up.

He stood before me and lowered his voice despite being the only two people here. "I'm trying to be good, but you are about to push me over the edge and ruin my plans." Kent slipped his finger beneath the thin strap of my dress and slowly dragged it over my shoulder. His glazed eyes focused on the soft skin he caressed, sounding more strained as he spoke. "You must not expect to go anywhere tonight."

"Would you really waste a pretty dress like this on a night in?"

"Little bunny, don't you know what happens when you tempt a wolf?"

I swallowed at the heat in his voice. "It's just a dress."

"On you, it could never be just a dress." He slipped my other strap down my arm. "No one is worthy enough to see you in this."

"Does that include you?"

"Especially me, nonetheless I'll claim the privilege for myself." He stepped away, putting unnecessary distance between us and leaving me bereft of his touch. "Now, you have a choice to make. You can go home and change, or I'm taking you upstairs, where you won't see another person for the next twenty-four hours. Maybe forty-eight, but seventy-two is also a possibility."

I stared into his fierce gaze, marveling at the muscle ticking in his jaw. With all seriousness, I said, "I'll take 'Fuck me, Kent' for a thousand, Ken."

"Jesus Christ!"

The quick trip upstairs flew by without me remembering how we ended up in the bedroom. As soon as Kent closed the door, time slowed. He took my hands in his and stared deeply at me.

"Tonight will be hard for me." When doubts shouted in my head and I tried to pull away, he tightened his hold on my hands. "I've struggled to be a gentleman with you, not rushing you, and tonight will be no different. Even if every atom in my body demands that I unleash the beast I've kept caged inside myself."

"What if I want your beast?"

Kent closed his eyes as if pained. "Not for our first night. Tonight, I want to cherish you with everything I have. Worship you for the goddess you are. Ruin you one kiss at a time the way you've ruined me."

"But I haven't kissed you."

"You're right. I stole our first kiss and demanded you give me the second. Regardless, I want more, freely given this time. Then after tonight, you won't be able to say you haven't kissed me." He pulled my arms over his shoulder and rested his forehead against mine, need and a pleading I couldn't deny shining from his eyes. "Kiss me, little bunny. Please."

My pussy clenched at the please that came from his lips. It damn near destroyed me. However, now that the moment was upon me, I understood Kent's intent. I wanted this time between us to last. I'd waited years to experience Kent's lips against mine, and I wouldn't squander the opportunity with a rushed crushing of lips.

Gently, I brushed against him, breathing in his air. I lowered my gaze until all I saw were his parted lips, waiting for mine. Our first kiss had been weeks ago, the memory of which had driven me wild every night since. Then our second kiss from last week only reminded me of a craving I hadn't satisfied. Both had faded now and Kent offered me another chance to refresh my recollection of his taste and the texture of his mouth. A chance I wouldn't let pass.

I licked his bottom lip, memorizing the firm softness as he opened his mouth wider. I tempered my desire to plunge inside, preferring to nip and savor and tease his mouth while his beard tickled my chin.

Kent gripped my hips, his fingers digging into my flesh as a moan ripped from his throat. "Little bunny, you're killing me."

"Shush, can't you see I'm busy?"

Before he could respond, I slipped my tongue into his mouth. The wait had been worthwhile. The smooth texture of his tongue coaxed me deeper and the minty mouthwash combined with his natural flavor intoxicated my senses.

Kent, unable to sit through my kiss as a passive bystander, firmed his tongue and dueled with mine. It was my turn to moan into his mouth. I hugged him closer, trying to meld our bodies together as I drowned myself in him.

Once upon a time, I thought I knew what desire was. Thought all those nights of using toys to ease a tension that never disappeared was lust in its purest form. What a fool I was. Giving and receiving was the ultimate experience.

"Kent," I panted as our lips parted.

He cupped my face. Like me, he found breathing difficult. And like me, he drew closer for another taste. Kent pressed his growing erection against my soft belly before pulling away.

"Kent?"

Seeing the confusion and disappointment on my face, he shook his head. "Before we go any further, I need you to understand there's no going back for me. I've only felt this strongly about one other person before, so if you have any doubts about where you see this thing between us going, we should stop now."

I laid my fingers against his lips, bathing in the security of his words. With a request to safeguard himself, he eliminated the questions in my mind about his motives.

"There was no going back for me ever since I turned sixteen." I slipped out of his hands and slid my dress over my curves to pool on the floor. While unsnapping my bra, I asked, "Haven't I waited enough?"

Kent gulped. "Were you ever going to tell me you weren't wearing panties?"

"Would you rather argue with me about what I wore, or deal with my situation?" I pressed my fingers between my pussy lips, then brought them up to show him the glistening digits.

"Fuck, little bunny, you don't play fair."

"This is no game, and I've been ready. How 'bout you?"

Kent removed his jacket and slowly unbuttoned his shirt. As each button slipped through its hole, his actions mesmerized me. His sturdy hands handled the delicate object with care, inspiring images of how he'd handle my body.

When he was fully naked, I marveled at his physique. Kent's suits downplayed his immense size. His arms and thighs were thick like tree trunks, and so was the beast pointing at me as the man stalked over to me.

"Kent?"

"Yes, little bunny."

"I need you to know something," I said, transfixed by the beast between his thighs.

"What's that?"

"My dildos haven't prepared me for you, so we might have a problem."

With a grin, Kent raised my chin until his face encompassed my view. "It's my job to prepare you, not some silicone stand-in." He lowered his mouth to mine before I could offer another objection.

Soon, I was clutching his biceps as he backed me onto the bed and pulled me up with his body until he lay on top of me. Under my skin, heat unlike anything I'd experienced before snaked up my limbs.

While still connected, he traced his fingers down my neck and over my puckered nipples to the dip in my belly button. Anticipation welled inside me as he continued his journey to my pleasure center and hovered over my clit. I raised my hips in search of contact, and he separated from our kiss.

With his breath fanning my lips, he said, "I want to see you come for me."

"Okay," I whispered, curious to see if his hands would succeed where mine didn't.

A fleeting touch brushed my clit, and my body shuddered in response.

"My little bunny is very responsive." Kent repeated the action, pulling the same reaction from me time and again.

Under his diligent attention, liquid seeped between my thighs. My breasts ached from so much need I couldn't ignore them. I pulled at my nipples, moaning Kent's name as he alternated the pressure he applied to my clit.

When I thought I was at my limit, he pushed two fingers inside my pussy. My walls clutched him, squeezing him tight as he withdrew and plunged inside me over and over.

"Kent," I begged as I writhed under his attentive caresses.

"It's okay, little bunny. Stay with me and I promise you won't regret it."

The build-up I was so used to came faster and more powerful. Would this time be different? Could Kent achieve where I'd failed?

My moans grew louder, and I squeezed my eyes shut, unable to withstand the waves of desire buffeting my body. Then Kent pinched my clit and my body exploded. For endless minutes, my body seized as pleasure washed me away. The intensity of my release consumed my senses.

Slowly, Kent's voice praising me brought me back to the bed, where he gently caressed my body. As awareness returned, I blinked my eyes open.

"Hey, beautiful. Do you think you can handle another one?" Awe filled Kent's face and voice as he continued to marvel at me.

Speechless, I nodded.

He left the bed but returned before I had time to miss him. In the brief span, he'd put on a condom. "Put me inside you when you're ready."

Before he finished his order, I reached for him, spreading my legs to welcome him.

"Slow and easy, little bunny. Tonight you're going to introduce me to my pussy, and I aim to treat her well."

I bit my lip as I welcomed him inside my body. Kent's head fell against my shoulder.

"Fuck, you feel so good." His breath fanned my neck. The strain from holding himself in check emboldened me.

"You, too." I hooked my leg around his hip, feeling him slide deeper inside me, filling and stretching me.

When he was fully inside, he raised himself on his elbow to look between our joined bodies. He swiveled his hips, dragging a deep moan out of me. "Stay with me."

Kent laced our fingers together, and without breaking eye contact, he made love to me. Between sweet kisses and the long drag of his dick inside me, pleasure enshrouded us in an intimate cocoon.

Because he'd primed me with an orgasm to end all orgasms, my next one came swiftly and brutally. My pussy clamped down on him, causing him to swear and beg from one breath to the other as my climax hauled him along.

Instead of pulling out once our bodies settled, Kent rolled us until I rested against his chest. "We have a problem."

I rose to watch his face. From his tone, I wasn't concerned, but I was curious.

He pushed my hair behind my ear. "There's no way I can be professional around you at the office when I'll want to be inside you all the time."

His confession forced a laugh from me, which caused my pussy to clench down on his dick. He met my startled gaze with a sheepish grin.

"Already?"

"I warned you we had a problem." He slipped out of me to put a fresh condom on his new erection. "And this time, I can't promise to take you slow and gentle."

"I told you before I wanted your beast. Nothing's changed."

"Good, because I don't care what time of day or night, work or home, when this pussy is in need, I will fill her up." He thrust into me. My walls clamped, swallowing him. "And she's in need right now."

CHAPTER 15

ent

"Move in with me." I winced as the words unceremoniously left my mouth.

Madison was in my arms after another round of passionate sex. I'd meant to broach the subject at a different time. The truth was, I'd wanted to raise the topic since Elsie's attack, but everything was so new with us I'd hesitated. I knew I was coming on strong and heavy-handed and most women would see my behavior as an emporium of red flags to avoid, but I couldn't let that stop me from going after my second chance at happiness.

"Is the sex that good that you want me at your disposal?"

I kissed an unmelanated spot on her shoulder. "I won't deny there's some truth to what you say, but I have a different reason for asking."

She twisted in my arms. "You sound way too serious for a naked conversation."

With a quick tug, I had her back in my arms. "Clothes won't change my reasons or my request."

"Move in with me doesn't sound like a request."

I shrugged. "So you agree you don't have a choice."

"*I* haven't agreed to anything, and before I do, I need to know where this is coming from. And you might want to explain with the swiftness before I take your bossiness some kind of way."

Understanding that Madison took my previous response as dismissiveness, I took her hand in mine and laced our fingers together. "We've kept the fact that we're seeing each other a secret until now. Even if I wanted to continue, I won't be able to hide what you mean to me."

"I'm still not getting how you went from zero to one hundred."

"Are you forgetting there's a serial killer on the loose targeting women I've slept with? You are more than a random one-night stand, which means you're in danger. Do you really expect me to let you walk away from me at the end of each day as if I won't spend the hours until I see you again worrying? I've lost one love of my life. I can't risk losing another."

"Kent..."

"No, little bunny. I barely survived after Lola, and although what we have is new, it's more intense and deeply rooted than what I shared with her. There won't *be* a me without you, so don't try to convince me everything will be okay."

This time, when Madison pulled away, I let her. She turned to face me, sitting cross-legged and with a frown to match mine.

"What will I tell my parents?"

"My vote would be the truth."

Madison shook her head, shooting my response down. "Not yet. You have to make amends with my mother before I can tell them we're dating."

"What's the worst that could happen if we tell them first and I make amends later?"

She arched her brow and twisted her lips. "Do not play with me."

I smirked at the unintended suggestion behind her response.

"And get your mind out of the gutter. You know my mother's reputation when you cross her professionally. You offended her personally. She will rip you to shreds before she'll accept you in my life. And this time, my dad won't be able to vouch for you."

"Fine, tell her you're taking me up on the offer I first made for you to stay in this penthouse because things at work are heating up and you'll be working longer hours. Mention it being safer for you to not be on the road late at night and you'll have her on board."

Madison hugged herself while contemplating my suggestion. "That could work. I wouldn't be lying…"

"Why do I hear a but coming?"

"What if Ife comes for a visit? We never discussed how to tell her."

"I won't hide you from my daughter. You aren't someone I'm ashamed to be with, and it would be better for her to find out from us in person, anyway."

"You truly don't care who knows about us?" she asked wonderingly.

I wrapped my hand around her neck to pull her closer to me. "Madison, when you aren't by my side, you leave an empty void I have no hope of filling. Why should I care what other people think if it means you're always with me?"

She pressed her hand above my heart and stared deeply into my eyes, drowning me in the warm abyss of her gaze. "Okay, I'll move in."

"Today."

"It is two o'clock in the morning. Can you let my decision percolate a little?"

"Today, little bunny. The sooner you're under my protection, the easier I'll breathe."

"Fine! I'll move in today, but I'm going to need some sleep."

"You can sleep after."

"After what?" she asked as I pulled her in for a kiss.

~

Two days passed since Madison moved into the penthouse. Although it was a temporary solution, I couldn't help soaking in that she lived with me. She was messy and threw her clothes everywhere. The bathroom sink was cluttered with her lotions, creams, perfumes, and more things than I could name. And I loved every bit of it.

She added a warmth to the penthouse I'd been missing, but there were still subjects we butted heads on. Disagreements were bound to happen, but I suspected she deliberately provoked me on one constant subject of our debates: her wardrobe.

Greed and selfishness were inherent in my reaction to seeing Madison's sexy office wear. Although I doubted anything could adequately tone down her natural attributes, was asking for her to wear less form-fitting suits too much? Now I was riled up and stewing.

The silence in my soundproof office did nothing to calm me as I waited for Madison to answer my summons. She was testing me with her lateness. The afternoon sun filtered through the window, marking the hour passing. As most people wound down for the day, I couldn't help but ask, why the hell wasn't she here?

The woman dominating my thoughts made a hasty entry seconds later, but at this point, she was incapable of placating my budding anger. How could she when everything she'd done today defied me? As she hurried inside, the suit currently molded to her curves increased my ire. That damn suit had made more than one man in the office leer at her as she passed them. It was supposed to be on a hanger in her closet, not on her body, causing distractions for me and all the unworthy bastards who worked for me.

"Sorry, I'm late. I had to go over the plan with Larry again. I think we agree now and won't have any more delays with execution now that you've refused to be seen with Elsie." Madison pulled the chair facing my desk out.

"Don't sit," I barked.

Startled, she met the fire in my eyes. "What's your deal?"

"What did I say this morning before I left?"

Madison furrowed her brow in thought.

I could tell the second she put the clues together by her straightening posture and the firming of her features.

"You thought I would take you seriously when you told me not to wear this outfit?" She sauntered over to me and I spun my chair to keep my body facing her direction. She didn't stop until she stood between my legs. "You can tell me what to do in bed, even the work I do for you, though I still reserve the right to overrule you. What you won't do is tell me what I can and can't wear while doing said work."

"Little bunny, you are pushing it."

She smiled and it gutted me. A little devil lived in the up tilt of her lips. This was the same smile she gave me before rocking my foundation. Being older than her, being her boss, and even being her best friend's dad, got stripped away in light of that smile.

"Let me tell you a secret," she whispered, although we were the only ones in the soundproofed office. "Not only did I ignore your arbitrary demand"—Madison grabbed my hand and slipped it under her skirt between her thighs—"I also didn't wear any panties."

The moment she finished the word panties, my fingers grazed the hot, wet flesh between her legs. On instinct, I sniffed the air and a welcoming scent greeted me. My mouth watered as her arousal suffused the room.

Too weak to ignore the temptation at my fingertips, I stroked her. "How long have you been this way?"

She leaned toward my ear and bit my lobe. "All. Fucking. Day. What are you going to do about it, Kent?" she dared me, enunciating my name with a crisp K and sharp T.

I glanced up at her triumphant smirk. Damn, she was gorgeous. And maddening. Now that she stopped calling me Mr. Luxe, hearing my name on her lips filled me with sweet agony.

Although we shouldn't be together for many reasons, her safety being the most important, she was a madness in my blood, demanding to take over my mental faculties. The enticement was almost too much to bear. I clenched my hands together as a reminder that this was yet another war we were fighting.

"Nothing, little bunny."

She pulled back as doubt clouded her eyes. "Are you punishing me?"

I firmed my lips and pinned her in my steely gaze.

"No, I won't accept that. You don't get to be mad about my clothes and withhold your dick from me. Remember your promise?" Madison snaked her hand under her skirt. When she retracted it, her fingers glistened in the afternoon sun. "You said, 'I don't care what time of day or night, work or home, when this pussy is in need, I will fill her up.' Well, damn you, it's time to do your job!"

"If you want my cock, you're going to have to take it. Take me so good that when I look at that damn suit, I won't remember why I'm mad now."

"You think I can't?"

"You think you can?"

She took two steps back to take all of me in. "You aren't going to provide any help?"

"I'm not moving from this chair."

She nodded the nod of someone who thought they were about to show someone up. "Alright, we haven't fucked in a chair yet. I guess I'll be the one to mark it off my list first."

Madison raised her hands and pulled the pins securing her corkscrew curls in an updo. As each strand fell, I sensed the battle ahead. I made no secret of what seeing her fluff her curls did to me, or having them feather across my face when she leaned over me. When everything about her was my weakness, how could her hair be the most potent? I couldn't explain it, but I knew I was already in a losing position the moment she hiked her skirt and straddled me on the chair, blanketing my face in her hair.

"Kent, you sure you don't want to fill my pussy up?"

I clutched the armrests beside me. The words to answer her, though, I refused to let pass my lips.

Madison swiveled her hips against my erection and I gritted my teeth against the pleasure. "I think I'm going to have fun playing with you so much. Every time you remember this suit, you'll remember how much I creamed all over your pants before I fucked your brains out."

I inhaled sharply, regretting the challenge I'd issued her moments ago.

"Maybe I'll make you come in your pants without ever putting your dick inside me. Think about all that wasted cum." She tsked, and that shit cut the last thread holding me together.

I pulled her head back by her hair. "Unzip me and take my cock out now, little bunny. You will regret toying with me when I have to carry you out of here with my cum leaking down your legs for everyone to see."

After our first night together, Madison said she wanted to feel me without barriers. I couldn't deny her even had I wanted to. Sinking into her, touching her walls without the latex shield, elevated sex with her to new heights. And filling her with my seed launched me to another level of nirvana.

"Promises, promises," she taunted me, but her quick movements releasing me from my pants spoke to her desperation. She fisted me and rose, on the verge of impaling herself.

"I don't think so." I pushed her back until she had to stand.

"What are you doing? I want my chair sex."

Instead of answering her, I turned her until she faced the darkening skyline in the distance, then pulled her onto my lap.

She leaned into me, rubbing her ass on my cock and causing the blood to rush to my head. "I can get with this position, too."

"You know the drill, little bunny. Put me inside you."

With her skirt scrunched at her waist, I watched her impale herself on my cock through the reflection in the window. Her pussy opened in welcome as she slid down my length.

"Mmm, Kent. Why do you have to make giving me the D so hard?"

"Why do you insist on challenging me?" I hugged her waist, feeling for the buttons enclosing her suit jacket and preventing me from seeing her breasts bounce as she took my cock. In her ear, I whispered, "Since you insist on being a brat, you'll have to bear the consequences." I ripped open her suit and scattered the buttons to parts unknown.

"Kent!"

"Don't move!" I thrust into her and grabbed the skimpy camisole she wore underneath the revealing jacket. "Right now, all you need to do is take this cock." I speared her over and over again, relishing in the sweet walls clutching me and her dulcet wails.

She put a hand on the fist clutching her shirt. As if that could stop me.

Rip!

That, too, came off, irreparable and lying in a crumpled mess on the floor. What remained of her clothing was a damaged jacket, a crinkled skirt, and a pink lace bra that enhanced the rich buttery brown and pink of her skin.

"Damn you, Kent," she moaned in ecstasy while thrashing her head against my shoulder. "I want more. Always want more of you." In the throes of passion, she fondled her clit, the momentary anger disappearing under her rising lust.

Her soft curls brushed my face, and it took all I had not to bounce her on my cock while holding her down to take every inch of me.

Fuck it. She wanted more, anyway. Why would I deny myself the pleasure? But first...

"Say goodbye," I said before ripping the lace fabric obstructing my view of Madison's magnificent breasts.

"Kent..."

"This memory I can live with." I caught her gaze through our reflection in the window, then I tugged on her nipples and rubbed around her areola.

She arched into my body, and her pussy tightened around me. I increased the power of my thrusts as I punished her with my cock. Her thighs quivered, the sign she was about to come. A good thing, because my balls tightened with the need to ejaculate into her womb.

As she sought purchase, waving her hands until she got a hold of the desk and my nape, her screams crescendoed, echoing in my ear. Her breasts heaved and her soft belly shook as she came for me.

So beautiful. So sexy. And so irresistible. I loosened the reins on my control and came inside her, pouring everything I had.

When our breathing calmed, she rose and headed toward the private bathroom.

"Did I say you can clean yourself?"

She paused mid-step. "I can't walk out of here with your cum leaking out of me."

I fixed my clothes and met her before she reached the bathroom door. Grabbing her hand, I took her to the hidden closet. "That's exactly what you will do, but since I ruined your suit, you can wear this one."

Inside the closet were extra suits for me and now for Madison. One thing I'd never do was allow another man to see what was meant for my eyes only, and since I foresaw more damaged suits in her future, I came prepared.

"This is nothing like the suit I've worn all day. People will know what we've been doing in your office."

"And your point would be what, exactly?"

"I can slip upstairs and find something else."

"There isn't time."

She folded her arms and stared at me in challenge. "Don't think this means I'll cede to your wardrobe demands in the future."

"We have somewhere to be, and I have another round ready for you. Now do you want to argue, or let me tend to my pussy?" I ushered her into the bathroom without another protest.

CHAPTER 16

adison

Our secret was out. At least at work. Apparently frosted glass and soundproofing meant nothing if Kent couldn't hide his satisfied smiles and possessive hold on my waist whenever we left the office together. And he made sure we didn't leave through his private garage. I should be angry, but I was secretly glad we didn't have to pretend in front of everyone. Despite his behavior in the office, when we were in public, we behaved as colleagues. I tamed down my clothes for our dates, though the way Kent stared at me in his unguarded moments, anyone would think I was seconds away from revealing my body for his personal enjoyment.

That more than anything else was what convinced me my parents were bound to discover us. Although Kent was inscrutable in business, he couldn't hide his feelings for me. I understood. He was the same way with Oyinlola and Ife. And now I get to walk around the world knowing he included me in his very small circle of people he'd given his heart.

Despite the risk of my parents finding out about us on their own, Kent and I hadn't found a good time to tell them about our relationship. We agreed it was best to wait until we'd cleared his name. Although Douglas PD exonerated him for the two murders he had an alibi for, they left the investigation regarding the other murdered women open, leaving a public stain on Kent's reputation. In my opinion, removing all reasons for my mother to object to Kent before he gave his mea culpa was more important than giving Nikita Montgomery the time and energy to eviscerate Kent and his apology.

"Hey Madison," Omar called out to me.

I hadn't realized I was on auto-pilot, walking between the other employees busily plugging away at their work, talking in small groups, and going back and forth from the printer.

"Hey, did you need something?"

"I bumped into Carol earlier. She wants you to call her."

"Did she say what about?"

Omar shrugged. "No, but I have other news to share."

Ever since Elsie's accident, Omar had volunteered to work with my team. He took over monitoring the BBD site and tried to identify who the users were that pushed the Kent was a murderer narrative. He proposed the murderer could be an employee. None of us wanted to credit his guess, but knowing for certain was better than living in ignorance. And since my long shot with Fred was a bust, I was on board for anything that could give us the answers we needed.

"Have you found something linking an employee to the murders?"

"I wish. You know how badly I want to find who cut Elsie." He beckoned me behind his desk to look at his monitor. "What I found though, makes me wonder if I've uncovered something else."

The user profile for @Nose2TheGrindstone appeared. I raised a questioning brow at Omar, not seeing what caused his alarm.

"From what I've been able to piece together, this person is Luxe Locations' general counsel."

"Hal?" I shook my head in disbelief.

"I know, right? That was my response."

"There's no way. I'm more inclined to think someone hacked his computer than to believe he would betray Kent this way."

"Now that you mention it, you're probably right." Omar picked up the receiver for his phone and dialed a number. "I'll get our IT department to dig into his login information. I would hate to have to tell Kent he's got a snake pretending to take care of the company."

"Okay, until IT either confirms or rules Hal's involvement out, don't tell Kent. That kind of suspicion without proof could ruin a friendship."

I left Omar agreeing with me and entered my shared office with Kent. As soon as I shut the door behind me, the transparent walls turned an opaque white.

"Do you know how much restraint I had to practice while I watched you talking to Omar?" Kent marched over to me and pulled me into his arms for an all-consuming kiss.

"I doubt you leashed yourself for long," I said, pulling out of his embrace. "You realize you aren't being subtle? Every time you block out the walls, you might as well put up a billboard sign advertising what we're doing."

"Ask me if I care."

"Why bother? I already know the answer." I headed toward my desk, but Kent's arm around my waist impeded my progress.

"Since the windows are tinted, why don't we take advantage of the few minutes we have free?" He pushed his hand beneath the waistband of my skirt and panties. "Wearing extra layers today?"

As I melted into his arms, his phone rang. "You better answer it."

"I can multitask." He hauls me behind him.

"No, Kent! You are not fucking me while you take a call."

"As long as you don't make a sound, no one's going to know."

Against my better judgment, I allowed him to position me over his desk as he answered his call and put it on speaker.

"What do you need, Mal?" Kent delved under my skirt and rolled my panties down my legs.

"I sent over the figures for the Hayden proposal. I wanted to walk through them before we meet with them next week."

As Mal spoke, Kent turned my face to the side and pressed his finger against my bottom lip. I opened without protest, and he pushed my panties inside. My lust had already saturated my underwear, and I fought back the moan attempting to escape.

I had no defense against Kent or his unquenchable desire for me. If he weren't in the same situation as me, I would probably cry at the imbalance in our relationship.

"Let me pull up the spreadsheet now." Instead of touching his computer, a metal clink sounded behind me, alerting me to the belt Kent unfastened.

In the silent room, the snick of his zipper lowering caused me to clench my thighs in anticipation.

"Have you found the file yet?"

"Not yet." Kent pressed his erection against my opening and I clung to the edge of the desk. As he pushed inside me, he fiddled with the computer. "Okay, it's wide open," He said before pushing all the way inside me.

I turned my face into my shoulder to stifle my groan.

"What was that?" Mal asked.

Kent slipped his hand over my ass and squeezed. "I didn't hear anything. Maybe it's feedback from the speakerphone."

While I tried to stay still and keep quiet, Kent plunged his dick in and out of my pussy. He wasn't gentle, but he took his time. Each powerful thrust pushed me further and further up on the desk. I was so wet and turned on; I knew I was leaking a trail of liquid as he pleasured me.

The magic Kent wrung from me as he spoke to Mal reduced my awareness. The control he exerted to sound calm, as if he wasn't fucking my brains out while challenging his CFO's approach to their partnership bid, pushed me closer to orgasm.

The signs of my impending climax became undeniable. My body tensed and my pussy's unending clenching of Kent's dick caused me to wave at him, signaling to him I couldn't contain myself or the scream that had been building in my lungs.

Did he not care, or was he too far gone to hang up? As I peaked, I let loose a tortured scream that my panties couldn't buffer completely. My release caused me to lift my body from the desk as spasms of pleasure ran through me.

When I dropped, Kent followed, his mouth beside my ear, feathering against me. Gone was the modulated voice talking over figures and pitches. Still inside me, my pussy continued to convulse around Kent, milking him as he filled me with cum.

As my senses came online one at a time, I heard Mal's voice calling Kent, who pushed away from me. I turned my head to watch him from the corner of my eye. With one hand, he unmuted his phone to respond. His other hand pulled the panties from my mouth and pocketed them when I reached for them.

"Mal, I like what you've put together so far. Make the changes we've discussed and let's go over the numbers again." Without waiting for Mal to respond, Kent hung up and hauled me into his arms for a kiss. "There is no tastier combination than your pussy and mouth at once," he groaned.

I sank into the kiss. My body had yet to recover from Kent's attention, and if I was honest, one of my favorite things to do was kiss Kent. We reluctantly parted.

"I have a few things I need to wrap up before my dinner meeting tonight," he said.

"It all makes sense now why you just had to have me."

He pressed one last kiss against my lips. "I don't need an incentive to feed my pussy what she needs. Knowing her, she'll be ready for dessert when I get home."

I had nothing to rebut him because it was true. My body craved him, whether he was near or far. He waited while I fixed my appearance. When I gave him the nod to remove the tint from the windows, I sat at my desk, the appearance of a professional in place. Omar's slick grin told me he wasn't buying my act. I shrugged and delved into my work.

An hour later, I remembered to call Carol, who'd invited me out for drinks. I didn't know what prompted the invitation, but time with her could help me pinpoint some of the BBD users bashing the company. Her position as a human resources manager meant she had a lot of insight into the employees, their complaint histories, and their overall impression of Kent. A couple of drinks wouldn't hurt, and I would probably return in time to see Kent off to his dinner meeting.

When the hour came for me to leave, I started packing my briefcase and forwarded my calls to my cell.

"Did Carol mention how many people were going out for drinks?" Kent asked, a frown on his face.

"No, but I doubt it's just me."

"Do you have the tracker I gave you?"

I pulled the dollar-coin-sized disk from my skirt pocket. The device was a compromise because I refused Kent's offer of a team of bodyguards. Valentino DeLuca had offered them to him as a present once he recognized the type of relationship Kent and I had. Kent would have accepted if I hadn't protested. Although he agreed to my decision, he grumbled about my choice every chance he got.

Now, Kent made a habit of asking me about the device whenever I left the house or office without him. Because I understood his fear about the very real serial killer on the loose, I never left it off my person.

As I got off the elevator, my phone rang. "Hey Carol, I'm about to get in the car. Did you need something?"

"I'm glad I caught you. I forgot to ask earlier, but would you mind if we carpooled? My boyfriend offered to pick me up after, so I won't have to limit my drinking tonight."

"Not a problem. I'll pick you up in front of the building."

"Thanks a bunch, Madison."

As I approached the exit to the garage, Carol ran up to my car. I stopped to let her in. "I told you I would pick you up in front of the building."

"You did? I must have forgotten, since I was scrambling to pack my desk up before leaving."

"Okay… Can you put our destination into the GPS? I didn't recognize the name of the bar. Douglas has changed a lot since I moved away. I hardly recognize any of the good restaurants anymore." I pulled out of the compound while Carol entered an address into her phone.

"I'm glad we're getting this chance to get to know each other better," she said. "It looks like you're going to be here longer than your contract from the way Kent looks at you."

I shrugged, feeling uncomfortable with the topic she chose to discuss. "I haven't made any long-term plans. My company is based in D.C. and so are many of my clients."

"Well, people make long-distance relationships work all the time. I'm sure you and Kent will figure something out."

While I followed the GPS directions, Carol kept the conversation going. When we approached a stoplight, I realized I'd driven into a sparsely populated area.

"Are you sure you put in the right address?" I asked.

Carol peered out the window and windshield. "Yes, this looks like the right spot. No one will think to look for you out here until it's too late."

"What do you mean?" I swung my head to face her.

At that moment, she pressed something against my neck. Jolts of electricity ran through my body, causing my muscles to seize.

"You ruined everything. Do you know how many years I've tried to get Kent's attention? I finally had a chance when he stopped sleeping around. Then you showed up, and you're nothing like his type. You're arrogant, Black, and fat. How could he choose you when I was available?" Carol shouted while continuing to press the Taser against me.

Her voice faded, as did her face. With no control of my limbs, I couldn't push her away or call out for help. Too late, I wished I'd taken Kent up on his offer of a bodyguard. As a tear slipped down my face and hope seemed to dwindle, I prayed Kent wouldn't punish himself for my mistake.

CHAPTER 17

 ent

"Hey, Kent. If you need nothing else, I'm headed out," Omar said from the door.

I checked the time. "Have you heard from Madison since she went to meet Carol?"

Although Madison said she would return before I left, she hadn't. Neither had she called to let me know she would be late. The sense of unease I had when she spoke to Carol on the phone earlier doubled.

"No, I haven't spoken to her since after lunch. Is there a problem?" Omar entered the office, concern writ on his face to mirror mine.

"She should have returned by now." I pulled up the app for the tracker Madison always wore. A steady light showed her at a railroad crossing.

No movement could have meant a freight train was passing, but if she went out for drinks, why was she in that area of Douglas? It was known for high crime, and I couldn't imagine a bar Madison or Carol would know being there.

I dialed Madison's number, but it went to voicemail without ringing. Already on edge, her lack of response drove me to act. "Omar, cancel my meeting and call the police. Tell them to meet me at the train tracks by Henderson Crossing. Madison's in danger."

I rushed to the elevator; the phone pressed to my ear as I tried Madison's number repeatedly. Although I raised the alarm, I couldn't contemplate her being in a serial killer's clutches. She had to be okay.

We were such a new couple, and I hadn't had enough opportunities to spoil her or prove to her I could be the man she needed by her side. I had yet to proclaim to the world that we were together. Then there was gaining her parents' acceptance, telling Ife, and so many more things on the list of things we had to do before we could truly enjoy each other.

Now was not the time to imagine Madison scared or worse. I would find her, and she would be safe. Despite my vehement hope, despair batted at me every second of the ride to the railroad crossing. The light telling me Madison's location hadn't budged, but I didn't know if that was a blessing or a cruel joke.

I broke every speed limit to make it to my little bunny. I needed to see her in her velour sweatsuit again. When I got to her, she was never leaving my arms, even if it meant I carried her wherever she needed to go.

I almost missed the turnoff. The car fishtailed before I corrected the course and drove down the street leading to Henderson Crossing. The map showing Madison's location was more detailed as I approached her.

When I arrived at the crossing, a black Chevy Suburban that didn't belong to Madison sat on the tracks. The car was bigger than my S-Class Benz. I didn't care that what I saw contradicted the app on my phone. The signal said she was in front of me.

In the distance, a horn shattered the quiet panic I'd been existing in. A train was approaching, and I had no way of knowing how far away it was. I ran out of my car to the silhouette on the driver's side of the SUV on the tracks. My heart stopped at what I saw.

Madison slumped over the steering wheel, unconscious. Her hands were duct-taped together and zip-tied to the steering wheel.

"Madison!" I tugged the door handle, but it was locked. Next, I banged against the window while yelling for her to wake up, but she didn't move.

I couldn't lose another woman in a car accident. I couldn't.

Frantic, I looked around for something big and sharp to break the window, but there were no rocks or sticks up to the job. The train tooted again, the sound closer than the last time. As I punched the window in earnest, the gate arm to warn oncoming vehicles that a train was approaching descended.

With time slipping fast, I doubled my efforts until the window shattered into pebbled glass. The sound must have jolted her awake. She groggily blinked, while I pulled at the zip tie holding her hostage in the car. No matter how much I tugged, I couldn't create a gap between the tie and the wheel.

"Kent?" her voice lacked the vitality I was used to.

"Hey, little bunny." I tried to inject a note of calm in my voice I didn't feel.

"What… where am I? Why does my body feel so sore?" She raised her head, but it fell backward against the headrest.

"Don't freak out, but you're trapped on some train tracks, but I'm going to get you out."

As the seconds passed, Madison became more alert. "Train tracks? Where's Carol?"

"No offense, but I don't give a shit about her right now. You're my priority. A train is coming and I need to get you out of here." As soon as I mentioned the train, another horn blew.

Now that Madison was becoming more coherent, her sense of alarm rose. She tugged her hands. "Oh my God, get me out! Get me out!"

"I'm trying, little bunny. I'm trying."

Broken sobs ripped from her chest as distraught pleas fell from her lips. A sense of helplessness tore through me with my lack of progress.

Madison turned her teary face to me. "Kent, the train is coming. You can't stay here. Save yourself."

"Don't say that. I'll free you. No matter what, I won't leave you." I looked down the train tracks. The sound was closer, and I could see the light as it traveled through the trees. Behind me, sirens wailed in the distance, but they were too far away to be of any help.

"I have an idea. Wait for me." I ran to my car as she screamed for me to leave.

With time flitting through my fingers, I crashed through the gate arm and used my car to push the one holding Madison captive. The wheels on my car spun, causing smoke to billow from under the tires. I depressed the pedal to the floor, but her car wouldn't budge.

The light grew closer and closer, shining brightly on us and halfway blinding me. Finally, her car moved. When she was free of the track, I glanced at the glaring light to my left, praying I'd have time to meet Madison on the other side.

CHAPTER 18

$\mathcal{M}$adison

"Why are you refusing to come home with me?" My mother stood beside the bed I shared with Kent. "Don't you know the emotional trauma your father and I have suffered? To think a serial killer is after you because Kent doesn't know how to channel his grief into healthier endeavors."

My relationship was no longer a secret from my parents. Even as a fixer, there was no avoiding my mom and dad discovering who my mystery man was. In the hospital, Kent refused to leave my side after our near miss on the railroad tracks, much to my mother's dismay. As the hospital staff checked me out, they got into a heated argument.

There went any hope of my mom giving Kent a fair shot. We would have to win her over the hard way.

"Mommy, Kent saved my life."

"Your life wouldn't have needed saving if he didn't endanger it to begin with." She fluffed a pillow that she'd fluffed two times already.

"And I'd like to remind you, they haven't caught that Carol woman, so your life is still in danger."

"And Kent has already gone overboard to make sure I have protection." I pointed to the man standing by the door.

Not only had Kent insisted on a bodyguard, but he also hired a company called Connors Elite Security Professionals. They were based in Bourbon, Texas, and they would supply a constant rotation of six guards. I would never be alone and vulnerable to attack again. After Carol, I gladly agreed to my new babysitters. I'd rather be watched and alive than alone and dead.

"Acting after the fact doesn't soften me up one bit."

"I love him." The simple words stopped my mother's next gripe. "And right now, he isn't taking what happened well. He came too close to watching me die in front of his eyes, and it brought up a lot of pain from when Oyinlola died. So, I'm not sorry that I won't be moving back with you."

Defeated, my mother plopped beside me and took my hand in hers. "You had to use the dead wife card to make me feel like a heel, didn't you? You are just like your father."

I shrugged. I'd use whatever weapon I had to make her back off Kent.

"Are you sure it's love?"

"Ever since high school," I admitted.

"Well, hell."

I patted her hand as she came to grips with the news.

"Are you ready for lunch?" Kent entered the room with a food tray. "I had Omar pick up food for everyone from Kori's Food Truck." He stared at my mom. "The food is on the dining table if you're hungry."

"I'll take that as my cue to leave you two."

I swung my feet over the bed. "I could have joined you. The doctor didn't say I needed bedrest."

"He didn't, but I do." Kent settled the tray on the nightstand, then kissed my forehead. As if he didn't believe his eyes, his gaze roamed over me until it landed on the bruise on my neck.

I raised my hand to cover the evidence of my attack that Carol left behind.

He grabbed me before I could hide it. "I promise you I'll make her pay." He slid behind me and settled me in his arms. "Until then, let me take care of you." He speared a piece of fried chicken and held the fork to my lips.

I rolled my eyes at his recent clinginess, but inside I loved the attention he lavished on me. After lunch, we remained in each other's arms, soaking in the reality that we'd both survived something horrific.

As I was about to drift off, my father knocked on the door. "Maddy, there are two detectives here to see you."

Detective Salinas walked in before Kent or I consented. My new bodyguard blocked him from getting too far into the room.

"Elijah, escort him to the den, please. We'll be right behind you." Kent rose and held his hand out to assist me out of bed.

Everyone, including my mother, was inside the den by the time Kent and I entered. The detective was trying to remove everyone, but Nikita Montgomery wasn't having it.

"As Madison's legal representation, I'm staying. And don't for once think I don't know about your reputation. I've worked with Douglas PD long enough to know how you operate with live victims. You waste time trying to blame them before you get to the job of doing your job."

"Ma'am, I'm here to follow up on your daughter's statement. I promise, we at the department are doing everything we can to catch Carol. The mayor has also expressed his interest in the progress of this case." A flush suffused Salinas' neck. He cleared his throat. "But there is one thing that makes no sense."

"And what would that be?" I asked, taking a seat beside my mother. Kent sat on my other side and held my hand, much to my father's chagrin. I sent my dad a conciliatory wink.

"In your statement, you said the car Mr. Luxe found you in didn't belong to you, and it wasn't the vehicle you used when you left the office."

"That's correct."

"Why are you asking her this? You found her car abandoned at a salvage yard about to be compacted." Kent's fingers tightened around mine until I rubbed soothing circles around his knuckles.

"The issue is Carol's weight. From her license, we know she's 110 pounds. Do you see our dilemma?" Salinas eyed me as if not coming out and saying the difference between her weight and mine was more respectful than his innuendo-laden voice.

"How shitty can you be at your job?" Kent's outburst brought everyone's attention to him. "Carol obviously has an accomplice. If you recall, Omar saw a man standing over Elsie. Whoever he is must have helped her transfer Madison to the other car."

"Have you tried reaching out to her boyfriend?" I asked.

"The problem is, no one who knows her has ever heard of a boyfriend. Right now, she's in hiding and we have no clues about who was working with her. So far, we've sent her photo to all the local and national news stations, but no one has called in with information."

"You should talk to the head of my human resources department. Deke was her date for a charity ball I attended," Kent said.

"I'll have my partner check him out. In the meantime, Carol's partner remains a mystery. With Ms. Montgomery being the only witness to identify her, you're in more danger than you were before."

Kent folded me into his arms. "Don't fear, little bunny. I won't let anyone get close enough to hurt you ever again."

Although the threat of Carol and her mysterious accomplice loomed above us, I took comfort in Kent's conviction. He'd risked his life to save me. He wasn't going anywhere, and I was damn sure going to stay by his side.

The name on my caller ID an hour later put my vow to the test.

Kent glanced at me, a question in his gaze.

I waved him off and took my phone to the study before the person at the other end disconnected. I sat on the floor, hugging my legs to my chest before taking a deep breath and pushing the green phone icon.

"Hey, Ife," I injected as much enthusiasm in my voice to cover the guilt eating me alive.

"Don't 'Hey, Ife,' me. How could you not tell me someone attacked you? Instead of hearing from you, I read about the danger you were in from an online Douglas Times article. I thought we were friends."

The hurt in Ife's voice doubled the weight of my guilt.

"Ife, things have been pretty hectic. I just didn't have a chance. You know I would have called." The lie slipped smoothly from my lips.

As a crisis manager, I was a professional liar; I was damn good at my job. But with Ife, I only ever lied to her about one subject. Her father. Since my attack had everything to do with her father, I had to keep the details vague.

"You promise?" She asked, amid shuffling sounds in the background.

"Of course... Ife, what's all that noise?"

She paused, long enough to make me suspicious. "Noise? I don't hear anything."

"Ha! Don't try me. You know I know when you're lying better than anybody."

"There's no... fine, I'm packing."

Panic and terror filled my veins. I swallowed twice before I managed a moderate tone. "Oh? Where are you going?"

"I'm coming to see you, silly. Someone attacked you," her voice wobbled and she sniffed. "And if not for me, you would be safe in your apartment in D.C."

"Ife, you are not at fault for other people's actions. There's no need for you to come running over here to look after me. Mom and Dad have me covered." So did your dad, but I wasn't going to say that.

Ife puffed out a disappointed breath. "Yeah, I forgot you finally have your mom and dad with you. How does it feel living under their roof again?"

"I don't know, Mom and Dad have rolled out the red carpet and being here feels a little surreal. I probably shouldn't admit this, but their constant need to pamper me makes me kind of want to be a kid again." I forced a giggle.

"I totally get that. Dad can't spoil me enough whenever I visit."

"True, but be honest, everyone caters to you. Your Insta is full of Ekele doing everything for you. He even took you to Nigeria to meet your mother's side of the family and introduce you to his."

"He did do that."

Her trip to her mother's homeland was nine months ago and she was excited upon her return. Up to six months ago she raved about Ekele's consideration and romantic gestures, but the lack of enthusiasm in her voice today warned me things weren't going well.

"Did something happen between you two?"

"I didn't call to talk about me." She injected fresh energy into her voice. "I need proof of life to reassure myself you aren't being held captive somewhere."

"Girl, please. If I were, would we be having this conversation right now?"

"What if you're an AI voice meant to deceive me?"

"Ife—"

"Maybe I do need to fly over—"

"Okay, okay." I rush over to the sliding glass door in the study because I wasn't sure if Ife knew the penthouse's design. When she switched the call to video, I accepted and made sure the camera pointed away from the building.

"You aren't at home?" Ife pushed her long hair from her face as she peered through her glasses toward the room's backdrop.

Thinking quickly, I made up an excuse. "No, Mom and Dad treated me to a spa day and a night at your dad's hotel." I crossed my fingers and hoped she didn't compare the small bit of skyline with one of the views from her father's hotel.

She eyed me up and down, and her smile fell. She pointed toward my neck. "She did that to you?"

I raised my hand to cover the bruise.

"There's no sense in hiding it now. I've seen it. And covering it up pretty much confirms she did it." Ife nibbled her lip. "Are there any leads?"

"Not yet, and honestly, I don't have too much faith in the police. I think they want to believe your father's capable of murder."

Ife's brow wrinkled. "Does this mean you're coming back home and handing off Dad to another company?"

Even if I weren't in love with the man, I wouldn't abandon a client in need. Not to mention D.C. felt less and less like home the longer I stayed in Douglas. I was falling in love with my hometown again, and would have serious qualms about leaving when I settled everything.

I think Kent has strong opinions on where you lay your head after every-thing is said and done.

I shook my head, not needing Kent and his intentions to confuse me while I had Ife on the phone scrutinizing everything about me.

"I thought you knew me better. Even if he weren't related to you, I wouldn't leave your dad in the lurch. I believe in him and if I can make those asshole detectives eat shit, I'm going to." I grinned until the frown lines cleared from Ife's face.

"You're right. And I can't thank you enough for being in my dad's corner. He's got a lot of business acquaintances, but I never trust if they're there for him out of a genuine sense of loyalty or they're looking to use him to enrich themselves."

"I get that. His circle is no more or less superficial than the ones in D.C."

"Which is why you don't see me rubbing shoulders with this heauxs."

"Ife, stop lying. All Ekele does is court that circle, and I've seen you by his side for many of those hoity-toity events."

"That's different, and how did we get off the subject of you again?"

"You have main character syndrome and can't help yourself?" I smirked into the phone.

Ife rolled her eyes, and the second of darkness I thought I saw overcome her features as she spoke about D.C. disappeared. "If you don't want me to visit, the least I can do is send you a care package. What do you want?"

I sighed. "Have I told you, you are the bestest friend in the world?"

"I mean, there's no maximum of times you can tell me."

"Of course there isn't." I snapped my fingers. "How about I send you all the Douglas stuff we used to binge during our sleepovers? I'll even add a few adult goodies to the box."

"You are speaking my language."

"Does this mean you believe I'm who I say I am and not an AI version of me?"

Ife closed in on the screen, in and out a few times with her eyebrow raised as if attempting to analyze every pixel on her phone. She eventually settled with the phone at a regular distance from her face. "Honestly, as long as I get my care package, I'd accept Mads.AI as my next best friend."

"That's cold."

"You know I'm spoiled. If I'm not going to get it from you, I'll—"

"Yeah, yeah, yeah."

Her airy energy shifted. "But seriously, Mads, you know I'll be there for you in an instant if you need me."

"Same here bestie."

We hung up, and my shoulders slumped. Keeping up the light-hearted act was more taxing than I expected because it was Ife on the other end of my conversation.

I strolled into the study to find Kent waiting on me. "You heard?"

"Not everything, but I can guess you didn't tell her about us."

I shook my head.

"We have to tell her, eventually." Kent pulled me into his arms.

As his heat permeated through me, I realized I'd been shivering from being outside.

"I know." I pulled my head back to stare into his concerned face. "But can we deal with one crisis before tackling another?"

Because no matter how many reassurances Kent gave, I didn't want to lose Ife. She was more than my best friend. She was there to help me pick up the pieces of my life even when she didn't know her father had broken me. She was my hand when mine were tied, my voice when I couldn't speak, and my favorite sweater when nothing but harsh wind cut through me.

And as I greedily soaked up Kent's affection, I remained more gluttonous. Because even as I knew my relationship with her father would destroy everything, I would hold off losing her until I had no other choice.

CHAPTER 19

ent

"Thanks for meeting me on such short notice." I sat in Valentino's home office, reminded of his wedding day three years ago.

That day business was the furthest from his mind, and based on his frequent glances toward the door where his wife slipped through moments ago, business was the last thing he wanted to discuss now.

"You asked for Sansone to meet us here. He should be here shortly." Valentino walked to his bar and poured two glasses without asking me my preference.

Not that he needed to. We'd had discussions over drinks enough to know what the other liked. He handed me my glass and sat on the sofa facing me. Because this wasn't an official meeting, we sat in the more comfortable couches in the corner rather than around his desk.

I waited a day after those asshole detectives stopped by before imposing on Valentino. I hated being away from Madison, however, I wouldn't allow my dependency on seeing her smiling at me to override her safety.

"Sloane, mi bella cognata, you're as beautiful as ever." Sansone's voice rang into the office. "What say you we ditch mi fratello, just you and me?"

"It was nice knowing you, Sansone. I'll make sure to leave a gorgeous bouquet of flowers on your grave. And I'll try to convince Valentino to make your funeral open casket, but I can't promise anything. You know how he gets about me." Sloane's voice gets louder the closer she gets until she appears at the door beside Valentino's brother. "Valentino—"

"I heard." Valentino stood and kissed his wife's cheek while his brother sauntered in with a cocky grin.

Once Sloane left us alone, Valentino turned to his brother. "It's time you found your own woman and left mine alone."

"But then I'd miss out on your reaction." Sansone grabs a drink and joins me. "So what was so urgent you needed me here?"

Valentino nodded toward me. "Kent needs a favor."

Sansone peered at me, studying me as if I hadn't done him favors in the past. Then he relaxed his face in a grin. "What do you need?"

"I have an employee on the run who tried to kill my..." I didn't want to call Madison my girlfriend. The term felt juvenile, something used to describe relationships with no future or substance with a partner barely out of college. Madison wasn't a girl in any sense of the word. She was two years shy of turning thirty, a powerhouse of a woman despite the difference in our age. And what we had wasn't a fling to last a season unless the season was the rest of our lives together. She was mine and no outsider was going to take her from me.

"My woman. I need this bitch caught. Alive." I turned to Valentino. "And I'd rather not have the cops on my back when I deal with her for touching what's mine."

Valentino grunted. "You dropped the ball when you let her over-rule you on the bodyguards."

"Moment of insanity I won't repeat." I sipped my drink, allowing the memory of Madison's brush with death to overtake me as the alcohol's smooth burn slid down my throat.

I didn't invite her to this meeting because my dealings with the DeLuca brothers weren't always above board. Despite Madison saying she accepted all aspects of me, including my darkness, she didn't know how dark I was willing to go for her. Or how dark I'd gone in the past. Valentino and Sansone did.

"Give me a description and I'll have my men on the lookout for whoever you need me to find."

I handed Sansone a card with an address. "When you've got her, take her to this address. I recently obtained the condemned property and am not in a rush to start development on it."

Sansone retrieved his phone. "This is an excellent location." He glanced up from the screen. "Mind if I use it for other matters?"

"Mi casa es su casa amico," I said.

Sansone drained his glass and slammed it on the coffee table. "This is why I fucks with you. But you can't just call me. Call this number." He wrote a number on the back of the card with the address I gave him and handed it to me. "This way whatever goes down won't trace back to me." He winked and smirked at me.

"Anything else?" Valentino asked as if understanding without being told I had more on my mind.

"I suspect there's another person behind Carol. For all their incompetence, the detectives assigned to Madison's case mentioned the possibility of an accomplice. Based on what went down with Elsie, I believe they're onto something."

"And you want them to get the Luxe treatment, too?" Sansone folded his arms and tapped his fingers against his elbows.

"He and that bitch abandoned her on train tracks. They intended for the train to kill her. No one walks away free." I glared at the two men.

I wasn't a member of the mob. Until these murders, no one suspected I could take a life. But these men have known me for years. Saw what I went through after my wife's death. They understood what despair did to a person, what it did to me. I wasn't willing to go back to those days.

And although I wasn't in the same league as Sansone and

Valentino, they'd seen me hold my own. Their respect for me glimmered in their eyes as we finalized our agreement.

With my back-up plan in place, I left the mayor's house on another errand. Valentino's comment on the bodyguards still rankled. Besides the men Madison knew about, I had two others following her less conspicuously.

I wasn't taking chances, which was why an hour later I pulled up to a farm. As I exited the car, my phone rang.

"Hello, beautiful."

"Don't beautiful me." Madison's voice, despite the attitude, was a welcome sound, speaking to the health of her strong lungs. "Did you tell my guards I wasn't allowed to leave the apartment until you returned?"

"Your safety protocol isn't fully in place yet. Until I don't break out in a cold sweat wondering if every time you leave my sight will be the last time, you'll stay at home." I rested against my car and waited for her next explosion, which I expected to occur soon.

"That is such a load of bullshit," she said, proving me right. "I have no idea where you are, but I'm supposed to pretend that you aren't in danger, too? Kent, Carol and whoever she's working with is escalating, but you don't have an issue with running these streets like nothing's wrong. I have men *you* hired to keep me safe. But I'm under house arrest?"

"Little bunny—"

"You are not going to little bunny your way out of this. Cute pet names aside, if we aren't partners in this relationship, we won't work."

I straightened my spine, all levity leaving my body. My voice lowered, and the darkness I kept from her leaked through when I said, "Did you just threaten to leave me?"

Madison remained quiet on her end.

"Madison…"

Click.

I stared at my phone in disbelief. She must have forgotten my warning. I checked the time and rushed through my last errand to get back to my stubborn little bunny. And when I got home, I would have her on her knees and apologizing.

CHAPTER 20

 adison

What did I just do? I stared in horror at my phone after I hung up on Kent.

Kent! The man I've been in love with for most of my life. The man I just told we wouldn't last.

I clutched my chest as I envisioned an atomic bomb exploding our relationship and ending us prematurely. I wasn't allowed to leave his penthouse, but I needed air. I fled to the balcony and slid the glass door shut. Because one thing I couldn't escape was the truth behind my words.

Kent and I wouldn't work as a couple if we weren't partners.

I wasn't blind to the imbalances in our relationship. He was twenty years older than me with more experience behind him. And although I was a successful crisis manager, Kent was a billionaire who ran an international conglomerate. There were already too many obstacles separating us.

I curled up on a chaise and tried to ease my anxiety. I'd come too far to sit and let life happen around me or allow Kent to dictate our future. While I contemplated what I would do and say when I saw Kent next, time passed. The sun sat lower on the horizon when the sliding door slid open.

"Madison, we need to talk," Kent said.

Without looking at him, I replied, "Then talk."

"No offense, but I think our talk is about to turn into an argument, and I'd rather not have an angry woman and a balcony so close together."

I glared at him but he stood resolute with an arm directing me inside.

Okay, if this is how he wanted things...

I stood and entered the room. Kent placed his hand on the dip in my spine and I walked away from his touch.

"Let's go into the bedroom, unless you want everyone to hear us."

I huffed, but turned toward the room because I didn't know what was about to happen and having strangers witness what might be my humiliation wasn't something I desired. On the way toward the back of the penthouse, two kennel cages caught my eye.

"What are those?" I detoured towards the cages to find a German Shepherd resting in each cage.

"The rest of your security detail. No one will mess with you when they see two of the most fiercely protective dogs surrounding you."

The two canines neared the bars of the cage to sniff my hands. Their size put them close to a year old. Big enough to make a stranger question approaching but young enough to train. The mix of gold and dark browns in their coat gleamed, speaking to the care they'd had before Kent purchased them. The dogs were cute, but I hardened my heart toward them.

I didn't know what the future held after my upcoming conversation with Kent and didn't want to get attached.

"You got me two dogs," I said without emotion, then continued to the bedroom. My prior anxiousness was on a back burner as my anger simmered over this manipulative tactic.

"Now, when I can't be with you, you can go wherever your heart desires." Kent followed close behind me, adding fuel to the fire.

He closed the bedroom door, and his neutral features turned granite once we were alone.

"You couldn't ask me if I wanted a dog, let alone two?" I rounded on him.

His nostrils flared. "You want to talk about dogs instead of the real problem here?"

I cackled. "If you don't see how this is part of the real problem..."

"Don't threaten me again with the ending of our relationship bullshit."

My anger fled. I sat on the bed and stared at him in despair. "Do I like dogs?"

"What?"

I repeated my question and he frowned.

"Don't you?"

"I've lived on my own long enough that if I wanted a dog, I would have gotten one for myself. I never did because they require so much time, and with my job I never had enough to give to an animal. And you chose one of the neediest breeds alive in terms of needing attention."

"I chose one of the best family-friendly, protective dogs alive to ensure your safety."

"Without discussing my needs with me."

"Madison—"

"No, Kent. You can't just decide for me and expect me to accept the results. I'm your girlfriend, not your employee." I raised my hand to stop him from pointing out what had brought me to Douglas. "Yes, you've contracted my company for a job, but I can fire you and return to D.C. I'm not beholden to you, professionally or personally, and I need you to understand that."

"Anything else?" he gritted while the muscles in his jaw ticked.

"I love you, but I don't want who I am to disappear because of my love for you. You've got me in a gilded cage that's more like a hotel than a home where I have to answer to everyone but myself for what I want."

"Madison, please. I've seen your selfies at your place in D.C. This apartment is homier than that blank space you live in." He arched his brow as if he won.

So what if he was right about the empty walls and lack of personality in my apartment? I was only there long enough to rest my head before I was off traveling for work or pulling in long hours.

"A cage is still a cage no matter how pretty the trappings."

Kent bobbed his head up and down but his expression gave nothing away. "You've made some good points." He flicked the top button of his shirt free from its hole. "However, I have one question for you. Am I your man?"

"Don't change the subject, Kent."

"Answer me Madison. Am I your man?" He shrugged his shirt from his shoulders.

"I don't see what—"

"Answer the question."

"Yes! You're my man." I hit the mattress with my fist.

"Glad we agree there. Now let me clarify some things for you. As your man, I have certain duties that I take to heart." He pulled his undershirt over his head and dropped it as he advanced toward me. "My principal duty is to provide. That comes in all forms. Security. Support. Stability. And most of all, love."

"You can do all that without excluding me from the conversation. Unless, it's not me you want but the idea of me. Because I'll never be the kind of woman who blindly follows just because you're leading."

"Is it because you don't trust me?" He paused with his hand on his belt.

I shook my head. "I don't assume you always have the information necessary to make every decision. But when you do, I trust you'll do what's right for you, me, and us. I know this isn't new for you." I stared into my lap and twiddled my fingers as I said, "You used to include Oyinlola in decisions that affected her."

The silence after I brought up his dead wife grew loud and pushed us further apart. A tear splashed on my finger, but I lacked the energy to wipe it away. I hadn't meant to talk about her. My relationship with Kent was different from his with her. Comparing how he was with her to how he was with me wasn't fair, but dammit, I wanted him to see me as someone deserving of an equal say in our relationship.

"You have a short memory, little bunny."

The barely suppressed anger in Kent's voice caused me to snap my head up and see his glare. He shed his pants and stood naked before me.

"What short memory?" I asked, right before he snatched my velour hoodie over my head and tossed it behind him.

"What are you..."

Kent pushed me onto my back, then targeted my matching velour pants next. A battle ensued where I wanted to keep them on and he didn't.

"You can't think sex with me right now will fix our issues." I twisted, trying to escape his firm grip on my clothes.

"Are you forgetting I let you talk me out of bodyguards to begin with? No offense, little bunny, but *I* can't trust you to keep yourself safe." He ripped my pants and underwear down my legs and hurled them as well. "But I will promise you this. I'll let you know my plans ahead of time so if you want to argue about it, you can. However, don't expect me to bend when the risk is never waking up to see your face or hear your voice again."

Kent moved to my bra, but stilled when I placed my hand over his. He glared into my eyes, but I met his glower with contrition.

"I'm sorry."

The heat fled his stare and he rested his forehead against mine. "What are you sorry for?"

I swallowed. His heat blanketed me, and his angry dick rested above my pussy. Was he warning me or punishing me? And if he was, what would either be? Was he showing me something only to deny me or was he keeping his hard-on close to my pussy to remind me he can fuck like a beast and I would be lucky to walk straight afterward?

"For picking a fight and not realizing what my actual issue was."

His silence pushed me to elaborate. "I was cooped up and restless and feeling out of place. Not being allowed out was kind of an excuse to blow up at you."

"Because you don't feel like this is home to you?"

I shrugged and looked away, but Kent captured my cheek and pulled until I met his gaze again.

"I built a home with Lola."

"I know," I groaned while staring at the ceiling and blinking back fresh tears. "It was in that home I saw your good qualities."

"And I intend to build one with you. From the foundation up. Our relationship is unique to us and only we can define it."

His response startled me into looking at him again.

"You want to build a home with me?"

"Little bunny, I obviously have to refresh your memory." He brushed his lips against mine.

I gasped as he licked the seam. He took advantage and pushed his tongue into my mouth to lick and devour me. While he greedily destroyed me with kisses, he kept his hands busy, divesting me of my bra.

I gasped again when he pinched, then rubbed my nipple, freed now from the cotton cups.

Sensations flooded my body, urging me to move. I rubbed my legs against his. My skin prickled as the hair on his limbs added to my sensitivity.

"Kent," I moaned into his mouth.

He separated our lips and kissed from my chin to my breast.

I clutched his head, sinking my fingers into his hair.

"I've told you once already, little bunny, there's no going back." He sucked my nipple into his mouth. "You can't threaten to leave me because I won't allow it." He drew on my sensitive bud and it zinged all the way to my pussy. "And since your memory isn't so good, I guess I'll have to remind you daily."

"Promise?" I writhed beneath him.

Need took over, making me incoherent in everything but the persistent ache between my thighs.

"Is my pussy wet?"

"You can feel how wet she is." I rubbed my wet pussy along his shaft but it wasn't enough.

"Yes, I can, but…" He dangled that but like a carrot, however, I was in no mood.

"Kent, don't tease me!"

"Is my pussy ready to be filled?"

"Yes… I need you inside me." I shifted against him, bumping my clit for the extra sensation.

"Then put me where you need me, little bunny."

I grabbed his shaft and placed him at my entrance. And I pulled.

He slowly sank into my body, stretching my walls with his girth.

I groaned in ecstasy.

"Fuck, you fit me like home," Kent whispered in my ear.

I crossed my ankles under his ass to pull him closer as he thrust into me. "I'll be whatever you need."

"You already are." Kent lowered his mouth to mine while he drove his dick in and out of me. While he tortured me with pleasure.

I clung to him, needing his strength to ground me while he tried his damndest to fuck me through the mattress. I writhed against him, reaching for that all-consuming end only he has ever provided. My pussy spasmed around his length and my thigh muscles shook with the effort to attain a powerful orgasm.

Then Kent fluttered his fingers against my clit and sent me soaring. My voice grew the higher I flew but I couldn't control myself. If I deafened him, I hoped he'd consider it a proud achievement.

"Fuck, little bunny. Keep milking me like that and I'll come before I'm ready."

"Come anyway. You and I know you're going to recharge and fuck me again in no time."

He chuckled. "You know your cock well."

I squeezed him again and he groaned into my shoulder and flooded my insides. I caressed his spine and rubbed my legs against his ass still clenching as he continued to empty himself inside me.

When he settled, he rolled us until I lay atop him, listening to his heartbeat slow. He rubbed my ass in gentle circles in the pleasant silence surrounding us.

"Are we good?" he asked.

"Are we partners?"

"Yes. I don't want nor do I need a door mat. I want you, Madison Montgomery. I want your stubbornness." He kissed my forehead. "Your fearlessness." Kiss. "Your heart." Kiss. "Your every goddamn thing." Kiss. "And I'll give you everything in return."

I sank into him, relishing his acceptance, his warmth, and although he hasn't said the words yet, his love. "We're good."

"Good enough that you'll sit on my face and feed me my pussy?"

I sprang up with a hand on his chest holding me upright. "You are never satisfied."

"Not yet, but I will be." He pulled my arm free and raised his head to meet me in a kiss, however barking from the other room reminded us of the recent addition to the household.

"I bet they need a walk." I pulled out of his arms and went in search of my clothes.

"Are you really opposed to having the dogs?" He went to don a more casual outfit than the dress shirt and pants he wore earlier.

I pulled on a fresh pair of panties and sweats. "They're here now." I peeked at Kent and slumped my shoulders. "And they're too adorable to abandon. I really didn't stand a chance."

Kent grinned and stood. "Good, and the burden of training them won't be on your shoulders alone. Remember, we're partners."

"Yeah, but if you had asked, I would have voted for a cat." I strode to the door.

"Cats can't protect you the way German Shepherds can."

I shrugged. "Still."

Kent ushered me out of the bedroom to tend the dogs. As soon as we appeared, they wagged their tails and barked.

"We shouldn't hold off the housing situation. Apartment living isn't ideal for GSDs." I kneeled down and opened the kennels.

"We'll find a solution that works until we build ours." He handed me a leash while he put the other on the second dog.

I peeked at him, wondering if this was a delaying tactic.

"Call me superstitious, but I want to capture Carol and her accomplice before we buy any property together. Something about having her negative energy surrounding us when we're supposed to be happy doesn't sit right with me."

I nodded, accepting his response. Carol was a problem. So was whoever helped her.

We left the apartment with my guards in tow. Would I ever get comfortable with so many men following me?

"What should we name them?" Kent pointed towards the dogs, dragging us in their enthusiasm to reach the park area built on the compound.

"How about Benson and Stabler? They were my all-time favorite duo on Law & Order: SVU."

We spent an hour tiring the puppies and beginning rudimentary training with treats. When we returned to the apartment, Kent disappeared while I sat on the floor, and played with them until they collapsed at my side.

From the corner of my eye, I glimpsed his profile. I turned to find him observing me, but like so many times, I couldn't read his expression.

"Why are you staring at me like that?"

He pushed off against the wall and closed the distance between us. "I'm wondering if you need another refresher."

I smiled, my heart lightened from my earlier burden. "I don't need a reminder."

"But that memory of yours..." He picked up the pups and placed them in their kennels.

"Isn't so short that I need a reminder so soon."

"Maybe I need one." He returned and held his hand out to me. Once I placed mine in his, he pulled me into a standing position.

"Yeah? I doubt it." I spoke with a whisper, although I had no reason to lower my voice.

With Kent so close and the determined glint in his eye, we were the only two people to exist.

He placed his pointer finger beneath my chin and pushed my face up. "Who's your man, Madison?" Kent asked with his lips a hair's breath from mine.

"You are. I told you before."

"Yeah, but you were mad when you said it."

"You're my man, Kent Luxe."

"Glad to hear it. And since you so boldly claimed me as your man, I'm telling you now, I'm claiming your future." He lowered his face until he also claimed my lips.

I didn't want to feel so giddy with the danger still surrounding us, but each glide of his tongue and the way Kent slid his hand to grab the back of my head to angle me for a deeper kiss... Well, the man had a golden tongue sweet enough to erase worries.

CHAPTER 21

ent

"Thank you, everyone for all the long hours you've put in over the past few weeks. We appreciate your dedication to the company's success while we navigate the speculation in the press." Hal closed his leather-bound portfolio and turned to me. "Kent, can I have a word?"

I settled into my seat while I waited for everyone from the legal and public relations department to file out of the conference room.

Hal rolled his pen against the tabletop. Back and forth. Back and forth until the last person closed the door behind them. I studied the head of Luxe Locations' legal team, wondering what had him so rattled he displayed his tell.

"Kent, I wanted to make you aware..." Hal cleared his throat. "Someone on the board is secretly setting up meetings with other members."

"Do you know the reason behind these meetings?" I leaned forward but kept my voice level, although I was keen to identify any disloyal member on my staff or board.

Hal flattened his lips. "I only have speculations. I haven't been invited to the discussions."

"Give me names."

"You should be more worried about why."

"Hal, I asked you why. You came back with you have guesses. Well, I can conjecture as well as the next man."

"Good, so let's get ahead of the message before more board members jump ship."

I steepled my fingers and looked at him over the tips. "You have a suggestion?"

Hal relaxed his stance and exhaled. "Yes. The woman you hired from the crisis management firm... She's bringing a lot of unwanted attention with the men who follow her everywhere. They're causing disruptions in the office."

"I hired them for her safety."

"But they don't work for Luxe Locations. They shouldn't have been given clearance to enter the building let alone terrify the employees."

"Hal, be honest. Those men probably make our workers feel safer."

"I have to disagree, Kent. But there is another solution if you don't want to remove them. Get rid of her. That way they'll continue to protect her without disturbing our work. It's not like she's up to the task. Her job is to revamp our image and she's failed." He held his hand to stop the objection on the tip of my tongue from issuing forth. "Look, Kent. I know you said she did a great job with that rockstar and prince, but from what I've seen, I wonder if she..." He lapsed into silence and pinched his lips.

"If. She. What?" I said each word with strained patience.

"If she didn't take credit for someone else's work. You can't deny she's the classic definition of a DEI hire."

The urge to leap across the table nearly overtook me. "In what way?"

"Come on, Kent! She's a woman trying to rehab a man's image. What the hell does she know? On top of that, she's—"

"Hal, you need to shut up and leave."

He jolted. "Kent, I'm trying to help save you from being ousted from your own company because an incompetent woman—"

I stood, glaring at my counsel. "If you don't walk out of here on your own, you won't be walking anywhere ever again."

Hal jumped out of his chair. "I hope the pussy is worth it when you lose your company."

I lowered the veil over my emotions, showing Hal who I was for the first time. His eyes widened and he fled toward the door.

Too late.

As rage fueled me, my fists pummeled his face. I didn't hear his screams, only his disparaging remarks about Madison. I didn't see his face as blood spurted from his mouth and nose, only the slimy, patronizing grin as he denigrated my woman's accomplishments.

I hit him, blow after blow feeding my fury until Madison's voice penetrated the fog and three pairs of hands dragged me away from Hal.

Madison's concerned face swam into view, clearing the haze. He cupped my face as her stare delved into my eyes.

"I'm good now," I said.

She sighed in relief. "Okay, now tell me what the hell this is." She pointed toward Hal.

His secretary assisted him into an upright seated position. His left eye was swelling fast, almost completely shut, his nose bent at an awkward angle, and blood made it difficult to see if there was more extensive damage.

I curled my fists again, wanting to ensure he hadn't gotten off lightly. If not for the gentle pair of hands raising my bloody hand to Madison's face, I would have charged over to Hal and finished what I'd started.

"Kent?"

"Something I'll handle." I kissed the tip of her nose then approached Hal. "I'll understand if you want to hand in your resignation. If not, don't think you can use this incident to threaten me. Use it to remember to mind your tongue. Got me?"

Hal glowered at me through his good eye for two seconds before begrudgingly nodding.

"And if you're in touch with those traitorous board members, make them aware that no one can take what's mine while I have breath in my body." I turned to Madison and held my hand out to her.

Without hesitation, she placed her palm on mine. Her immediate acceptance despite the blood still dripping from my knuckles was more proof, not that I needed any, that I needed her by my side.

As I left the conference room, more faces came into focus. Omar, Mal, Deke, and a few office workers. Given what I'd done to Hal, I'd have to engage Quarren's firm to keep everything under wraps.

As soon as we entered my office, Madison fled to the bathroom. She returned with a small first-aid kit and a roll of paper towels in hand. I stared out of my glass walls to observe my employees as they pretended not to avidly watch us. With a disgusted tsk, I stood to my desk and frosted over the glass for my privacy.

Madison followed and laid bandages, antiseptic wipes, saline solution, gauze, and the roll of paper towels beside me before taking my right hand in hers. With her focus on my bloody hand, she asked. "Are you going to tell me what made you go fight club on your lawyer's ass?"

"He made a suggestion I didn't like."

She raised her face and quirked her brow. There was no judgment in her eyes, just a need to understand.

"He thinks having you around is bad for business. Even implied I might face a coup over you being here. Nothing I'd ever entertain." I smiled at her, trying to reassure her, but the corners of her mouth fell and sadness entered her brown eyes, distorting them with an unwelcome shadow.

She bowed her head over my fist and flushed the blood from my hand with saline, exposing several cuts I wasn't aware I had. "Maybe you should," she said to my hand.

I stilled. "Maybe I should what?"

Madison shrugged, still without looking me in the face. "Consider not having me around."

"Try telling me that shit to my face."

She glared at me, a sheen glimmering over her eyes until a tear spilled onto her cheek. "If someone or a group of people are actively working to take your business from you, don't let me be the reason they succeed."

"That memory of yours is doing that shit again," I growled about to rise and show her why this conversation was a nonstarter.

"I'm not suggesting we break up. We can go back to keeping our relationship a secret. Instead of working in the office, I'll work upstairs." She cupped my cheek and pressed her forehead against mine. "Pretending will buy you time to find out who's working against you."

"And how does it help you on your quest to exonerate me?" I inhaled her scent, allowing it to settle in my lungs and calm the adrenaline running through my blood at the mere possibility of ending our relationship. "Didn't you say the man working with Carol might be on my payroll?"

"Yes, but I have a plan that doesn't require me to be in the office."

I arched my brow, needing more than a vague plan to ease my sense of loss at the thought of not looking up from my computer to see her head bent over hers.

"Remember, you asked Omar to help me on that end? He's pretty dedicated to getting Elsie justice."

I grunted, not entirely pacified but curious, nonetheless. "They're getting serious? He works fast."

Madison peered up at me from lowered lashes. "Right because me moving in with you a few weeks after working for you would be considered a slow burn romance?"

I smirked. "There goes that memory again. Must I remind you how many years it took me to see you?"

"Only if you want to sleep alone on the top floor tonight." She dropped her hand and pulled away.

I grabbed her around the waist until she landed in my lap.

"Kent, you're going to get blood all over my clothes."

"Can't have that, can we?" I dragged her blazer over her shoulders, smearing Hal's blood on her blouse..

"This is the opposite of helping." She writhed in my lap, awakening my cock every time her ass rubbed against me.

"The change of clothes in the bathroom would beg to disagree."

She opened her mouth to protest, and I swallowed it and her moans as I worked her body to a fever pitch of need. I wanted no more talk about her spending time away from me or pretending we weren't together while I planned a future with Madison.

We hadn't discussed the future of her business in DC or how to tell Ife about us. So many unknowns still surrounded us, but one thing I wouldn't relent on was having Madison facing our troubles proudly by my side.

CHAPTER 22

$\mathcal{M}$adison

Words swam before my eyes, the sign I needed to take a break. Without Kent sitting across from me, work engrossed me to the point of ignoring basic bodily functions. Eating and going to the bathroom took a backseat if it meant I was closer to finding clues about Carol and her accomplice.

Maybe I focused on her because I didn't want to express my genuine fear.

I almost died.

She almost cut my life short when I was finally about to join that elite club so many woman aspire to. The same one my mom's been part of for most of her adult life. Where I found success in my profession and relationship without sacrificing one for the other. And fucking Carol and whoever she used to transport me into that other car were trying to put a damper on my wins.

I refused to let them.

I stretched my neck and decided to take a break. If Kent checked up on me, I didn't want him distressing over my missed lunch, even if I enjoyed his punishments a little too much. The release I got put me in a blissful, aroused state without the tension and stiff muscles. But what I valued the most was the aftermath, when he would hold me in his arms. I'd never felt more cherished or safer than in those quiet moments.

After washing my face and eating, I returned to Benson and Stabler mewling at me. They had been good all morning as they slept at my feet while I worked. I walked them in the park, escorted by my guard. Since the hour was late for lunch, only a few employees took advantage of the outdoor space for a little fresh air. Their curious glances made me flush with embarrassment although I had nothing to be embarrassed about. I refused to give them more fodder for the BBD site after Kent's fight last week with Hal.

Thankfully, I had little time to dwell on them as wrangling Benson and Stabler under control diverted my attention.

Reinvigorated by the workout with the puppies, I returned to the penthouse and my earlier task. A report from my second-in-command, Emily, snagged my interest, and I needed to dig deeper. She'd tapped her contact at the NSA for information about Carol.

Although the person had nothing new to pinpoint where Carol could be hiding, I was learning a lot about the woman who abducted me and who we suspected of killing Kent's former dates. For example, Carol was an alias. Although shocking, learning the woman who abandoned me on an active train track went by a different name made sense. Born Jennifer Aselworth of the New England Aselworths, a prominent family with generations of wealth, Jennifer displayed unsettling signs of erotomania because of an underlying bi-polar diagnosis. There was mention of other families connected to the Aselworths. One name sounded familiar but I couldn't place it. Instead, I focused on Carol/Jennifer's diagnosis.

Erotomania? What the hell was that? I sidelined the report to research the diagnosis, growing more concerned with each new question I had. At the top of my list was, did her obsession with Kent begin when she began working for the company, or did something else trigger her?

Suddenly, my vision went dark. My heart rate spiked. Why hadn't I heard anything? No one should have been able to enter the penthouse with the guards stationed outside. I raised my hands to feel silky material covering my eyes.

"I have a surprise for you," Kent said, calming my rising panic.

"You scared me!"

"I called your name a couple times but you must not have heard me." The hair from his beard tickled my neck, then his firm lips pressed against the underside of my chin. "Forgive me?"

"Maybe. Your surprise isn't another set of puppies, is it?"

He withdrew with a disgruntled frown. "Have a little faith."

I eyed him with a narrowed glare but allowed him to pull me from my chair and lead me to the living room. A black bag sat on the coffee table. Mesh panels on the sides revealed an indistinct silhouette inside.

"Kent, what did you do?"

He passed me to unzip a panel on the top. A tiny feline head popped out and I gasped. The orange and dark brown marks of a tabby surrounded two green eyes but from its cute pink nose to its chest was the fluffiest white fur I'd ever seen.

"You got me a cat?"

"You said you prefer them." Kent shrugged with a sheepish grin so endearing I stared in wonder. "As long as I have breath in my body, I'll give you everything you want." He stroked my cheek.

"When I said I would have voted for a cat, I didn't expect—"

"Lesson learned. Expect more from me. Expect that when you tell me what you like or what you want, I'll provide those things. I pay attention to everything you say, even the casual comments."

I peeked at the cat that's been observing the surroundings during my conversation with Kent. "What's its name?"

"Up to you."

The cat leaped out of the bag and strutted to the edge of the table like he had already laid claim to everything he saw.

As I neared him, he peered at me with a sense of superiority I couldn't help but find adorable.

"What made you choose him?" I asked.

"He was fluffy without being too fluffy." Kent stood beside me as I reached out my hand for the cat's inspection.

The feline sniffed me, then meowed as if demanding something. All without budging from his spot.

Benson and Stabler barreled into the room as if I hadn't exhausted them during lunch. They jumped at and sniffed the new arrival, their curiosity and eagerness to meet the cat almost tangible in the air.

Without hesitation, the cat launched himself at Stabler. His paws hugged the dog's throat, and he twisted, slamming the puppy to the ground. Stabler backpedaled and ran behind Kent's legs. The cat leveled a glare at Benson, and he hied to join his brother.

"I seem to recall you disparaging a cat's ability to protect."

Kent stared in amazement at the feline. "Obviously that cat's been here before. If a don were a feline, it'd be him."

I wrinkled my nose. "He's too cute to be a Don. I think I'll call him Tyger. He's pretty fierce in a gorgeous package." I kneeled down to pet the cat, wondering if he would treat me similarly to the dogs.

He peered at my hand then my face then decided to approach me. Surprised, I waited, but he didn't stop at my knees. Instead, he crawled into my lap and curled into a ball while meowing at me the entire time. When he glanced expectantly at me, I asked Kent, "Did you buy him treats?"

"Among other things." Kent handed me a small pouch.

I fed Tyger who quieted after the first treat. He pawed at my face until I lavished him with pets.

"I take it I've earned your forgiveness."

I quirked the side of my mouth while sidling a glance at Kent. "You've earned more than my forgiveness."

Heat immediately enters his blue eyes. "Yeah? Give me a hint."

"A pussy for a cat?"

"I don't know if you're trying to be sexy or funny. Regardless, I intend to collect."

CHAPTER 23

ent

I took Tyger, who was surprisingly long for a tabby, from Madison's lap. Her offer wasn't one I intended to take a rain check on. I grabbed her hand, pulled her up, and began stripping her.

She laughed. "Kent, the bedroom is—"

"Too far. And you're overdressed, little bunny."

"You just have a problem with me and clothes. Nothing I wear is suitable."

"Because everything you wear belongs on the floor." Once naked, I spun her to face the couch and directed her with a hand on her spine onto the cushions and in position. "Spread your legs for me, little bunny."

She peered at me over her shoulder. Desire raged in her eyes, her irises darkening to an almost molten black.

I kneeled behind her until my face was level with her thick ass and brown lips peeked through her thick thighs. Shiny pink treasure begged me to do more than look, an invitation I'd never deny. I grabbed the back of Madison's thighs and buried my face between her legs and breathed her in.

No scent compared to Madison's lust. She filled my lungs, driving my thirst for her higher. Unable to hold my hunger at bay any longer, I spread her cheeks and lick from her clit to rosette. Her flavor hits my tongue in an explosion.

"Ooh." Madison's body shivers under my tongue.

"That's right. Coo for me, little bunny. Let me hear how well I'm treating my pussy." I almost lost myself in Madison, so caught up with eating her out I barely registered the sting from when she reached behind herself to grab my hair. Hell, after the first time she came on my tongue and I lapped up her juices, I went in for another until her thighs shook and she cried out, "Mercy!"

She collapsed onto the back of the sofa, her body shaking as she tried to catch her breath.

I kissed her shoulder and caressed her spine, paying extra attention to her ass. As large as my hands were, they barely covered half her rear and I'd never stop trying.

When her breathing calmed, I turned her face to kiss her. I sank into her lips and her taste until she began writhing against my cock.

"Ready for round two?"

She moaned and nodded.

I rose onto the couch behind her and took myself in hand, dark in color and hard in anticipation of reuniting with Madison. I sank into her and she accommodated my girth by spreading her legs wider.

"You always feel so good on that first stroke," she groaned.

"And you always feel good on every stroke." I curled my fingers into her ringlets and brought her face closer to mine.

Madison lowered her eyelashes but I glimpsed the white of her eyes as they rolled into her head.

"Who do you belong to, little bunny?"

"You. I've always been yours, Kent," she said breathlessly as I plunged inside her.

"And this pussy?"

"Yours like everything else."

I rubbed her ass as it jiggled with every thrust. "And will you let me claim this ass next?"

Without hesitation, she said, "Absolutely."

"Dad! Mads? Oh my God, I'm going to be sick."

At the threshold of the living room, Ife stood covering her mouth. For a second I didn't recognize her without her signature long hair. She now sported a razor-sharp bob.

"Ife?" Madison froze in horror.

"Shit!" I pulled Madison onto the couch, out of Ife's view, and covered her with a throw.

"What... Why? Oh my God, why?"

"Ife, wait in the study. I'll explain what you need to know, but allow us to get dressed first." I pointed her toward the room.

Although my daughter stayed our family home whenever she visited, she worked with the designers who decorated the penthouses. Once she stomped down the corridor, I turned to Madison. She seemed frozen as if a hellish scene played out in front of her.

I cupped her cheek until she focused on me. Guilt and shame filled her eyes and she stared at my chin instead of looking at me directly.

"Little bunny, we knew she'd find out eventually."

"Not like this. Never like this. What are we going to do?" Tears welled up on Madison's lashes before sliding down the sides of her face and into her hair.

"I'm going to talk to her. Make her understand." I stood and pulled Madison from the sofa. "And you are going to put some clothes on and wipe the guilty look off your face. You have nothing to be sorry for, and Ife can be reasonable."

"Okay," Madison said in the smallest voice I'd ever heard from her. I pushed her toward the bedroom, but she stopped and picked up our discarded clothes.

I helped, putting on mine in a rush before heading toward the study. Ife, my baby girl who wasn't a child anymore, paced the study and wiped her face. She reminded me so much of her mother. From the her deep brown complexion to the way she stomped whenever

156

someone or thing frustrated her. This time I was the source of her problems.

I entered the room. "Ife…"

She swung around and pointed toward the door behind me. "What was that, and don't tell me it wasn't what I think it was. I heard… How long has this been going on behind my back?"

I leveled her with a pitying stare. "First, you aren't a child so I know you understand what you saw. Second, only guilty people would say to someone without vision problems they didn't see something they clearly did." I reached out my arms to capture her shoulders and hold her still because she continued to tread back and forth.

She evaded my hold with a grimace.

"Third, I never intended to hide my relationship—"

"Relationship? No, whatever is between you two is not a relationship."

"Are you going to listen or interrupt everything I say?"

"When what you're saying isn't making sense, of course I'm going to chime in and tell you about yourself."

"You obviously have some things you want to get off your chest before you'll allow me to respond." Despite the anger flooding my veins, I folded my arms and sat on a leather-bound chair to patiently wait her out.

The moment was already fraught with high emotions. I channeled the skills I used as a CEO whenever conflicts arose at the company that I was willing to handle with more logic. Although whenever Madison was involved, I tended to lead with my feelings, doing so in this instance would hurt my daughter.

"Why her? Why Mads? You could have any woman in the world." Ife looked expectantly at me, but I refused to add flames to our argument until she got all her bile out. She huffed and rolled her eyes, probably remembering other disagreements we had where I used this tactic.

"I never said anything when you hoed yourself around and became community dick—"

"Don't disrespect me just because you're mad. I'm still your father, whether or not you agree with my choices."

"Fine! I never objected with the other women you were with because I knew you were lonely after Mom died, but… Mads is different. She was mine first. My best friend. My safe space. Why'd you have to take her from me when I needed—"

"I haven't taken her from you, sweetheart. Madison will always—"

"You just don't get it, do you? When you dump her like the others, how am I supposed to act around her?"

My face firmed and the fierceness I felt at the possibility of a life without Madison must have escaped and been visible on my face because Ife reared back.

"No. You can't be serious."

"There will be no dumping Madison. I will mar—"

"Don't you dare finish that sentence. You can't expect me to accept your relationship as if everything is normal when it can never be the same." Ife shook her head, her pacing became more erratic as she mumbled, "Whatever fever dream you two are in can't be serious. She just got here. There's still time to end it before it's too late, and maybe just maybe there will be something to salvage between us." She stopped and turned, a feverish light in her eyes. "That's it. You end this… nonsense now. I'll try my best to forget I walked in on what I walked in on and heard what I heard. She'll go back to D.C. and things will eventually return to normal."

I frowned, very opposed to the idea of Madison going anywhere without me. "And what happens when she returns to Douglas?"

"Why would she? She avoided coming here for years. She stopped visiting her parents once, she can do it again."

Suddenly, the enormity of Ife's words hit me. *I* was the reason Madison disappeared whenever I visited Ife. I was also the reason she never came home. No wonder her parents fawned over her so much. They didn't know the next time they would see her after her assignment was over.

And Nikita… The reason she didn't push harder against our relationship when she still harbored hard feelings against me was most likely because Madison was more likely to stay in Douglas if we were in a relationship.

My little bunny loved every moment she spent with her parents. I'd thought before there was a desperation underlying the visits she made when she wasn't busy working herself to an early illness. All because I rejected her when her heart was at its most vulnerable, Madison had cut as many ties to Douglas as she could for a clean break.

However, as I looked at my daughter, I realized there was one tie Madison couldn't sever. She left everything that represented safety and love and protection, yet kept the one connection that would always remind her of her heartache. She endured eight years of painful reminders every time she spoke, visited, and saw Ife. And she did it because her love for my daughter was the only thing keeping her together when she faced everything alone.

I couldn't let my relationship with Madison be the catalyst for ruining their relationship after the damage I'd already done to Madison. "Sweetheart, I thought Madison was your best friend. What you're asking isn't fair to her."

"Fuc—to hell with fairness. The second she let you stick your dic—your you know what—inside her, all fairness went out the window. God! I'll never get that image out of my head." Ife scrubbed her face as if trying to cleanse her memory, but what she saw wasn't something anyone could forget.

On her next pass in front of me, I snagged Ife's wrist and halted her manic pacing. She pulled, but my grip was strong and my will stronger. She eventually stopped resisting to glare her fury down at me.

"We need to find a way to work things out." I loosened my hold.

She yanked herself free and backed away. "There's only one way to figure things out, Dad. You have to choose. Me or Madison."

I lurched from my seat and rounded on Ife. "You must be forgetting who the man who raised you is. Who changed your diapers, who read bedtime stories to you, who was there to comfort you when you had nightmares, who scared off all the bogeymen, and who was there at the drop of a dime to support and praise you? I was there for every accomplishment you made and I will be there for all the new ones. You will never not be my daughter, and I'll never stop loving you. And I will always show up whenever you ask or need me."

She nodded, her face becoming calm for the first time since she arrived.

"And Madison will be by my side for all your future endeavors."

CHAPTER 24

$\mathcal{M}$adison

I sank to the floor outside Kent's study after hearing Ife's ultimatum, my heart shredded and bloody in the hands I curled against my chest. Not even Kent's defense of me eased the pain as Ife stormed out of the office without seeing me, screaming, "Don't expect to talk to me until you get rid of her!"

Memories bombarded me, silencing the questions about how she knew where Kent was or how she got into the penthouse. Those were insignificant compared to our years together. Years of us huddled side by side from childhood to adulthood as we shared secrets turned to ash on my tongue. Years of adventures we had no business going on, trips, coffees, late-night conversations, sleepovers for the hell of it, crying sessions, calm-down sessions where we talked each other off a bridge—mostly I did most of the talking while Ife did the threatening —binge sessions whether it was food or movies, or our favorite K-pop idol, Woo Do Kang, being sighted in the wild.

Ife was my person from the time we entered kindergarten and

she saw the light skin patches on my face and said, "I wish we could be sisters. Since we can't let's be best friends and punch the dummies who keep pointing and making weird faces whenever they see you."

Yeah, Ife was my warrior and my safe space just as much as I was hers. And now I had to contend with destroying that.

Kent walked out of the study and noticed me curled in on myself on the floor. He kneeled beside me and cupped my knee. "Little bunny, she'll come around. She just needs time."

I shook my head and opened my mouth, but a sob escaped. One became two, then three until I lost count and poured my heart out because it was breaking.

Kent used his strength to pick me up and carry me to the bedroom where he held me until I passed out from the emotional upheaval.

Hours later, I woke to him holding me in his arms as if he hadn't moved from the spot for hours. The room was dark, probably three in the morning. I blinked, feeling the pressure to cry building up behind my eyes again as my new reality hit, but no moisture appeared to help my outpouring. I was a dry lakebed about to fossilize the relics abandoned in its depths when it was once full. Emptiness engulfed me as the realization hit again.

I was no longer Ife's person. She'd relegated me to a 'her.' As if I was a stranger, unworthy of being in her vicinity.

"I think, deep down, I knew something like this would happen," I whispered brokenly to Kent. "That's why I was so against her finding out about us. Even with all the madness surrounding us, I wanted to hold onto what we were becoming for as long as possible because I haven't felt happiness like this ever in my life."

Kent twisted my body until I looked up into his face. His lips were a firm line and I imagined brackets framing his mouth if not for the covering of his beard shielding the telltale sign from me. Even without that indicator, Kent who always appeared younger than his age, wore his forty-eight years and then some in the wrinkles at the corners of his eyes and the ridges in his brow.

"Little bunny, I promise I'll dedicate my life to making you happy again. I'll convince Ife what she's doing is hurting herself as much as she's hurting you, and I'll make her come around."

At his mention of his daughter's name, I glanced away. The teenage me never thought twice about the consequences of starting a relationship with the man I loved, and the adult me was just as guilty because I avoided thinking about them for my own selfish ends. But now...

Kent pinched my chin and turned my face to look at him again. "I understand how important Ife is to you, and as long as I have breath in my body, I'll give you everything you want," he said, repeating his vow from yesterday.

A time when the only thing on my mind was being seen, heard, and appreciated by the man I'd hero worshipped as a child.

"But now's not the time. She's not receptive to any overture on our parts."

"No, I can't accept that. I have to talk to Ife. Maybe if she heard..."

What? That I'd pursued her father while he was married to her mother? Or how about years later, how I taunted him, intending to seduce him as a way to exact my revenge for hurting me, but ensnared the both of us in my trap instead?

"Maybe you're right." I sagged against Kent, dispirited and unable to see a way for us to mend this rift. "But how long do you think we'll have to wait?"

Kent wrapped me in his arms and kissed the side of my neck. "I don't know, little bunny, but we'll have each other to lean on until the time's right."

Would we though? One day, if Ife never forgave us, Kent would grow to resent me. Ife wasn't just his daughter. She was Oye's, too. A part of his wife. Ife was the embodiment and the living proof of his life with her mother, and I never wanted to be the reason he lost that reminder. Ife was also his princess. His little girl that he'd spoiled from the moment she was in her mother's womb all the way until before she caught me and her father together. I grew up on stories about how Mr. Luxe went from an ice-cold business man to a puddle of water whenever Oye rubbed her stomach, his concerns always about his wife's and unborn daughter's needs. Then as I grew, I saw him interacting with Ife firsthand.

Even my dad didn't pamper me as much as Kent indulged his daughter, and I was a daddy's girl. Still am. Just like Ife. So I knew from the years I'd stopped visiting my parents how hard life would be for Ife, and I'd maintained communication. For her to tell Kent she was cutting him off from that minimal of contact would devastate them both.

"Maybe I should move back in with my parents until—"

"That's not an option I'm willing to entertain, little bunny. We're a unit now, and units don't live apart."

I snuggled closer into Kent's warmth, wishing I had his conviction while not arguing with him. I wanted what he wanted too much, even knowing that under enough stress, any unit could crumble to the eventual pressure. I didn't want that, but I also didn't want Kent to turn into a man full of regrets for not repairing the fractures in his and his daughter's relationship. As I lay huddled within the loving embrace of the love of my life, I silently vowed I would do whatever I had to do to mend Ife and Kent's bond. Even if it meant enduring the unlivable.

CHAPTER 25

 ent

I slammed my phone in its cradle as I stared at Madison's empty desk. Despite understanding why she decided to work upstairs and avoid how her present reinforced the boards recent thirst for my ousting, I wished she were close.

Although only a day had passed since my confrontation with Ife, Madison's presence soothed me, and I needed calm now as Ife ignored my calls and messages. I had Omar call her on the hour, every hour and transfer the call to mine, but all I got for my efforts was a custom voice message saying until I ended things with Madison the call would not go through.

While I brooded over my love life, Hal and Mal barged into my office. I glanced at Omar whose back was conveniently facing me then to my digital calendar that showed I had the rare hour free.

I glared at the two men, suspecting my free hour was by design. "Hal," I barked. "Brought Mal in for reinforcement?"

Hal leveled a sheepish smile at me and shrugged at Mal. "I came to apologize."

"With a buffer." Mal sauntered over to me and studied my glower. "Saw Ife run out of here yesterday. Is that the cause of the storm building on your face?"

"What are you talking about?" Hal, forwent the safe distance he'd kept between us to approach.

"Hmm, did she learn about you and Madison?" Mal rubbed his chin as he voiced his thought.

I switched my glare to him, silently confirming his assumption and the motherfucker laughed. "My life is funny to you?"

Mal shook his head while hugging his torso. "No, but the irony is."

"What are you talking about," Hal asked.

"Don't you remember the day Madison showed up, you and I expressed interest and our boss over here declared he wouldn't protect us from Ife's wrath when she murdered us for touching her best friend?" Mal chortled with unholy glee.

Hal, exercising a little more intelligence, covered his mouth to hide his amusement.

"Laugh and I'll double the beat down I gave you when you spouted the shit you said about Madison." I cracked my knuckles to remind him I was ready to go any time and place.

He raised his hand in surrender and wiped the smile off his face.

He was still on my shit list and hadn't redeemed himself, even if the apology he alluded to was for his insults to my future wife.

No, I hadn't asked Madison yet. I wouldn't be. She already made her choice when she agreed to be with me, and I would accept nothing less than her becoming Mrs. Kent Luxe.

I turned my attention to Mal whose shoulders hadn't stopped shaking. "I can give you a taste of what I gave Hal."

Mal straightened and shrugged off my threat with a grin while grabbing my arm. "Follow me. We can't do much about what went down between you, Ife, and Madison, but we can help you take your mind off it for a few minutes. Plus, you've been a real shit today."

"Really?" I glanced at Omar who avoided meeting my gaze as Mal and Hal sandwiched me between them and steered me to the main office elevator. "I wonder who gave you that idea."

"The janitor I found weeping in the men's room after you glared in his direction." Mal pushed the button for the elevator.

"I did not." I shrugged their arms off and straightened my suit.

"I was there. He was the reason I came to apologize to you."

"Apologize? For what specifically?"

Hal eyed me. "Let's get a few drinks in you first. No offense, but I'd prefer to say what I have to when you're more mellow, and you're nowhere close enough to that state of mind yet."

"You risk me forgetting all about you begging my forgiveness once I sober up."

Hal waved away my warning. "Not only will I have a witness," he pointed at Mal, "But I've seen you shit faced with clients before who thought to get one over on you and you had perfect recall the next day. We've been working too long for you to think I'd take advantage that way."

"Hmph." I entered the elevator as soon as the doors opened. Not because I wanted to spend time with my legal counsel and CFO. I desperately needed that drink to get my mind off Ife's rejection.

They took me to Refresh, the lounge bar in the downtown Luxe Continental hotel. As soon as we walked through the doors, the hotel staff perked up and met us with the first-class service famous in my hotels. They ushered us to a private room off the lounge that we could close by sliding the pocket doors or leave open to observe the main room.

We chose to leave the door open. I drank the first three drinks in silence while Mal and Hal made small talk.

Once some of the tension melted from my shoulders, I turned to Hal. "Alright, let's hear it. Maybe this time my punch will straighten out the knot I put in your nose."

"If you drop the hostility, you'll hear what I have to say."

I quirked my brow as I waited, though I couldn't imagine what he'd say to erase the way he denigrated Madison's and her accomplishments.

"Look, I know there's nothing I say that will excuse what I said about Madison. I let my concern for the company blind me to being a decent fucking human being, and I'm sorry for blaming her."

"That it?" I asked, remembering the worst of what came from his mouth.

"I should never have implied... what I did about her body or that you would have risked your legacy because of it."

I stared stonily back at him for seconds on end.

Hal gulped his drink but held my gaze.

"Alright, put me out of my misery. Are you going to beat the living shit out of Hal or forgive him?" Mal shoved himself against his seat and folded his arms in a pout.

"Why do I think you want the former?" Hal asked.

"Because you think I'm as bloodthirsty as Kent. Although, if you had spoken about my woman the way you spoke about Madison, I doubt you would have walked out of the office." Mal smiled. "Good thing, I'm like Kent before he met Madison. No ties but many straps." He winked and Hal and I groaned at his corny take.

"Well, before you decide on forgiving me, I have a confession I didn't know I needed to make until Mal mentioned Ife's upset departure yesterday."

I closed my eyes and squeezed my empty glass. "What. The. Fuck. Did. You. Do?"

Hal poured himself another drink from the bottles we'd ordered and swallowed the contents in one go. He repeated the action and I grabbed the bottle from his hands. "I saw Ife yesterday. She mentioned going to the house but it felt like no one had been there in months when she stopped by to surprise you. You weren't in your office and Omar told her you didn't have a meeting scheduled."

"Hal..." I ground the words between my teeth.

"I mentioned you could have been in the penthouse. I swear, I didn't mention which one."

"No, you just told her the code to get into it." I stood over him, shaking with wrath.

"How was I supposed to know she would catch..." His lie shriveled under the heat of my glare.

Although no one brought it up, everyone gossiped about the times my office walls turned opaque when only Madison and I were inside. It was all over the BBD site, but I ignored the chatter for Madison's sake. Maybe everyone's excuse for not turning against Madison was because she was an outside consultant and not an employee threatening someone's job. As long as no one disparaged her, I didn't address the site. A part of me didn't because I reveled in everyone knowing she was mine.

Hal wasn't ignorant to what Madison and I did, had even had the audacity to use her as a bargaining chip to save me from the board. He could never convince me he didn't suspect what Madison and I would do in the privacy of our home.

"Look, Kent, I swear, the penthouse slipped out. I wasn't thinking when I told her about it, and I didn't even give her the code at first."

I squeezed my fists, reliving the horror on Ife's face and our subsequent fight.

"Kent, she tried your private elevator on her own. When it didn't work, she sought me out and badgered me until I gave her the two codes. And before you ask me why I didn't give her only one, she specifically asked for both. She wouldn't leave me alone until I gave her what she wanted. What was I supposed to do? Have security escort the owner's daughter off the property?"

"Man, leave." Mal shook his head in disgust. "If I were in Kent's shoes, I can't say I'd forgive you for any of the shit you pulled. Especially because if she came to you, I know she went to Omar first and he didn't fold."

"I will, but before I do..." Hal turned beseeching eyes on me. "You've got to fix your relationship with Ife. If the board and the public see you as a united front, her presence would combat the negative press you've received. She'll rebrand you as a family man and not a lady's man, and the board—"

"Hal, take a few days off. Work from home if you must, but if I see your face or hear your voice again in the next two minutes, I can damn well guarantee the police will arrest me for your murder, and I'll say to hell with my public image."

Hal shakily rose from his seat and backed out of the private room as if he were facing off a king cobra poised to spit venom in his eyes and bite him with an extra dose of the lethal serum.

If I had the ability, I would. Because of his handling of my daughter, Madison was in pain, and I was the cause. My daughter was in pain, and I was the cause. I was in pain, and no matter how I looked at my situation, there was too much hurt and not enough healing to go around while Ife refused to give me the time of day.

"Kent, man, I'm really sorry your situation is so fucked up." Mal poured me another drink before serving himself. "If there's anything I can do, just let me know."

I swallowed everything in my glass. I wished I could feel the burn as the alcohol went down, but Mal had poured the smoothest cognac we carried at the lounge. I stared at my empty glass. "Because Ife walked in on me and Madison, my daughter's cut herself off from her support network." I shook my head, hating that I'd turned into a villain in my baby girl's eyes.

"Maybe she just needs time."

"That's what I told Madison. The problem is Madison has me and her mom and dad. Ife's alone."

"That's a real shitty hand you've been dealt. If I had a sister, I would send her to be Ife's sounding board. Unfortunately, I only have an older brother, and he's busy working for on the Second Family's detail. Not that I'd expect you to want my brother anywhere near your daughter."

"You're right. I don't know him, and I'd need more than you vouching for him before I'd ever ask him to look after my daughter when she's vulnerable."

"Do you want me to give you the name of a good therapist? I slept with... I briefly saw a therapist a few months ago. She might be able to help Ife put your and Madison's relationship into perspective."

I stared at Mal as an idea popped into my head. "You stayed away from Madison after I warned you."

"I took her to lunch."

"Because I was being a dick to her. Plus, the minute I mentioned work you forgot she existed. I knew then you were fucking with me and had no intentions toward her."

"True, getting one over on you does entertain me. So, what does that have to do with Ife?"

"I can trust you to be the shoulder she needs until she gets her equilibrium back. You'll listen to her problems and be the ear she needs without crossing the line."

"What? No. What you're proposing sounds a lot like babysitting. I've got my own life and playing support animal and pseudo therapist to a heartsick woman is not my idea of a good time."

"Mal, I'll owe you big if you do me this favor. If Ife spirals because she's never dealt with a loss like this, I don't know what I'll do."

Mal's horror at my suggestion turned to pity. "You could mitigate her loss. Put her above Madison. You said yourself, Madison has her mom and dad. You and Ife would have each other in the fallout."

"If only." I shook my head. "If I choose my daughter over Madison, Madison will also lose everything for the second time, but worse. She'll move away like she did after high school and she'll never return. This time, she won't have Ife to serve as a buffer for her loss. For years, Madison endured pain because of me. I can't be the reason she goes back to that nonexistence. Please, Mal, do me a solid," I begged, trying to protect my daughter and the woman I loved at the same time.

"Fuck me." Mal poured himself another drink.

"Does that mean yes?"

He raised his glass. "Farewell bachelorhood. Hello CFO nanny." He downed his cognac with a grimace that wasn't due to the drink but the coming days as he gave my daughter what I couldn't.

CHAPTER 26

$\mathcal{M}$adison

Work.

Work was the cure in times like these, I reminded myself. School work in college was how I distracted myself while I licked fresh wounds from Kent's rejection. Afterward, work during my internships, my first official job, and when I decided to branch out on my own saved me from dwelling on things I couldn't change. The long, sleepless hours I sacrificed were worth it because I built a successful business.

The playbook helped me in the past; it had to help me in the present. So, I buried myself in work. For days at a time until Kent's frustration boiled over.

I was on my second week of trying to work my pain away when Kent walked through the door to see me pushing my exhausted body beyond its limits again.

He didn't punish me, though. He never did anymore. Kent pinched his lips and without a word pulled me from my desk and led me to our bedroom, where he held and petted me like a wounded animal until I broke down and cried. It was our new routine.

My outpouring set off our menagerie.Benson and Stabler howled and Tyger mewled in sync with me.

I felt sorry for Kent's poor ears because the animals refused to quiet. They snuck into our bedroom and leaped onto the bed, pitifully wailing along with me. The dogs deferred to Tyger and only the feline trod forward to nudge my arm until I cleared a path for him to curl into my lap. Once the cat settled himself, Benson and Stabler found space on my legs and circled until they, too, curled into a ball with their heads on me. Calm now, they shared concerned glances with each other before turning their sad eyes on me and licking the parts of my body they could reach. I couldn't move under their combined weight, not that I would. But the combined heat of Kent's body behind me, the purring engine in my lap, and the thick, double-coated German Shepherds guaranteed I would be drenched in sweat.

I couldn't recall a time when I had so much love surrounding me, then I remembered... Ife was only one body, but she did as much for me as three pets and a man was doing for me right now. However, she had no one to do the same for her.

And the tears started over again, as did the concert of lamentation. And my sweet Kent, refused to leave my side or make me feel guilty for my feelings. He's said he understood what losing Ife meant to me. I didn't believe him. How could he know? But with the way he showed up for me, maybe he did. Had I told him? No conversation came to mind. Then again, he said he never missed anything I said. Maybe this is what that meant.

When grief wrung me dry, my eyes grew heavy.

"Oh, no you don't." Kent shook me awake. "I know you skipped lunch. I won't let you skip dinner."

"I don't have an appetite." I batted his hand away.

"I'll make you something light to eat. Regardless, there's no sleeping until you've eaten and I've given you a bath. You can't be comfortable having sweated so much." He slipped behind me with great difficulty.

Tyger protested being jostled and the dogs became alert at his escape from the bed. When I didn't move, Kent reached out to me.

"You can't disturb a cat when they're comfortable. I think I read somewhere it causes permanent trauma."

Kent rolled his eyes and lifted Tyger despite both of us protesting. "We'll pamper his bad memories away. After a few treats, he'll forget where he was."

Tyger's glare, directed at Kent said otherwise.

"I don't know. You're risking your life displeasing Don Tyger this way."

Kent sneered at me, then the cat. "You're here rent free because of me. Show a little gratitude."

Tyger launched himself at Kent who barely dodged the attack.

"You were saying?" I said as Tyger resumed his position on my lap.

"Dinner in bed works, too." Kent left the room, shaking his head.

The dogs watched him leave and whimpered their dilemma. Who should they choose? In the end, they also stayed with me.

The moment of levity passed, leaving me traversing through another episode of sadness. I must have dozed off because Kent shook me awake. The four-legged weights holding my body to the bed were no longer in the room, though how Kent achieved the miracle, I didn't have the energy to guess.

"Here. I made you some soup."

"You made this?"

"I'll have you know, I learned from Lola. I couldn't have my wife and daughter eating food from someone who didn't have a vested interest in them getting better when they were sick. I know I became a shitty husband to Lola the last years she was alive, but I remembered what it was like to take care of someone I love."

I nod and took the tray with the soup from him. The aroma was familiar.

Scent leaves.

Along with the poultry scent, the strong, pungent anise-like aroma wafted on a steam wisp as I inhaled.

Oye came from Nigeria and often seasoned her soups with scent leaves. She grew it in her backyard during the brief summers and inside during the rest of the year. Kent must have continued growing it.

My mouth watered. Not even Ife knew how to make her mother's soup and the last I had a bowl was many years before she died. Even though I had no appetite, I couldn't pass up the opportunity to try Oye's soup.

I dipped my spoon in the bowl and slurped my first spoonful. Familiar heat from the peppers bloomed on my tongue, warming me from the inside. One spoon became another until I emptied the bowl.

"Want another?"

I sheepishly nodded.

Kent stood and exchanged my bowl with his. "Take mine." He had yet to touch his soup. Before leaving the room, he kissed the tip of my nose. "I'll be right back."

I devoured the second bowl at a slower pace than my first, savoring each bite as I ate with Kent this time. When the last of the soup disappeared, I sagged against the bed. The warmth inside my body lulled at me, but Kent pulled me from the bed and marched me to the bathroom for a cool shower and fresh set of pajamas.

Neither of us acted on the desire thrumming below the surface. It was too soon after Ife to think about doing the very thing that splintered us. So we returned to the bedroom and clung to each other.

Two hours.

I sighed, realizing my reprieve was at an end. I fell asleep two hours ago but was now wide awake with a mind I couldn't turn off. I peeked at Kent. He was deeply asleep.

I slid from the bed, as had become my habit after Kent put me to bed. I'd be lucky if he stayed asleep the rest of the night, but he inevitably missed my weight pressing against his and would come in search of me. I glanced at the clock. One A.M. I had two, maybe three hours before he became restless and realized I wasn't beside him.

I snuck into my office and booted my laptop. Tyger soon joined me. The dogs were in their crates and I wasn't letting them out. I stood strong against their puppy-eyed stare, feeling like the worst owner alive. I comforted myself knowing when they turned two they would have their freedom.

I turned to my computer and opened the mail application. A message from Omar caught my eye.

IT confirmed Hal hadn't been hacked but couldn't verify if he was @Nose2TheGrindstone. There've been no messages posted to the BBD site for weeks.

I wished the news made me happy, but Hal was still an unknown. I hadn't felt one way or the other toward him until he suggested Kent and I split. He was now a permanent fixture on my shit list, but that didn't make him guilty of abducting me. Why would he? I always came back to motive and I'd found none.

I went back to the BBD site to search for posts about Kent. The most recent ones no longer centered on his connection with the murder victims. Instead, they speculated on our relationship. I took Kent's employees not looking at him as a potential suspect as a win despite the embarrassment of having my personal life be fodder for the gossip mill.

As I scrolled the backlog of conversations and used my search engine to optimize what I was looking for, I noticed a pattern with a few user names. @Officevixen69, @Peoplepleaser13, and @In_the_-know stopped posting around the time Carol disappeared.

Had she created multiple profiles to smear Kent at the office?

I wouldn't put it past her. Her actions were unfathomable to most people. Maybe her erotomania manifested itself this way. If so, ruining a man's reputation wasn't so extreme she would see it as going too far. Convinced I had proof of her plotting, I needed to dig further.

Before me was a loom and warp threads waiting for me to weave the weft into a clear design. However, I couldn't see the image clearly. How and why did Carol target Kent and the women she murdered?

Did she do the actual murdering or was it her male accomplice? What beef did the man have against Kent?

There were still so many unanswered questions, but little by little, I found reason to be hopeful. I clung to it since hope was in little supply these days.

"I hope you found something useful to make you losing sleep worth it."

I jumped with a squeak as Kent's voice shattered the silence.

Tyger stood and glared balefully at Kent before sauntering off to lay claim to another part of the apartment.

I glanced at the time at the top of my screen. Two and a half hours. I sighed as I silently said goodbye to the last half hour of work I wouldn't be doing, then swiveled my chair until I faced Kent. I shared my findings and suspicions with him but his demeanor remained... inexplicable.

He held his hand to me. "Let's go back to bed so you're fresh when you start again in a few hours."

"That's the excuse you're going with?"

He arched his brow. "Oh? And I thought you were tired of me complaining about the other reason."

I tilted my head to observe him from another angle. Rumpled, with tousled hair and pillow wrinkles embedded in his cheeks, Kent appeared softer than when he concentrated deeply on any subject. Despite his lowered guard, there was steel in his blue eyes as he willed me to bend to his will.

"Little bunny, come back to bed. You know I don't do well when I don't get sufficient cuddles before I start my day."

"You do start more mellow in the first couple hours." I took his offered hand, allowing him to lead me back to bed.

"If my staff only knew, they'd also petition you to stop skimping me on my necessities."

"I'm a necessity now?"

He swung around and glared at me. "If you question that, I'm not doing something right."

I arched my feet until I stood on my toes, then I kissed his cheek.

"Consider me corrected. You do more than enough." As I sank to the floor, I raised his hand and kissed his knuckles. "Let's go to bed."

I managed another ninety minutes of sleep wrapped in Kent's arms. This time he added his legs to the embrace, entangling our limbs as if to add an anti-Madison escape detection system to our sleeping arrangement. The alarm clock blared at six and I was surprisingly refreshed, although my sleep was choppy.

CHAPTER 27

ent

"Omar, call Mal and tell him to bring his laptop. Then join us in the office when he arrives."

"Will do."

I disconnected my call with Omar and stared at my blank screen. I'd allowed a situation to sit for too long, but now had to make a move.

"What's going on?" Mal entered my office with Omar trailing behind him.

I nodded toward the chairs in front of my desk. "I need a list of all our shareholders."

Mal and Omar shared a glance.

"Is this about Hal?" Mal asked.

"Indirectly." I rocked my chair back and forth. "The excuse he had for going after my relationship with Madison was someone on the board is scheming behind my back."

Mal frowned. "This is news to me."

"Which is very concerning. When I asked Hal, he played off my question, claiming he didn't know who was behind the move."

His deflection from the day I tore into him still fueled my rage. Although he was never close enough for me to consider him a friend, he'd worked with the company for decades with a compensation package that rivaled bigger corporations. I would never understand a man willing to throw so much of his life's work away. What did he aim to get from his betrayal? As if I didn't have enough on my hands with running and growing Luxe Locations while handling a ruinous public relations nightmare?

Thank God for Madison. Her tactics had gained traction. Then her attack happened. I wished I could embrace the pivot from the media and police, but Madison almost died to clear my name, and I didn't take the risk of losing her lightly. However, with the heat off me, I could focus on the snake in my midst.

"How's that possible?" Omar crossed his leg over his knee and frowned. "Isn't there a master list of shareholders?"

"There are, but not all the names on the list belong to individuals." Mal opened his laptop and rested it on my desk. "We have about two thousand shareholders with varying ownership levels." He clicked some keys before falling into silence.

"How many of them are trusts or LLCs? We need to focus on them to find the culprit." I tapped my forefinger on my armrest.

"I sent you and Omar our updated list from last quarter's board of directors' meeting. It will take some time to go through everyone to differentiate the anonymous LLCs from the others."

Omar opened his laptop on his lap. "Why does it matter if the LLC is anonymous?"

"As the name implies, the person behind doesn't have to identify themselves. They can use an agent to represent them and their interests, making it difficult for me to find whoever wants to oust me from Luxe Locations." I accessed my email to find the list Mal sent.

"Am I correct in assuming your request isn't just for the list? You want an investigation?"

I allowed the tense silence to grow before nodding. "A very

discreet investigation. With two thousand shareholders, I have to assume we begin with the largest entities, then figure out what combination of holdings could give someone the idea they could sway others into siding against me."

"But don't you own the majority shares in the company? Can anyone truly pose a threat to you?" Omar hadn't looked up from his screen since accessing Mal's email. His intense scrutiny was one reason I've stuck with Omar since taking the chance on a kid with a past that could have ended his life early if not for his determination to improve his circumstances.

"My shares, combined with the shares Ife inherited when her mother passed does make me untouchable."

The tension in the room skyrocketed to another stratosphere. Shock came over Mal and Omar's faces.

"Kent, I know Ife isn't happy with you right now, but she's your daughter." Mal leaned away, his tone one of a person handling a psych ward patient on the verge of a psychotic break.

"She is my daughter, which means she understands leverage. I won't allow her to use the company I built to interfere with my personal relationship."

Omar slowly raised his eyes to watch me. "Are you... declaring war?"

I stood and rounded my desk until I was inches away from a glass wall, contemplating the busy workers on the office floor. Mal and Omar's wary eyes pressed on me, and I hated it.

"Once the rift between me and Ife becomes public knowledge, someone will approach my daughter." I placed my hands in my pocket, hiding the rage shaking my fingers from sight and modulating my voice for Mal's and Omar's benefits. "I have to preempt their attempts. If Ife never learns of the opportunity, I'll have a chance at salvaging our relationship."

"We don't have much time." Mal returned his attention to his laptop. "Hal knows about your fight, and if he knows, he's probably told whoever put him up to—"

"You understand my urgency." I tightened my hidden hands into fists.

"Are you certain Hal knows the reason behind your problems with Ife?" Omar met my gaze in wall's reflection. "Maybe—"

"He knows. Worse, although he hasn't come into the office, he still has access to company files." I rubbed the tautness in my nape.

"If you suspect him, why haven't you made a move before now? We need IT to limit his access and spy on his work." Mal joined me by the wall, anger radiating from him. "Do you understand the shit he could be stealing under our noses at this very second?"

I glared at my CFO from the corner of my eye. "Hal hasn't bene-fited from his position since Madison saved him from a worse ass kicking than I wanted to give him. However, he hasn't incriminated himself yet, so now we need to root out his backers."

"You think there's more than one?" Omar asked.

"I'm being cautious."

"What about calling an emergency board meeting to replace him?"

"Mal, you know the waves that will cause internally and externally. We can't just hire anyone to be our counsel. I'll need a candidate ready to replace Hal, and no one inside the company is qualified enough to offer as an interim or permanent solution."

"But you have feelers out?"

I side-eyed Mal for pushing this point. "I have headhunters sending me candidates as we speak."

Omar snapped his fingers. "No wonder why I've been forwarding so many calls from Bishop Works lately."

Mal raised his brows, impressed at the name of the elite hiring company I contracted to find our next head lawyer. "Alright, with that in the works, I'll concentrate on the shareholders and work with Omar. One thing."

"Spit it out."

"I'd like to get an analyst to help. Their ability to code and statisti-cally analyze large data could narrow down our options to something more manageable."

I peeked at Mal. He was correct. Someone with the technological know-how could reduce how long it took us to find the person out for me. Unfortunately, it wouldn't be easy. To pinpoint the person involved might involve looking at months or even years worth of shareholder activity. Mal could do it, but he had other more important tasks as the CFO.

I nodded at Mal. "Choose someone trustworthy. Tell them you'll reward them for their discretion."

The sooner we identified the culprit, the sooner I'd breathe easier.

While I hadn't taken my eyes off the employees diligently working to make my vision of Luxe Locations into reality, I silently plotted what I would do if I found Hal's involvement in ousting me wasn't as a mere puppet but mastermind.

No one took from me and walked away.

CHAPTER 28

$\mathcal{M}$adison

The enameled glass and wood door from my past loomed like a giant before me. The quiet stillness of the suburban neighborhood did nothing to dispel my dread or the roiling ball of acid and anxiety in my gut. Although this was a safe space for many years of my life, today it reminded me of another time I exposed my vulnerability to a member of the Luxe family that nearly destroyed me.

I breathed deep and raised my hand to ring the doorbell. Before my finger made contact, it opened, revealing Mal's surprised face. I stepped back.

"Mal? What are you doing here?"

He glanced behind him, then at me. "Just catching up." Without another glance at me, he raised his hand. "I'll see you around, Ife. Madison." He got into his car and drove away as if his presence was normal.

I turned my attention to the person I was here to see.

Ife stood still, hugging herself with eyes almost as red as mine. Had she poured her heart out about me and her dad? I had a hard time believing she would because I'd never heard of her and Mal having anything deeper than an acquaintanceship.

"Why are you here, Mads? Your theft not complete until you snatch my childhood home, too?"

I swallowed the barb, accepting it as my punishment. I deserved her anger and would endure however she needed to lash out. Her response was my penance from the years I'd coveted her father's love.

"Can we have this discussion inside? Or would you rather give your neighbors a real-life Telenovela episode?" I glanced around the houses surrounding the Luxe home. Although the street was silent, there were many stay-at-home parents living in this subdivision who would relish witnessing and gossiping about their neighbors' drama.

Ife stood aside and allowed me to enter.

The last time I was here was after Kent punished me for the first time. Despite his reservations, he'd brought me here to the place he'd shared so much with his wife. I'd tested him then, knowing if he kept his life with Oye to himself, only sharing anecdotes of their lives together, he would never be fully mine. And he'd passed. He'd let me inside, and the memories of my times in their household were full of bittersweet moments. I understood his need to keep her memory enshrined in the house and never asked him to put me before his remembrances again.

However, as the past again enfolded me with sounds of Ife's and my running through the rooms to admonishments of no running in the house, as we grew older and our antics changed to plotting ways to gain the attention of Ife's crushes, and the dreams we shared of being in each other's lives as aunties to each other's kids, it was Ife's turn to either slam the door on our history or allow our story to continue.

Please don't let our relationship end here.

"Please try to understand. Ife, you're my best friend."

"Am I?"

"Ife... Why would you question what you mean to me?"

"Then tell me how long you've felt this way about my dad? You've only been back a few weeks. There's no way you fell for him in such a short time. So? How long?"

I avoided her gaze, unable to admit I'd been in love with Kent for half my life.

"As I thought," she sneered, her judgmental gaze stripped me bare and pushed me against a burning pyre. "I was nothing but a convenient tool for you to get close to my father." Ife's eyes glimmered.

"What? You can't believe our years of friendship boil down to me using you. For so much of my life you've been my only family. I love you so much."

"You love me so much you want to replace my mother?" A tear slipped down her cheek as she stared at me with heartbreak in her eyes.

"What? No! I never saw myself as—"

"No? So, tell me how this works Mads? What do I call you?"

"Mads. Madison. What you've always called me. That won't change."

"Maybe not… But you can't expect things to be the same between us. I saw you fucking my dad."

"I know, and I never wanted you to see us like that. I-I didn't know how to tell you, and that's my fault, but you have to believe me when I say you are important to me."

Ife stared at me in stony silence, the muscle in her jaw ticked the same way Kent's did. She broke off eye contact to gaze at the ceiling and she took a deep breath. "Do you have a rule with my dad never to discuss me?"

"Well, no…"

"And you expect me to trust you?"

"I don't understand why you'd think you can't."

"You can't be this naïve Mads." At my vacant look, she scoffed. "So when Dad and I have a fight, do I become pillow talk? What does the conversation look like? Are all the secrets we've shared over the years now currency for you to prove to my dad he can trust you? Do you take my side when I'm with you and his when you're with him? Do I have to live each day wondering when you'll spill the things I've told you in the past, when I was at my worst or most vulnerable?"

"Ife, I would never betray something you've told me in confidence. I never have and never will." I reached my hand out to her but she slapped it down.

"How do I know that?" She shook her head, her disillusionment and hurt sliced through me. "I don't know anything anymore." She turned her back and walked deeper into the house, not stopping until she reached the kitchen. "If you've said what you had to say, you can leave now." She pulled open the fridge and took a bottle of cola before slamming the door and leaning against the stainless steel surface.

I stood before her, bloodied from her accusations and hurt feelings, wanting to discard my pain to help her through hers. "I haven't, actually, but you're not ready to hear me out so I'll leave. Before I do, there was a topic I wanted to ask you about."

Ife slammed her bottle onto the island countertop in front of her, and froth spilled over the mouth onto her hand. She snagged a towel to wipe the moisture dry.

"Not related to my relationship with your father. I promise." Her silent glare compelled me to continue. "I came here because you asked me to help rehab your father's image. Although Carol exposed herself as the murderer, there are shareholders of your dad's company trying to unseat him. I think someone will reach out to you. We need to know if they're the mastermind or who they're working with. Will you join me to expose them?"

Ife grabbed her drink and pushed past me, a calculating look overcoming her features. I'd seen that look too many times to let it go. When her brows furrowed in this way while she chewed her lip, nothing good came of it. Too many times, I wasn't able to talk her down from a scheme destined to get her in hot water. And too many times I sat beside her when shit flew everywhere, hitting us in the face with consequences and regrets.

This time felt different. This time she shut me out.

I followed, earnest in my desire to protect Kent. "Ife, you know the sacrifices he made for the company. It would kill him if the people plotting his demise succeeded. I know it would mean the world to him if you overlooked our recent strife for his sake."

We entered the formal living room Oye used only for special occasions. White Queen Ann furnishings sat on a Persian rug while delicate porcelain figurines stared in their frozen pose. The room was the least welcoming in the house. Ife sat on the sofa, stretched an arm across the seat back, and sipped from her bottle.

"How do you know someone will reach out to me?" Ife asked, crossing her legs and idly dangling her foot up and down.

Her interest, though mildly expressed, gave me all the encouragement I needed.

"There's someone who knows you and your father aren't on good terms right now. There's a chance he'll use the discord between you to either get your shares or your vote."

"Oh? How'd the gossip mill become privy to my fight with my father?" Ife tilted her head.

"If you think I spread the rumor, you're wrong. Hal saw how you left the penthouse."

"Hal's worked as the company's lawyer for years. He knows how to keep a secret, so why would he say anything?"

I swallowed and dipped my head, unable to maintain our stare. "Your father and he had a disagreement about me that landed Hal in the hospital."

"So you haven't just come between me and my father. You're also causing him issues at work."

"Doesn't your father deserve love?"

"Not from you."

"I get it, Ife. You don't approve." I held all my pleading inside. The many ways I wanted to beg her to forgive me and let me back inside her circle, however, I wasn't here for me, I reminded myself. "Now can we get back to ensuring your dad remains the CEO and president of Luxe Locations?"

She narrowed her eyes at me, pain and anger mixed together and adding a sheen to the warm brown eyes that once beheld me with compassion and love. "Hal already approached me."

"He did? What did he say?" I sat beside her, my knee bent on the sofa facing her.

Ife glared at how close I came to almost touching her, then she shrugged off the mild disgust and rose to sit in a side chair. "He said he had a way to make my father see reason. Then he offered to buy my shares."

Dread filled me as I asked, "You didn't sell them to him, did you?"

She sneered at me and rolled her eyes. "I told him I'd think about it."

"Thank you, Ife. You have no idea how much—"

"I don't need your thanks. And I didn't agree for my father's sake. I'm still mulling over how siding with him benefits me."

"But... If you do this your father will never understand. He'll feel so betrayed—"

"Maybe then he'll understand what the sentiment feels like."

I rose from the couch and kneeled at her feet. "Please, Ife. He could survive many things, but not a betrayal from his daughter."

She folded her arms and looked away, making it clear my begging and pleading offended her. Ife maintained her position for a full minute before sighing. "Mads, you sit there pretending like you aren't the one with all the power here."

"Me? How? I don't own any shares, nor do I have influence over the other shareholders."

"But you have sway over two important ones, don't you? And for you to get those votes aligned, you only have to do one thing."

Her implication horrified and broke my heart in the same blow. "You're willing to leverage your shares if I leave your father?" I forced the words past my dry lips.

"Now you get it. If you want to know if there's someone pulling Hal's strings, you have to promise to walk away from us. Forever."

CHAPTER 29

ent

I checked my reflection for the tenth time in twenty seconds, despite the curious hostess waiting to seat me. I'd refused her offer, preferring to wait for Ife's arrival before going to our table. As I waited at my daughter's favorite restaurant, I hoped this meeting would give me the opening I needed to begin reconciling with her.

Not a day went by that I hadn't lamented the closeness we had. She still hadn't shared what had brought her back to Douglas. In other visits, I would have spoiled her with shopping trips, dinners, and other bribes to tempt her to move home and seriously consider her future at my company. Although I never pressured her to take over, I would be overjoyed for her to continue a tradition I started.

"You came." Ife's voice held a note of surprise that hurt.

"Of course. I told you, I'll always show up for you." I reached out to her but she stepped away, and I allowed my hand to fall.

Ife caught the hostess' eye. Without a word, the woman led us to a private dining room. Ife arched her brow at me but said nothing.

I explained the choice anyway. "For privacy."

She hummed her understanding. If things became contentious, we wouldn't become fodder for Douglas' society gossip magazines.

After the hostess sat us, we stared at each other in silence. Ife wore an invisible armor I hoped to breach while I hid nothing from her penetrating gaze.

"Have you changed your mind about Mads?"

I snapped my napkin open and laid it on my lap. "Starting off strong, I see." I reached for the menu. "I wonder what tonight's specials are."

"Why don't you stop deflecting and answ—"

She stopped mid sentence as our server arrived. We quickly gave him our order while Ife watched him leave until the door closed behind him.

"Dad, I deserve an answer."

I slammed the menu closed, irked by her demand. "And what do I deserve, Ife?"

She paused while reaching for her water goblet. "What do you mean?"

"Exactly what I asked."

She changed her selection, and instead of sipping from her water, she drained her wine. "I still don't understand your purpose."

"Your mother died eight years ag—"

"Don't you bring her into this." Ife slammed her hand against the table. "I know more than anyone else how long she's been gone, all the things she missed out on." She inhaled a shaky breath. "I still talk to her, you know."

"As you should. It took me years to get to where I could say her name without breaking apart. Now, I have conversations with her. Mostly about you. How proud I am of everything you've accomplished, as well as my concerns as your father."

"But you moved on. You found companionship with other women."

"No, Ife. Those women allowed me to hide from myself. They

never touched me in any meaningful way. And companionship? They were never close to offering me that."

"But Mads does? She's young enough to be your daughter."

"You think I don't know that? I'm very aware of our age difference."

"Then why, Dad? Why her?"

"Because she showed me how to live again. For the first time in a long time, I had more than you and my company as my reasons to live."

"And so where does that leave Mom?"

I rose and kneeled by Ife's side. I took her hands in mine as I peered into her hurt eyes. "Your mother will always be a part of me. I don't shy away from my memories with her now, and part of the reason is Madison. She loved Lola almost as much as you."

"I can't listen to this. Please, stop." Ife hugged herself while rocking in her chair.

I sighed and retook my seat. "One day, I hope you'll change your mind."

"But there are so many women out there who could do what Mads does for you and more."

"Sweetheart, I wasn't looking for love when she came walking through my door and read me for filth."

"She did what?"

"Yeah, the woman you sent to save me didn't hold back from challenging everything I did and exposing me as an asshole. But I realized pretty soon, she made me unreasonably angry because I was fighting a losing battle with myself. I'm not blind to her faults. In fact, I've been very critical of her, and I need you to understand because when I say I'm in love with her, I'm not confusing what I feel with lust."

The server returned with our food, his smile dropping as he took in Ife's sad expression.

"Sorry, but can you pack this in a to-go container? I won't be staying."

"Ife—"

"Dad, I've heard you out. And as much as I want to be in your corner and cheering you on because you deserve to have love again, I can't get over the person you chose is Mads. It feels like the deepest betrayal, one I need more than a few days to get over. And if I'm honest, I'm not sure I'll ever get over losing what I shared with either of you." Ife stood to leave.

"You can at least wait until your food comes." I tried again to keep her.

"Take it with you. I don't have the stomach for it anymore."

She made it to the door before two men I had nothing but disdain for came barreling into the private dining room.

"Detectives, I'm trying to have a meal with my daughter. Can you harass me with your conspiracy theories another day?"

Salinas smirked. His aura oozed malicious intent. "Kent Luxe, you're under arrest for the murder of Carol Prosper. That's right, you asshole. We've got you on the hook for her, and soon we'll get you for the other murders."

"That's impossible. My father couldn't kill anyone." Ife blocked Salinas from putting handcuffs on me.

"Ma'am, I understand this may come as a shock, but we're only trying to do our jobs." Glass took my daughter by the shoulders. "If you continue to obstruct us, we'll have to arrest you, too."

"Get your hands off my daughter." I sidled around Ife's body to show Glass why touching my girl was a terrible choice.

Because I took my eyes off Salinas, I was unprepared when he snuck up behind me and put me in cuffs. As he read me my rights, I stared stonily at Glass until he removed his hands.

"Ife, call Quarren and tell him to meet me at the station." Salinas began dragging me from the room, but I had one more thing to say. "If you see Madison, reassure her and let her know I'll be out soon."

"Don't count on it." Salinas dragged me out of the room and through the restaurant, preening like a peacock.

Quarren met us at the precinct's entrance and followed us into an interrogation room.

"Detective Glass, you better have a good reason for arresting my client after the months of harassment perpetuated against him by your department."

"Counselor, I understand you're paid big money to defend and deflect, but there's no doubt your client is guilty."

"How? You haven't even asked if I have an alibi." I glared at the two men who've caused me endless irritation.

"Because you'll use Madison Montgomery, and she's no longer credible. She might even be in the cell beside Mr. Luxe if we prove they conspired together."

I shared a confused glance with Quarren before returning my gaze to the detectives.

"Please explain. Ms. Prosper abducted Ms. Montgomery and left her to die on railroad tracks. Are you forgetting?"

"Ahh, yes. The abduction that cleared Mr. Luxe of the serial murders and gave him the perfect alibi." Salinas grinned, his joy at my demise spilling into his sarcasm. "See, we found Carol murdered like the other women, and all the clues we gathered painted a pretty clear picture. She was Mr. Luxe's patsy. He was the man behind—"

"Officers, I don't mean to interrupt, but the attack on Elsie destroys your argument. The witness who found her never identified my client as the man standing over her."

"You mean the man employed by Mr. Luxe? Funny you should mention him. We found a large deposit into Mr. Evans' account shortly after that attack. A payoff from an employer with something to hide."

"This is ridiculous. I didn't bribe my assistant, never attacked Elsie, and never found Carol, though I wish I had. She had a lot to answer for."

"We agree on that point, Mr. Luxe." Detective Glass opened a folder. "And hopefully we can come to another agreement with your confession about how you killed her and the other women who fit your sick profile."

For hours, they interrogated me, trying to catch me in a lie while feeding me bits of evidence to confuse me. However, Quarren was on their asses, clocking their shady questions. Despite my lawyer's presence and his attempts to name drop the police chief and mayor, they refused to release me until my arraignment.

"Sorry, Mr. Luxe. But since it's late on a Friday night, you won't see a judge until Monday morning the earliest. I hope you don't mind the humble accommodations." Salinas led me to an austere cell where four other men of various backgrounds waited. Each person glared at me and the cops before turning their attention inward.

Whatever their problems were, they found it more important than investigating the newcomer, a blessing I hoped would last me through the weekend.

"Kent, I'll do what I can to get you out of here before Monday," Quarren said before leaving.

I stared at the walls, seething. Until I recalled my last words to Ife. Madison wouldn't take me not coming home until Monday well. Hell, I wasn't taking my situation with any equanimity. My place at night was beside my little bunny, nowhere else. But now I faced charges that seemed made to frame me and no way to fight them.

CHAPTER 30

$\mathcal{M}$adison

Three A.M. and still no word from Kent. I threw the blankets aside and slipped out of bed. For the first time, I understood Kent's insistence on having me at his side at night. Our bed wasn't as welcoming without his body heat and his warm breath fanning my forehead through the night.

Despite the late hour, I called Quarren's number. I had no hope of reaching him, but I needed something to distract me. When his voice asked me to leave a message, I nearly tossed my phone against the wall.

I desperately needed my best friend. Any other day, she would welcome my presence because she would be as anxious as I was, but I was persona non grata in Ife's eyes. With her off limits and my desperation growing with each passing moment, I packed up the animals and went to the only other place guaranteed to welcome me.

As I freed my pets from their carriers, my mother's incredulous voice came from the stairs, "Maddy? Do you know you scared me nearly half to death?" She sped down the staircase, but her first good look at my face transformed her relief at knowing I wasn't an intruder. Instead, concern furrowed her brow and dragged at her mouth. "Baby, what happened? Why're you crying?"

"The police found Carol."

At the sound of my distress, Tyger, Benson, and Stabler encircled me in a protective circle.

Mom frowned. "Isn't that good news? Now she can face the consequences of hurting my baby."

I hiccuped and shook my head. "She's dead."

"Not the fate I would have chosen for her, but not one worth your tears." Mom maneuvered between the dogs to get close to me. She cupped my face and swiped under my eyes.

"I'd agree with you if the police hadn't arrested Kent for her murder." I hurled myself into my mother's welcoming arms and broke into sobs.

Benson and Stabler whimpered in commiseration while Tyger pawed at my leg.

"Honey, do you know what time it is?" My dad came grumbling down the stairs. "Your ass belongs in bed, not—Maddy?"

"They arrested Kent, Dennis." My mother's arms shifted but with my face buried in her neck, I had no idea what she was doing until my father's heat joined hers.

"Baby girl, what do you need?" Dad's voice changed from joking annoyance to concern in the blink of an eye.

"K-K-Kent, I need Kent."

Nikita sighed and pulled my arms from around her neck. "Alright, baby. Bawling ain't never solved nobody's problems. We'll go to the jail in the morning, but in the meantime, tell me everything you know."

I relayed what Ife told me, which wasn't a lot.

"Cops love throwing their weight around, especially when dealing with wealthy people like Kent. I bet they sat on their arrest warrant to ensure Kent spent the weekend behind bars." Mom brushed my hair out of my face and wiped the moisture from my cheeks. "Since there's no sleeping for the rest of the night, let's use those skills of yours to manage this crisis. Or did you forget what put you on the map and kept you thousands of miles from home for so many years?"

Nikita's much-needed reminder stopped my crying more effectively than telling me to stop. I couldn't believe I cracked under the pressure when I'd never faltered before.

"Thanks, Mommy." I straightened with new determination and got to work. Kent needed me more than ever.

Once the sun rose, I was ready for any challenge dumb enough to fall in my way. My confidence remained until I reached the jailhouse and encountered Ife. Her eyes were as bloodshot as mine, but she didn't have an ultimatum hanging over her shoulder the way I did.

"Figures you'd be here," she muttered and turned her back on me to address the officer at the entrance. "I'm here to see my father, Kent Luxe."

The woman glanced at her and yawned. "You're here really early for a Saturday morning. This guy important?"

"He is to us." I stepped forward. As much as I respected Ife's right to see her father, I was too impatient to see him for myself.

The woman checked something on her computer. "Sorry, don't see a Kent Luxe." She shrugged and returned to her previous activity of watching the monitors on her desk.

"How's that possible? I was there when the cops took him into custody?" Ife banged her fist against the officer's desk.

"Don't know. He's not in the system."

"He has to be. Check again," Ife insisted.

The woman swatted Ife's hand away. "He's not here. Now, leave."

I narrowed my gaze on her and peeked over her desk at the monitors. Because the images were upside down, it took me a few seconds before I found him on the fourth monitor. "That's him right there." I pointed to Kent's face. "Now, you can either allow us to see him, or I'll make this weekend one you'll regret. Even if I have to call the mayor himself."

"People like to drop his name all the time because they're taxpayers." She leaned closer to me. "But let me let you in on a secret. Just because your taxes pay his salary, doesn't mean you have him on speed dial." She settled in her chair with a satisfied smirk.

"You would be correct if I were a mere taxpayer." I pulled my phone out of my handbag. "But you see, here's the difference. A Joe-Schmo taxpayer wouldn't have Valentino's personal number on speed dial, or rub elbows with him at fancy events like this one." I turned my screen for the woman to see.

Her tanned complexion paled.

"Now, do I press this number that clearly states Valentino DeLuca Home? Or do you do your job and get me in to see Kent Luxe, who by the way, is also good friends with Mayor DeLuca?"

Within two minutes, Ife and I stood in front of an interview room. She hadn't stopped staring at me since I bullied the officer out front.

"You should go first," I said. "Kent will be worried about you since you saw them take him last night."

"That...performance you put on—"

"Ife, I know you don't want to understand my feelings, but what I did was no performance. Kent has become my world, and I'm going to do everything in my power to make sure he keeps everything he loves."

"Does that include me? You're going to make sure—"

"Ife? Madison? You shouldn't be here," Kent said. He raised his cuffed hands toward us, the sheen in his eyes belying his harsh words.

Two guards stood beside him. "You each have twenty minutes." They escorted him inside the room and Ife followed.

As time ticked by, I wondered what they were saying. I rested my head against the door as whispered prayers fell from my lips. All of a sudden, the door keeping me upright swung inward and I almost fell on my face. Before I had time to recover, Kent pulled me into his arms and stole my breath with a desperate kiss. My body began softening until I remembered we had an audience.

I pushed at Kent's muscular arms caging me in, but he wouldn't relent until I twisted my face away and whispered, "Ife's watching."

My conscience wouldn't allow me to look in her direction. Instead, I hid my face in Kent's neck.

He loosened his arms but didn't release me. "Ife, if you have a problem with me showing Madison my feelings for her, turn your back."

"Kent!"

"I'll wait for Mads outside." A soft click of the door told me she left.

"Little bunny, how is Ife going to get used to us if we hide our relationship?"

"There's hiding and then there's flaunting. You sticking your tongue so far down my throat you almost touch my stomach isn't the best way to get her used to us when she feels we've betrayed her." I patted his chest while searching his face for signs of mistreatment. "Did they do anything to you?"

"No. The accommodations weren't the best, but I was more worried about you." Kent brushed the skin under my eyes.

No amount of concealer could fully camouflage the dark flesh, proof of my sleepless night.

"I bet you didn't even eat before you showed up here, did you?" Kent frowned.

His concern for me when he was the one in jail pushed at the tears I'd tried to hold back.

"I'll have you know, Nikita Montgomery stuffed me with a proper breakfast before she allowed me to step foot outside."

"You weren't alone. I'm glad." Kent pulled me over to the lone desk and sat me on the surface. He wouldn't stop touching me. My sides, my hips, my face. As if he hadn't seen me in years rather than hours.

"You didn't sleep last night either, did you?" I smoothed his beard and caressed his lips.

"You know I can't when you aren't beside me."

"So what the hell is Quarren doing to get you out? I've tried calling him, but I only get his voicemail."

"If he's earning his retainer, he's figuring out the bullshit that's going on." Kent explained everything the cops accused him of last night. "But that is neither here nor there. I need you to do something for me while Quarren works on my case."

"Of course. I've already started compiling character witnesses, dossiers on the detectives—by the way, my employees are not happy with me for putting them all on your case—mmph."

Kent's mouth smothered mine, preventing me from continuing. Since I'd interrupted our first kiss, I savored this one. He pulled my body until our torsos met and I wrapped my arms and legs around him. Anything to get closer to him and share my heat with him.

His dick grew hard, poking my pussy and serving as a reminder of the time we missed with each other last night.

"Little bunny, I wish we had more time." Kent pressed his forehead against mine while staring into my eyes.

"Me, too." I cleared my throat and shook the lust free from my brain. "But we have planning to do."

He rubbed his thumb against my lips, then trailed his hand to my nape where he stroked the fine hairs and made me shiver. "Quarren has the legal side handled, but there are other matters I trust only you to find out for me."

"Whatever you need, I'm here for you."

"I'm sure news has leaked about my arrest. Hal or whoever's behind him will make their move. They'll probably call an emergency shareholder meeting to vote me out. Get my proxy documents together."

"But if you'll be out by Monday, there won't be a need. Even an emergency meeting takes at least a week to organize. Wouldn't my time be better served looking for the real culprit? I already have my private investigator leaning on his DPD contacts to find out what's in Carol's file."

"Little bunny." Kent sighed and stepped free of my embrace. "Listen to me carefully. I don't want you anywhere near Carol's investigation."

I opened my mouth to protest, but he swiped his hand in the air, cutting me off before I began.

"Carol was murdered, Madison! Probably by the person she was working with. They already tried to kill you once. Don't give them another chance to murder you and don't ask me to watch you die."

And just like that, anything I would have said to argue him to my side died on my lips. To protect his heart, I would never force him to relive another loss like Oye's.

"Okay, I'll get your documents together, but only as a contingency. You will get out on Monday and be available for any nonsense Hal and his people try." I walked into his arms again, desperate to make as much of the little time we had together.

"Promise me you won't do anything reckless while we're apart," Kent said into my hair.

"I promise," I said and silently added the caveat: unless I'm protecting you.

Enclosed in his embrace, I could forget almost anything, and I hoped he gained more from our hug than I did.

"Times up." The officer who'd led Kent here entered the room to escort him out.

Behind him, Ife stood, staring at me and Kent, still in each other's arms.

I stepped back, bereft of his absence but with a new mission.

"What will you do now?" Ife asked once Kent and the officer left.

"Take Hal down. Do I have to do it alone?"

"Your priorities are whacked. My dad's in jail for murder." Ife sneered at me, and I felt it slither down my spine and settle in my heart.

"You don't think I know that?" I whispered fiercely, upset by her accusation. "Kent wants him handled while Quarren takes care of the case. And I only want him focussing on getting out of here, so I'll take whatever task he needs me to take off his plate as quickly as possible so I can spend all my energy on proving his innocence."

Ife folded her arms and avoided eye contact with me. "So what's your plan?"

I glanced at our surroundings. "Not here. I'd rather not have anyone listening in."

"How about Dad's old penthouse?" At my frown, she puffed a put-upon breath and rolled her eyes. "We agree we don't want to be seen talking in public, right?"

"Right..."

"I don't want you in my childhood home. I don't want to be in your love nest. So the top penthouse makes more sense."

Instead of addressing her acerbic tone about my current home, I brought up a potential issue. "Someone might see you on the grounds. Without knowing who Hal has in his corner, I'd rather not risk you showing up on the property."

"Then where do you suggest, Mads?"

"No need for the attitude, Ife. We both want to look out for your father. How about my mom and dad's place? We can trust them, it's private, and I doubt anyone would check for you there."

"Your parents know about you and my father? They approve?"

"After Carol abducted me, Kent and my mother had words about my living situation. There was no hiding our relationship after that. Plus, Mom's approval comes with conditions. You can ask her yourself when we get to the house." I passed Ife, having had my fill of her judgmental looks and silent accusations.

Part of me wanted to escape before she brought up her ultimatum again. I never answered her the first time, however, the what-ifs kept intruding on my thoughts.

What if Kent and Ife never reconciled because of me, could I live with the consequences? I would be depriving him of a relationship with his future grandchildren, and that would be unforgivable. What if the stress from their estrangement destroyed his love for me over time? Could I survive after sharing a life with him? I was confident in his devotion, but love wasn't always the solution, and I never wanted to be the reason he lost anyone he loved.

At my parents' house, Ife disappeared into the kitchen to help my mom. When she reappeared, we brainstormed various ways to expose Hal's dealings with the mystery shareholder until we landed on one.

Exchanging ideas almost felt like the days we used to plot shenanigans we had no business being up to, or dream up our future lives and how we'd always be a part of each other's families no matter what.

Hope kindled in my heart that Ife could one day accept my new role in Kent's life.

"This is the most perilous option," Ife said with a satisfied sigh. "You'd bear all the risk if he caught you. Maybe we should hire someone to do the dirty work."

Her suggestion stumped me. "Do you have someone in mind you can trust? After all, we're talking about the company your dad built from scratch. Your inheritance. I don't know about you, but I doubt anyone but us would work as hard to ensure he keeps his life's work."

"You have a point." Ife bit her bottom lip as she contemplated our plan. "Okay, but nothing you said saves you from the risk you'll take."

"True, but as long as you distract him, I know I'll find what we require. So all we need to decide is when you approach him." I stretched out on the floor, surrounded by Post Its.

Ife twisted her lips. "That's not all we lack to decide."

"Huh?" I raised myself into a seated position, surprised I'd missed something.

"Without me, this plan won't work. And everything else we thought up and discarded, we did so for a reason. They were shitty ideas." Ife sat back on the sofa and folded her arms with a gotcha smirk on her face.

"What am I missing, Ife?"

"My price."

And there it was. The ultimatum I'd avoided at the police station.

"Ife, this is your dad's comp—"

"I'm not leaving here without a definitive answer, and I won't play along unless I know that once everything is done, you're out of our lives."

With the finality in her voice, the little flame of hope I held dear dwindled into smoke before extinguishing.

"I-I—"

"No more prevaricating, Mads. I know you've thought about it."

"If I agree, will we have a chance to be friends again? Even if it's long distance and only by phone?"

Ife blinked and swallowed multiple times in the silence after my question. As the quiet extended, I understood the true cost of my selfishness. I'd once heard that breaking up with a boyfriend was less painful than a friend, but I was looking at losing both at the same time. I couldn't tell which hurt worse.

Her suggestion to hire someone rose in my head. If I placed my faith in someone else's hands, Ife's ultimatum would be useless. Despite my heart surging at this possibility, I knew I would be on borrowed time. Ife would find another reason to push me out of Kent's life. However, the stress of waiting for the next warning paled in comparison with trusting a stranger to care about Kent as much as I did.

In Quarren's case, although I didn't know him well and hadn't evaluated his ability to free Kent from the murder charges, I had my mother as a backup. If Quarren made one misstep, I would convince Kent to hire Nikita as his counsel.

With all the back and forth in my head, in the end, I hung my head low in defeat. "Okay. Once we've rooted out all the threats against Kent, I'll disappear." The words barely passed my lips, and I couldn't believe they came from my mouth. They were weak. Defeated. Hopeless.

"Alright. I'll set up a date with Hal right now." Ife retrieved her phone and walked out of the room, an odd sound slipped past before she disappeared from view.

It could have been a sob, but I shook the thought from my head. She'd been so adamant, she couldn't now be regretting pushing me this far.

"Hal said tonight works," Ife said while avoiding my gaze and hugging her body tightly.

"Okay. I'll get ready."

We parted ways after going over our plan again. My investigator, Sam, picked me up and drove us to Hal's house while Ife met Hal at a restaurant downtown. Sam was my best PI. A former Navy SEAL, he had many specialties that could land him on the wrong side of the law but on the right side of my clients.

We sat in a nondescript vehicle across the street from Hal's place. A wrought-iron fence separated us.

"You know, I could do this myself," Sam said.

"We only have about two hours to search his house from top to bottom. The more hands we have, the faster we get out of here and back to safety. Because one thing for certain, two things for sure is I don't intend to end up in a jail cell tonight." I urged him out of the car, pretending I wasn't scared shitless about the crimes we were about to commit.

While Sam remotely disconnected Hal's alarm system and opened the gate, I drove the car further down the road. Once I joined Sam at the gate, he led me toward the there-story mini-mansion Hal called home, using his flashlight to avoid obstacles. I turned mine on as we passed rooms with opulent furnishings.

"We need to search his study, office, and library. I doubt Hal would keep records anywhere else in his house." Sam opened an app on his phone. On it was the blueprint of Hal's home.

"What about the basement?" I pointed to the large space beneath us. "Don't guys like to keep their secrets hidden in dark, unexpected places?"

"Madison, look at this place. Why do you think any part of this building is dark?"

"Good point." I nodded and followed him to the office.

Four wooden filing cabinets matching the rest of the furniture lined the wall. Each had four to six drawers.

"We'll be lucky if we have time to search other rooms." Sam swung his flashlight across the room.

"Let's split the cabinets first, then regroup. He might have a secret compartment in his desk. Your expertise will be best used to ensure we don't leave any traces behind."

"Let's get to it." Sam proceeded forward and chose the cabinet furthest from me.

I went to the other end. As we rifled through the cabinets, we would meet in the middle. We got to work in what I imagined was companionable silence for Sam but for me, fear filled the void and screamed in my ear. Files filled each drawer to the max. Tax filings for the last fifteen years, investment statements, and a lot of miscellaneous documents that had nothing to do with the information I needed to help Kent.

Forty-five minutes passed before I finished going through all the files in the first cabinet. I glanced at Sam.

"Found anything yet?" I slid another drawer closed, trying not to lose hope while another worry piled onto the one that had ridden my back since Ife and I came up with this plan. Because there was a possibility I would leave here with nothing to keep Kent at the helm of Luxe Locations. Ensuring his future was worth the price Ife demanded, and I would gain no pleasure in seeing our venture fail.

"I'm not sure, but I think I found something promising. In case this leads us to what we need, I'll take pictures. You should too." A flash followed his statement, followed by many more.

The next cabinet called my name. Unlike the first, this one didn't open when I pulled the handle. I searched for a locking mechanism by running my hands along the surface.

"Sam? I'm having difficulty finding where to open this."

He interrupted his search to join me. "Hmm. This might have the jackpot we're looking for."

"Because it's locked?"

"Not just locked, but it has a hidden mechanism." Sam ran his hands along the front and sides. "If it isn't easily visible, then we'll check the back." His muscles bulged while he struggled to shift the cabinet.

Who knew papers could be so heavy?

My phone dinged.

Things are not going well. Hal's getting ready to leave and I don't think I can buy you more time.

"Shit!"

"What's the problem?" Sam grunted under the strain.

"Our time got cut short by fifteen, twenty minutes tops." I bit my lip as the pressure from Kent's future pressed heavily on my shoulders.

My heart thumped against my ribs, drowning everything except my doubts.

"Found it." Sam fiddled behind the cabinet until a soft click sounded. "Here you go. Don't bother reading, just take pictures."

"Right."

He returned to the files he was working on and I turned my attention to the folders in front of me. The closest three confused me. They were empty. When I checked the label, the blood in my veins iced over and the folder slipped from my numb fingers.

"Madison? Why don't I see your camera flashing?" Sam asked.

Right. I was here to find evidence, but the empty files creeped me out. Regardless, I photographed the labels and placed them where they were. The next file sickened me and gave me hope. As I swallowed my bile, I sped through the files while taking photographs of the contents. There were so many. Awful images bombarded me, but I snapped picture after picture, knowing the more I had the better off Kent would be.

"Madison, if we want to get out of here undetected, we need to clean up and leave now." Sam cupped my shoulder, and I jolted at the contact.

Sweat dotted my forehead, and my breathing came out in pants. I nodded and made way for him to put the cabinet back to rights. As we were finishing, car lights passed over the windows. Sam lunged at me and we fell to the ground.

I fumbled with my flashlight until I turned it off. "Do you think he knows someone's in his house?" I whispered.

"If he doesn't, he will when he doesn't have to disarm his alarm. We've got to leave, now." Sam grabbed my hand and we ran while crouched toward the garage.

I didn't ask him any questions, though our destination was risky. If Hal's headlights landed on us, we'd be lucky to only land in deep shit.

Sam paused at the alarm panel while I tried to control my shaking limbs. "Alright, the security system will be up and running in five seconds. Pray he hasn't opened the garage by then because that's our best exit point."

"God, Sam, how the hell are you so calm right now?"

"Madison, I've survived war zones and special ops missions. Shit isn't bad until it's bad."

"Right." I nodded though I had zero confidence in my agreement.

How could I when prison bars filled my vision? Terror had my limbs in a chokehold and every movement was a constant negotiation.

"Alright, let's go." Sam grabbed my arm and pulled me along as we entered the garage.

"Where do we hide?" I scanned the dark area.

Like the house, the garage was huge and filled with shadows.

"My eyes have adjusted. Yours?"

"Not quite." All bravado fled from my voice, but I relied on my faith in Sam.

He squeezed my hand. "Then follow me."

We rushed toward a destination I couldn't see. We were still in motion as the garage door began to rise and a car's headlights beamed into the space. For a brief moment, I glimpsed a row of cars before Sam yanked me to the ground behind a tarp-covered vehicle.

Sweat now slid in a river down my back and I pressed my hand against my mouth to quiet my harsh breaths.

The car door opened, and Sam tugged on my hand again. Crouched, we quietly sprinted toward the exit, and barely cleared the door before the hinges of the garage door engaged and started to fall closed.

Once outside, Sam and I ran like Dobermans were on our tail and about to rip us apart. At the gate, Sam quickly did his magic and we slipped through before Hal would know we'd been on his property.

When we arrived at the car, I fell into the passenger seat and shook. The text I sent Ife informing her we got out was probably full of gibberish because I couldn't control my body long enough to send a coherent message.

Throughout the long ride to arriving at my parents' doorstep, my body rebelled at the thought of portraying a calm facade. There was no way to slip past my mother in this state. And if my father caught me, I would unintentionally activate his overprotective mode. Either way, I was screwed.

"Looks like your parents aren't home yet," Sam said.

"What?" I turned toward the house, blinking away the haze of my hysteria. The house was dark, but it was too early for Mom and Dad to have gone to bed. "Oh, you're right." I breathed a little easier, but my body remained shaky as I opened Sam's car door. "Thanks for everything you did tonight."

"No prob. I'll email you the pictures when I get home. I'm sure we'll find something to trace Hal to the secret shareholder you're looking for." Sam waited until I got inside and shut the door before driving off.

As soon as my door clicked, the hours of terror leading up to what Sam and I had escaped took their toll. I ran to the downstairs half bath, dropped to my knees, and emptied the contents of my belly. Tyger, Benson, and Stabler crowded the entrance, watching me and mewling in concern as I heaved even when I had nothing but stomach acid left to come out.

How long I spent on the floor, I didn't know. But I hugged my animals to me as I tried to scrub the images I'd seen at Hal's house from my mind and reminded myself I was safe in my childhood home where guards patrolled and my dogs would protect me with their lives.

For more hours, even after I went to bed hugging my animals, I watched the door and jumped at every slight noise until my body rebelled and shut off without my permission.

CHAPTER 31

ent

Douglas' district attorney, DA Kemp, stared across the table at me. His smug smirk rankled my every nerve.

Detectives Salinas and Glass who sat on either side of him wore similar expressions.

"Now that you've been arraigned and denied bail, would you like to issue a confession?" Kemp folded his hands over a folio, his eagerness to put me away clear for everyone to see.

Kemp's story made Douglas' news last year. He came from a low-income background. Despite his hard work, the upperclass circles he found himself in ostracized him and relished every opportunity to remind him he didn't belong. As his success grew, his grudge against the upperclass ballooned and he openly went after people with wealth like mine.

His bias didn't exclude me although I wasn't born into wealth. My struggles to make Luxe Locations into what it was today didn't factor into his vendetta, although we both fought for our success. For Kemp, he went after anyone with a checkbook larger than his, and unfortunately he had me in his sights. I'm sure Glass and Salinas stoked his inferiority complex with their own as they'd been hostile to me since the first victim showed up dead.

I glanced around the court house meeting room as I reminded myself not to give Kemp anything. "You've made a big mistake. The real murderer is still on the streets but you're wasting resources on a flimsy conspiracy theory that won't hold up in court."

"Oh? Am I missing something in your bio? Nothing here says when you passed the bar." Kemp opened his file. "No, all I have are seven murder victims and you on the hook for them."

Quarren rested his hand on my shoulder, a reminder not to let my anger get the best of me. "Kemp, your case is a mountain of circumstantial evidence I can debunk in my sleep. If you take this to trial, know my client won't be the one the jury judges. It will be you and the police department for your targeted and continuous abuse of power and vindictive harassment against my client. You're on record for targeting men of means because you don't think they deserve their wealth. Once I wipe the court with your snotty noses and win, I'll sue you and the city of Douglas for gross negligence and emotional distress. But you have the opportunity right now to correct your mistake before you dig yourself a hole so deep you wind up on another continent. Drop the charges and let my client go."

During Quarren's comeback, Kemps face grew redder and redder. Steam emitted from his quivering nostrils.

I sat back and folded my arms, satisfied with Quarren's approach. He understood when to attack and when to play nice. I was done with the Mr. Congeniality role after spending three sleepless nights away from Madison.

Although she visited me every day, she was keeping something from me. When I saw her next, I wouldn't allow her to hide the truth from me.

"Quarren, you can try putting me on trial, but a jury of Luxe's peers aren't the billionaires. They're working class to middle class men and women who'll look at your client as an over privileged individual who thinks the world should stop for him. I'll get his employees on the stand to paint him as a ruthless, exploitative employer who thinks women don't deserve to live."

I clenched my teeth, certain he'd find a few. After all, there was that god awful website where employees shit on me for being a demanding boss.

"And I'll counter with the good he's done in the community and other workers who love working for him. Trust me, Kemp, I and my client will come out looking better than you." Quarren opened his briefcase. "And on that note, here's my motion to dismiss." He handed kemp a brief and shut his case. "We'll see you in court."

I followed Quarren out of the meeting room and stopped short at Madison's anxious face.

CHAPTER 32

$\mathcal{M}$adison

Everything in me screamed to tell Kent what I found, but I couldn't. Anything coming from me or Kent would cause the prosecution and cops to consider us with suspicion. With the way the prosecutor went after Kent in the courtroom during his arraignment, I wouldn't put it past the DA to claim we'd planted evidence.

Not telling Kent was one secret on top of another. I also couldn't confess to the bargain I'd made with Ife. Knowing the bombshell I had in my lap would free Kent in a matter of days dampened my happiness. From the concern turning down Kent's eyes, he probably suspected I was hiding things, but right now I had no choice.

"Little bunny?"

I ran into his arms before the police put handcuffs on him again and led him back to jail. "Kent, I'm so sorry the hearing didn't go as planned."

He squeezed me and kissed my forehead. "Me, too. I wanted to make up for not being by your side every night."

"Oh." I stepped out of his embrace. "I have the proxy documents you asked for." I pulled an envelope from my purse and handed it to him.

"Good. I'll make you my proxy—"

"No, I don't want that."

He wrinkled his brow in confusion. "By giving you my proxy, I'm protecting you."

I cradled his face in my hands. "I understand the thought behind the gesture, but you need to give them to Ife. Think about the optics. If I show up with your votes, I'll only fan the flames of your opposition rather than oust them. Ife has history voting, and more of a stake in keeping you in charge."

"My daughter is in a lot of pain right now and lashing out. She didn't even show up in court today."

"True, but deep down, she's not vindictive. She knows cutting you out of your company is a step too far."

Kent breathed in and looked to the ceiling before meeting my gaze. "Do you trust she's on my side?"

I nodded, keeping the fact I'd removed the biggest obstacle to getting her agreement a secret.

"Alright. Ife will be my proxy." Kent signed the documents and handed them to me.

I drew his face to mine for a much-needed kiss. A clock ticked in my head, counting down every moment we had that I needed to log into memory for when I wouldn't see Kent's face or hear his voice again. I intended to stockpile every second so when the pain became unbearable and the loneliness drove me to despair, I'd have a part of Kent to keep me sane.

"Hey Quarren, I can't delay any longer. The transport's about to leave and I need your client on the bus."

I pulled away to find an officer talking with Kent's lawyer. The man turned to us, his handcuffs ready to click around Kent's wrist.

"Get some sleep little bunny. Quarren will surely win his motion tomorrow. And give the kids an extra treat for me," Kent said, talking about our pets.

We didn't linger over goodbyes. A good thing because I was close to breaking down. He chucked me under the chin and allowed the officer to cuff him. He soon disappeared from view.

My throat ached with the need to cry, but I had many days ahead of me to weep. For now, I needed to fight for my man's freedom.

After leaving the courthouse, I called Ife. "Meet me at my mom's." I hung up without extending the conversation. Not that Ife would want to chitchat given the current state or lack of one regarding our friendship.

When I arrived at the Montgomery house, my dad greeted me. "Things didn't go as planned?"

"Not even close. But Kent's lawyer is doing his best."

Dad squeezed my arm and pulled me into his arms. I breathed in his familiar scent, taking comfort in the strength, warmth, and acceptance I'd always found with him.

"Alright, baby girl, Ife's waiting for you in the living room. While you two are busy, I'm going to take my granimals for a walk. I doubt they got a proper exercise following you around all day."

"You're right. The guards try to keep them distracted but they've grown attached to me and want to be around me all the time."

"Like that cat. He struts around here like he owns the place until you get home. He turns into molasses so fast, I get whiplash." Dad kissed my nose, leaving me with the task Kent gave me.

I straightened my shoulders and entered the living room.

"I've been looking over these pictures your investigator took and I think he found something," Ife said as soon as I crossed the threshold.

She sat on the ground with printouts surrounding her in various piles.

"Here. These are for you." I handed her the envelope with the proxy.

She opened it with a frown. However, as she read, her eyebrows raised. "Isn't this a bit drastic? After all, he's getting out today."

"Actually, he's not. I just came from the hearing."

Ife checked her watch. "Shit! I can't believe I missed it. I was deep into these documents." She rocked back on her heels. "He must have thought the worst of me for not being there to support him."

"Your father is more understanding than you give him credit." I cleared my throat, reminding myself now's not the time to fall apart. "We're expecting an announcement for an emergency meeting to come out soon, so look out for an email."

Ife studied my face. "There's something else on your mind, isn't there?"

I kneeled beside her and booted my laptop, where I'd transferred the photos I'd taken. "Sam's not the only one who found something."

"Oh my God, Mads!" Ife blanched, her warm brown complexion took on an ashen undertone. "You got these from Hal's house?"

"Yeah, which means he's the one who's been killing all these women."

"But there are more here than are connected to my dad. We have to get these to the police."

"We can't." I stalled her from leaping off the ground and explained why they would doubt any evidence we brought to them they didn't find on their own. "I can't even call in a tip without worrying they'll trace the call back to me."

Ife slumped down but perked up a second later. "You have staff with random connections. Can't they call in a tip?"

"I thought about that but haven't figured out how to point the police to the exact location without sparking an investigation that will uncover my employee. On top of that, there were other files I found worrying. And I'm sure you'll share my concerns when you see why." I located the image of the three empty files I found and showed it to her.

She crinkled her brow and switched from studying the photo to me. "Am I understanding what I'm seeing?" She pushed my laptop away to pace. "Hal labeled the folders with the other women by their surnames. Two of those folders have our surnames on them."

"I think you need to hire some bodyguards," I said as she paced, her energy more manic as she dwelled on the threat.

"I had dinner with Hal. He could have—"

"But he didn't, and I think it's because he still needs you."

"If that's the case, why is your file empty? He seems to have it out for you, yet he hasn't made a move since Carol."

I shrugged, although I had a theory. "I think Hal deeply hates your father. He'll either wait for him to be released, which is tenuous right now, or he'll engineer the perfect moment to inflict the most emotional damage."

"Does my father know about this?" Ife plopped beside me, and her openness and proximity were painful reminders of other times we worked toward a common goal.

"Not yet. I don't like the idea of him knowing and not being able to act on the information while he's behind bars. Honestly, I just want him out."

"Alright, if Dad's out, and your people are out, we might need bigger guns."

"Bigger guns, huh? You know, the way your father's arrest went down never sat right with me." It was my turn to pace the room. I cupped my chin as I thought about the timeline of events. "They arrested him on a day and at a time when any city official worth their weight was off the clock to make Kent stew in jail. What if their purpose was to prevent him from contacting someone with enough pull to get him out?"

"Someone like…"

"Valentino," we said in the same breath.

"Why didn't I think of him before? I was quick to drop his name to see Kent. I should have gone to his house—"

"I thought you were bluffing when you talked to the officer."

I sent her a sheepish grin. "I was. Kent knows him like that, I don't."

"Well, I guess the two of us are going to get better acquainted with him because neither of us wants my dad to spend another night in jail."

CHAPTER 33

ent

Anticipation and anxiety filled me. I hadn't had a good night's sleep in days. Every time I saw Madison, she looked like she was working herself into exhaustion on my behalf. The one worry I didn't have was her tendency to skip meals. With her staying at her parent's house, Nikita and Dennis wouldn't allow her to drink meal replacements as she worked.

I'd always admired Nikita's strong will and dedication to her family when Ife and Madison were younger. Now, my admiration skyrocketed for how Madison's mother continued to care for my woman while I was incapable.

I closed my eyes and breathed through my frustration. Today's meeting with Judge Alderton was my chance to get home and reassure myself Madison, Ife, and my company were out of danger.

Quarren, Kemp, and I sat in the judge's chambers surrounded by oppressive, dark brown furnishings. Was the point to leech any semblance of hope from the accused? Or was the decor to send a warning to both sides of the bleak days ahead?

"I'm ready to hear your arguments." Judge Alderton and his clerk entered the room. The judge removed his robe before seating himself behind the heavy mahogany desk while the clerk sat to take notes.

"There's a motion to dismiss. On what basis?" Alderton glanced at Quarren then Kemp.

While my lawyer and the DA went back and forth about the reasons, precedents, and other legal jargon for whether the case had merit, my mind wandered to the two women waiting in silent support in the halls. Tension separated them, and although hopeful, I doubted their distance was only because of my circumstances.

"Alright counselors. I've heard your take. I'll issue my decision tomorrow."

"Tomorrow?" I lurched from my chair.

"Yes. Tomorrow. Unless you'd like me to deny the motion right now?" Alderton arched his brow and looked toward my chair.

I took his silent suggestion and sat, seething about yet another delay.

While he rattled off instructions, I listened with half an ear. My next move was to involve Valentino. His wasn't a name I liked to use lightly. Favors with DeLucas came at an expense, and I already had a future debt I owed them. Although Carol's murder halved the debt, the man behind her was still out there, and Quarren's defense strategy wasn't to find him or raise reasonable doubt through another party. Regardless, I wanted the name of the man making my life into a nightmare.

Quarren patted my shoulder, and I glanced around the room to see Kemp on his way out. I rose and followed my lawyer through the exit.

"Can you negotiate some time for me to speak with Ife and Madison?"

He checked his watch. "Let me see if there's a room available." He went down the hall.

Before disappearing, he paused to talk to Madison and Ife. Quarren pointed in my direction and left. My daughter and her best friend approached. An aircraft carrier could dock in the space between them. Despite the distance, their steps had a bounce and a lightness surrounded them.

"You two seem oddly optimistic. What do you know that I don't?"

They shared a glance, but Madison spoke first.

"We don't want to jinx it."

"Jinx what?" I asked.

Ife hugged me instead of answering, a smile wobbling on her lips. "You'll see soon enough."

I crushed her to me. The last time my daughter hugged me like this, she was moving to D.C. to conquer the world. It was the first time I realized she didn't need me to fight her battles. I was at a loss because Lola's passing was still fresh and my daughter would be half a country away.

"Dad, I can't breathe."

"Sorry." I loosened my hold.

Quarren strode toward us, and Ife sidled beside me. I held my hand out to Madison and pulled her to my other side. Despite the fuckery, I relished having my love and my daughter standing beside me. It gave me hope for the day Ife and Madison would reconcile and make more moments of us coming together like this the norm rather than as a result of tragic circumstances.

"Kent, I found a room. You have an hour." Quarren nodded toward a closed door across the hall.

As soon as the door closed behind us, Madison charged toward the desk while extracting a blue folder from her bag. "Since we only have an hour, we need to go through these files for clues." She withdrew another folder, this one was pink. "Ife and I read through several documents already and started digging into some of these LLCs and cross-referencing them with the list of shareholders Omar sent over. However, Hal had a lot of contracts and other documents we still need to get through." The last folder she removed was purple.

"What do you mean Hal had a lot of contracts? And how exactly did you obtain these files?" My voice was strained as I picked up the purple folder.

Madison didn't… couldn't mean to imply she had an active role in gathering this information.

She folded her arms and glared. "Kent, would you rather argue about my methods or find the asshole trying to steal your company? I know what my priority is, but maybe you need a refresher?"

Ife's eyes widened at our confrontation, however she wisely bit her lip and shuffled through the pink folder.

I stood over Madison, uncaring of my imposing stance. "No, little bunny. You need the reminder." I grabbed her chin and matched her glower. "You are my priority. Your health. Your safety. Your life. Everything else takes second chair."

She lowered her lashes, hiding the brilliant brown eyes I loved to lose myself in.

I jerked her head up. "Whatever shit you did to get these files, don't do it again."

She nodded and I punished her for her recklessness with a fierce kiss. I was just getting started when Quarren cleared his throat.

"Do I have to remind you we have a time limit?"

I separated from Madison with one last peck on an un-pigmented spot on her cheek. "Let's get to this."

Quarren and Ife brought out their laptops, making the research into some LLCs go faster, but Madison had collected a lot of information. When I checked the time, twenty minutes had passed and I was still researching the first LLC.

"This is odd," Madison said.

We all raised our heads, curious about what caused her outburst.

"Hal has a contract for the sale of an LLC but the buyer and dates are blank."

"Why's that odd? If he's the owner of the LLC, he could be using the contract as a template," Quarren said without looking up from his pile of documents.

"Mmm, I'm not sure. I feel like I ran across the name of the LLC before and it's not one of his."

"Let me see. It could belong to Luxe Locations." I reached for the contract.

My company owned a lot of LLCs. Although I didn't have them all memorized, if it belonged to me, the name should look familiar.

The name of the LLC did look familiar, but not for the reason I'd hoped. I rifled through the papers I'd spent the last twenty minutes skimming. "I need a laptop." I snapped my fingers.

Ife reached me first.

There were a few windows up. As I minimized them, one struck me. It was an image of file folders. One had my surname on it as well as a couple others. Although I found it strange, I minimized the window to open a search engine to find what I needed. I keyed in the name of the LLC and followed the clues until I got to a person. I clenched my fists as rage filled me.

"Dad, you found something?"

I was about to answer her when a knock interrupted me.

Quarren rose and answered the door. "Kemp? What are—"

"You've got your damn dismissal." He stalked into the room, his glare pointed in my direction. "You're lucky Mr. Luxe. We have another suspect in custody."

Madison and Ife shared a glance and their lips tilted up slightly.

"Who is it?" Quarren stepped around Kemp and folded his arms.

"Luxe Locations' legal counsel, Hal Hannity."

"Hal? A murderer?" I asked, finding it hard to believe the man I'd worked with and whose ass I kicked was the same man capable of killing Carol.

"For the Carol murder or all the murders you suspect my client of committing?"

Kemp's lips thinned. "All of them. We've prepared the paperwork for Mr. Luxe's release." Kemp handed a sheaf of papers to Quarren.

"I appreciate this." Quarren began scanning the documents and Kemp turned to leave. "By the way, you aren't going to try to connect my client to another conspiracy theory now that you have the actual murderer in custody are you?"

Kemps shoulder stiffened. "No, we no longer have reason to believe Mr. Luxe had any involvement."

Once he left, Madison and Ife's smirk grew into full-blown grins.

"You're coming home today," Madison croaked as her eyes gleamed.

I was still in a state of disbelief. Kemp's appearance and disappearance were so sudden after dropping the good news.

"Did you two have something to do with this?" I stared between the two women.

In turn, they glanced at Quarren who shrugged and packed his laptop. "I think my presence may complicate things. Congratulations, Kent. If you want me to look into these files some more, I can."

"Thanks." I shook his hand. "But there's no need. I found who I've been looking for."

Shock filled Ife's and Madison's faces. "You did?" they asked in the same breath.

Madison stepped forward. "Who's trying to steal your company?"

"Someone I'll handle." I cleared the search history from Ife's computer and closed the windows before returning it to her.

"Does this mean all your problems are handled?" Ife asked while staring at Madison.

The light in Madison's eyes dimmed, and her curious smile fell.

I peered closer between my daughter and my lover, understanding there was a message exchanged in a language I didn't speak, and I had no translator available to clue me in on the real topic.

"Not quite. I still have unanswered questions, but I expect life will return to normal soon."

"I like the sound of that. A return to *normalcy*." Ife hugged me but it was unlike the earlier one she shared.

Beneath her glee was a sinister satisfaction that left me unnerved. Especially as Madison stood farther away than I liked during Ife's mini-celebration.

CHAPTER 34

$\mathcal{M}$adison

"What are you doing?" Kent asked as we rode from the courthouse to our home.

I had my head bowed over my phone while my fingers flew over the screen. "Finalizing plans for your rebranding tour."

"My what? I'm not a rockstar performing for avid fans."

I rested the phone on my lap and gave him my attention. "No, but we finally have amazing PR to benefit you and your company. I'm pushing to do this now to stall the company-stealing bitch ass hoe from making moves. Plus, I'd already had the framework mapped out. All that's left is for my team to execute my vision."

I tried to hide my anxiety. Ife's not-so-subtle reminder of my promise put a doomsday clock over my head. The countdown to when I wouldn't see Kent again was on, and I intended to relish every moment we were together.

His lips quirked. "And I don't get a say in this tour?"

I took a subtle breath to brace for the act I was about to put on.

Once I felt confident I wouldn't make Kent suspicious, I arched my brow. "You trust me. Why do I need your input?"

"Good point. And honestly, how the public views me and my company isn't at the forefront of my mind right now." He pulled me from my position beside him and sat me on his lap. "Now this... I haven't had a good fix of my little bunny in days."

"Is this why you had the guards take Benson and Stabler in a separate car?" I sank into him, pressed my nose against his throat, and inhaled his scent.

He wasn't alone in missing our closeness. I'd longed for the nights when he and his smell wrapped me in safety, or whenever he needed a reminder that I existed in this world, which occurred multiple times a day.

"Innocent eyes should stay that way."

"Ha!" I poked his chest. "The dogs don't count and those body-guards aren't innocent. They play the role because letting their employers know they've accidentally walked in on or by as their employers fucked is not the discretion you pay them for."

Kent stilled, and a dangerous note entered his voice. "Are you telling me they've seen you naked?"

"Did I just activate your possessiveness?"

"Little bunny, don't toy with me. I want to know who else has seen the gift you've given me. The second most cherished treasure you've handed me."

"Second?" I straightened in his lap, preparing myself for my over-heated reaction to the insult I expected with his response to my next question. "What's the first?"

"Don't change the subject. Who's seen your body? Was it while I was inside you, pleasuring you? Did you have that look on your face? The one that would drive men who conquered empires to leave the celebrations hailing them as heroes in a mad rush to return home bloody and scarred to see. Because if they did, we only have a few minutes before the cops put me in cuffs again."

"Nice deflection, but you forget who you're dealing with. What's the first most cherished thing I've given you?"

"I can't believe you even have to ask." He laid his hand on my chest. "Your heart is the gift I covet above all others. I must not be doing something right if you didn't know."

I blinked back tears. Instead of the affront I wanted to have, he'd reminded me of the sad future ahead. "You know you can never return it to the sender, right?"

He snorted. "Consider me a hoarder. I'm never letting your heart go. Now, give me a name."

I choked on a giggle. "Sorry, I was too distracted by what you were doing to me to pay attention to anyone's face."

Kent grunted, but his active mind was probably plotting how he would catch the man who dared glimpse my body.

"It's your own damn fault. If you weren't so impatient, we could make it to the bedroom and behind closed doors, but nooo, you have to have me when and where you want me." I twisted my torso to rest my spine against his chest while he clutched my hip in his large hand.

"Thanks for reminding me I've been deprived of more than my freedom. How're you going to make the hardships I faced up to me?" He rubbed and gripped my flesh from my hips to my butt as his dick lengthened beneath me.

I spun in his lap and lowered my head to his ear to whisper, "I had this whole welcome home party idea I wanted to try."

"Yeah?" Kent's voice deepened.

"Oh, yeah." My register lowered to complement his.

"Tell me more."

I flicked my tongue on his earlobe and sucked the morsel into my mouth with a moan. "I bought this pretty little dress I know you won't wait to rip off me."

"Describe it to me." Kent moved his hand to the zipper at my nape.

"It's black."

The muted hiss of the zipper protesting as Kent lowered the slider turned me on as much as the soft brush of his finger against my bared skin. A shiver ran through me and my breath hitched.

"It's sheer."

"And how does the underwear you're going to have underneath

look?" Kent unsnapped my bra and pulled the material of my dress and bra over my shoulders and down my arms, exposing my breasts for his view.

"What underwear?"

"Jesus Christ." He grabbed my neck from the back and buried his face below my chin.

His beard teased my skin as he licked and sucked. So many sensations at once caused everywhere in my body to tingle. My nipples hardened and tiny sparks set off in my clit.

"The dress has lace appliqués for my naughty bits." I gasped as he sank his teeth into the flesh above my collarbone.

"Straddle me, little bunny. Let me pet my pussy and show her how much I've missed her."

As soon as I raised my body to do his bidding, he latched onto my breast and sucked. I muffled my cry into the hair on top of his head.

He trailed his hands up my thigh, bunching my dress the higher he went.

"And after you see me in my dress, I'm going to get on my knees."

Riiip.

"Kent!"

"What? I'm giving you a head start so you don't have to worry about panties when you put on the dress. Now tell me what happens after you get on your knees. I'm dying to hear what's next." He squeezed both my ass cheeks, pushed them together then pulled them apart over and over as he resumed his attention on my breasts.

"I'd unbuckle your belt." I reached for his belt and demonstrated my intentions. With my dress around my elbows, I worked his belt free with limited mobility. "Then I'd unbutton your pants and unzip you."

Kent groaned around my nipple as I put action to my words. Then he speared me from behind with his fingers.

Now, I was the one moaning as he added another finger into my slippery depths and stretched me. I needed the preparation to handle Kent's monster dick. Especially after almost an entire week without him inside me.

"What are you going to do next, little bunny?"

"What I would like to do is rip your boxers off the way you treated my panties, but…" I shrugged. "I'm not that strong, and my movements are limited at the moment. So, I guess I'll have to do this instead."

I pulled his dick free and it sprang up between our bodies, hitting my waist. I wished for a better view, Kent obstructed my vision as he fed on my breasts as if I were his first meal after a long fast. I couldn't blame him, either. If I were better positioned, his dick would be in my mouth while I did my best to suck his soul dry.

I stroked his length. Sticky fluid spilled over my hand. "Then I'd lead forward and lick you from your balls to your tip. Swallow every drop of pre-cum before welcoming you into my mouth."

The pressure on my breasts eased.

"Look at me, little bunny."

When had I closed my eyes? My lids were heavy as I raised them as if I were intoxicated from his touch. When I finally met his stare, he had a feral glint in his eyes.

"We don't have to wait until we get home for you to give me my welcome home gift." Kent freed my arms and gently pushed me to the floor of the car.

I silently forgave him for leaving my pussy empty once I saw the dark hue of his engorged flesh. His mushroomed head called to me as pearlescent fluid pooled at the top. Saliva pooled in my mouth.

"Little bunny, look at me."

I dragged my eyes to meet his. Kent loomed over me, a king on his throne. A hungry, demanding sovereign who looked at me as if he would sacrifice everything he had for one lap of my tongue.

I smiled and reached out for him. Without breaking eye contact, I dragged my tongue against the heavy weight under his scrotum before I greedily sucked his balls.

He hissed at the first contact.

"Like what you see?"

He lowered his lids over his feverish blue eyes and caressed my cheek with his thumb, adding tenderness to the heated moment.

"Like? That's such a tame sentiment for what seeing you, hearing you... touching you does to me. Haven't you realized by now little bunny? You are the sun to which I gravitate. The food that sustains me. The water that gives me life. The very blood that flows through my veins. You are my purpose, and I am your servant, ready to receive your blessing."

"Blessing? You give me too much credit, but now I have something to aim for." I reached for his hardness and slowly licked until I got the treasure at his tip.

Kent's breathing deepened. His eyes narrowed as his anticipation built, surrounding us in a cocoon of overwhelming desire. "Your mouth feels so good."

I engulfed as much of him in my mouth as I could handle, but Kent's dick was long and wide. He filled my throat as I bobbed up and down, uncaring that I sounded like a glutton. I wanted... No; I needed his salty emissions, the same way he professed to needing me.

"That's right, little bunny. Suck me off. Take what you need. Take what belongs to you."

I hummed at his encouragement. Filled my throat with him until I almost forgot to breathe. Spit ran from the sides of my mouth, coating him as I relished his velvety texture. I reveled in his manly scent and doubled my efforts to make him come.

When he combed his fingers through my hair, I knew he was close. Muffled curses issued from his mouth, but I didn't stop. I wanted his explosion. I wanted to lap up everything he had to give, and I wouldn't let him hold out on me.

Soon, his fingers curled into my hair, almost pulling the strands from my scalp. The sting added to my pleasure as the first burst of fluid hit the back of my throat.

Kent groaned as he released and released the nectar I'd craved for days. I'd felt so cold without him by my side. Now he warmed my insides with the sign of how much he missed me. I licked and swallowed everything he gave, not missing a drop. Even after I'd drained him, I tended to his dick while he moaned his pleasure.

I was so engrossed in him, I protested when he dragged me from my prize. He quieted me by plundering my mouth until I wouldn't dream of objecting. Why would I have reason to after he grabbed my ass and used it to control my body? He pulled and pushed, ensuring my wet pussy and clit dragged against his softened dick until he hardened again.

I pulled away, needing a second to catch my breath from being overstimulated.

"Little bunny, put me inside you and shower me with more blessings."

"Give me a second." I gasped for air.

"Sure." He pulled my torso close and sucked my breast into his mouth, not giving me the time I needed to catch my breath.

My body pulsed screaming its need to be filled louder than my need for air. My pussy clenched on nothing while weeping its despair at its emptiness. I gave up the fight to breathe normally and slid him inside me. As wet as I was, he still stretched my walls.

"Mmm, Kent, you feel so good inside me," I said once he was all the way inside.

He cupped both sides of my face until my glossy gaze met his fierce one. "Thank you for welcoming me home." He thrust from below, pushing himself deeper inside me.

Not once did we break from peering into each other's eyes as we fucked to completion. When he came the second time, filling me inside with his cum, emotion inundated me to the point I began to tear up.

I leaned forward, wrapped my arms around his neck, and buried my face in his chest to hide from his piercing view. Moments like now, I had to hold close because they would soon end.

I couldn't even confide in Kent. He was too stubborn and possessive to let me go, even for his benefit. So I had to be the bigger person. And fuck, did it suck.

CHAPTER 35

ent

"If you keep stalling, we'll miss our appointment." I grabbed Madison as she passed by and pulled her onto my lap.

All morning, she packed the files she'd accumulated in her home office from her unauthorized investigation into Carol. She'd already filled two boxes while I watched from the small sofa.

After days of not seeing Madison, I'd found myself orbiting her space to watch her do mundane things for the joy of being in her sphere. I returned to work yesterday, but have already cancelled meetings to be near her, and I took today off to spend with her. All for the sake of experiencing her and basking in her presence.

"Please, all you have to say is we're running late and they'll bend themselves backward to accommodate *the* Kent Luxe." She kissed my cheek and tried to rise from my hold, but couldn't escape my unbreakable grip.

"Have you changed your mind about finding the property where we'll build our dream house?" I peered into her eyes.

She averted her gaze and gave a half-hearted laugh. "What made you draw that conclusion?"

The sense I had from before that she was hiding something grew. At first, I thought it had to do with Kemp dropping my case, but what if there was another explanation? She changed the subject when I brought up the topic.

"Maybe because you deflect or distract me when I ask you something that makes you uncomfortable. You couldn't be more obvious that you're hiding something from me."

Madison glanced at me while nibbling her lip.

My gut sank at her guilty expression. I could almost see her mind racing as she thought up a lie to appease me. She opened her mouth and I shook my head, stalling her.

"I'd rather you stay silent than lie to me."

She gasped. "I wasn't going to lie to you." I released her and was about to lift her from my lap when she said, "I was trying to tell you without setting you off."

My brow twitched. "Are you... afraid of me?"

"As if." Her immediate scoff put me at ease.

My pride wouldn't be able to handle if the woman I loved feared me. "Then what is it?" I turned her face to have full access to the emotions flashing in her brown orbs.

I fell into her depths, almost losing myself and forgetting the reason I needed to see her eyes. The effect this woman had on me... There's no wonder I would do anything to keep her by my side.

"Well." She dragged the word out, then sped through the rest of her reasoning. "I found the evidence used to free you and asked Valentino to make sure the police got an anonymous tip that didn't implicate you."

She sat stiffly in my arms as she awaited my response.

The twitching that began at my brow moved to my eye. My throat swelled under my tight restraint, otherwise I couldn't control the volume of my voice. "Where did you find this proof?"

"In Hal's home office?"

I closed my eyes and prayed for patience.

"I wasn't alone. I had Sam with me. And remember, we found the files you needed to block the anonymous shareholder trying to take over your company. And right on time, too, if I say so myself. The vote is next week. So, do us both a favor and ignore my method and celebrate the results with me instead." Madison kissed me on my cheek with a grin wide enough to blind the sun and attempted to hop off my lap.

I had other ideas. "What evidence did you find?" I asked while barring her escape.

Her smile dropped into a disturbed frown, and she shivered. "I don't want to talk about it."

I rubbed her arms, wanting to comfort her but needing to know everything she'd done while I was locked away. "Then show me. I assume you took pictures like you did with the files we went through."

She bit her lip and left me in doubt for a few heart-pounding seconds before nodding and whispering, "Okay."

I released her, and she slipped away. Within a minute, she returned with her laptop.

"Before I show you, know I had a plan to distract him. I didn't just break into his house. Of all the ideas we had, Ife—"

"Ife was in on this?" I rubbed my temple while my blood pressure rose and pulsed beneath my skin.

"Well, no one considered him to be dangerous. Not...even...you..." She petered off at my glare and pushed her computer toward me. "Here's everything. And as a reminder, you love me." She backed away and I let her.

My throat ached too much from all the admonitions I wanted to set free on her, but before I did, I needed to know the extent of the promise she'd broken. Because in her word salad of logic, she failed to admit she'd acted recklessly.

While she continued to box up her files on Carol, I turned to her laptop. Among gruesome images of the women I'd dated, there were photos spanning what looked like over a year's worth of other victims. Included were state IDs or other items that I guessed belonged to the dead women. I hadn't gotten through many when one image froze my finger above the next arrow.

Three familiar surnames drew my interest.

"Madison, did your photos of the LLC files get mixed up with these?" I peered at Madison, hoping I'd drawn the wrong conclusion.

She hesitated before putting another folder into a box. "No, why do you ask?"

"Because there are files labeled with our names on them. And if they were in the same place as these murder victims—"

"Then we should be happy Hal is in jail and hopefully on his way to prison."

"Okay." I stood and marched toward her. "If this is the way you want to play in my face. I'll play."

Alarmed, she spun around to face me and clutched the desk at her back. "Kent, what are you planning to do?"

Without answering, I bent down and threw her over my shoulder.

"Kent! Put me down." She wiggled until I almost lost my grip and dropped her.

In response, I spanked her once as I carried her to the bedroom. "You've more than earned a punishment for the shit you pulled behind my back, and as God is my witness, you will remember this lesson for the rest of our lives."

I dropped her on the bed.

"Don't you think you're overreacting? You're out of jail, I'm safe, and the person who wanted to harm me is locked up."

I flipped her onto her stomach and dragged her pants and panties over her ass and down her legs. The first hit caused her butt to jiggle in delicious ripples.

"Kent!"

"You promised you wouldn't be reckless."

"I wasn't—"

Spank.

"Ow! If I had known he was a murderer, I wouldn't have broken into his place. Probably," she muttered the last word as if I wouldn't hear.

Smack.

"Why are you punishing me for trying to save you?" The first sob broke from her, halting my hand in mid-air.

I spun her onto her back. "Madison, I have an obscene amount of money at my disposal, which I can use to pay people to risk their lives. Why do you think I wouldn't hire someone who specializes in covert operations to ensure your safety? What do I have to do to get it through your head that your life means more to me than jail?"

"I'm sorry." Tears spilled from her eyes, and she launched herself into my arms. "I'm sorry I didn't talk to you first about the plan, and I'm sorry I went because I was terrified the whole time and when I saw the pictures and the file with my name and I realized he intended to add me to his victims—" Violent sobs broke from her, cutting off her manic apology.

As her body shook mine, I realized she'd been holding all this in for my benefit. Instead of the unaffected role she played, she'd been deeply traumatized and the spanking didn't help. I hugged and pressed her body closer.

"I'm here and I won't let anything happen to you," I whispered reassurances while rubbing her back and comforting her as she wept.

This wasn't her usual outpouring after a punishment I administered and the longer she cried, the worse I felt for forcing her confession this way. As she clung to me, I rearranged our bodies to lie on our sides.

"Forgive me. Please, don't hate me. Don't hate me. Please." Over and over, she repeated the phrase.

Her distress broke something in me. No amount of patting and rubbing circles into her back eased either of our torment.

"Little bunny, nothing you do could make me withhold my forgiveness from you. Can you forgive me for pushing you too far?"

Madison's grip around my neck tightened. "Not your fault."

I pressed my nose into her hair and swallowed the ball of guilt choking me. I wasn't a good man. I didn't deserve her absolution, but I'd take it. Fuck, I'd rejoice in anything that would return the look on her face that told the world she felt safe with me.

Hours passed with her face pressed against my neck, dampening my skin until a chill ran in my body as her tears cooled against me.

I refused to let go or push her away. She'd latched onto me with a desperation I didn't understand but I recognized the anguish in the tightness of my embrace. I feared I'd broken something special between us and I wouldn't know until she looked at me again. When she fell asleep, I separated our bodies, tucked her under the covers, and placed Tyger beside her. He looked toward me, then Madison. Without a meow, he crawled between her arms and began purring, making his preference known.

With my thoughts in a jumble, I ambled around the penthouse but nothing stuck and I decided to keep my hands busy. I walked into Madison's office and saw the files she had yet to box. I filled out what I could of her archiving form and I piled the boxes by the door in preparation for the storage company to pick them up. On my way back to double-check I had gotten everything, a note torn from a pad caught my eye.

It had a list of questions. From what I gathered, they were subjects Madison wanted to research, like erotomania. Her notes for the questions she found answers to explained a lot that I ignored or took for granted because Omar did a great job as my executive assistant. One symptom people diagnosed with erotomania exhibited was sending intimate to unhinged communications to their obsessions.

I recalled receiving a letter from an anonymous woman declaring her love for me. After the first unhinged piece of mail Omar showed me, I'd told him to trash them in the future, and I'd never seen another cross my desk since.

If I'd recognized the pattern earlier, could I have saved the women who died? Then I remembered, Carol didn't kill them. Hal did. His motive remained a mystery to me. Had he revealed his reasons to the cops?

I continued reading Madison's notes until I saw her question about the name I saw on the third empty file folder. My mind made many connections to too many instances and an urgent need drove me. I didn't care what time it was. I was sick of not having answers.

I dialed a number I'd memorized by heart, praying it was still good.

"Do you know what fucking time it is?" Sansone answered from the burner phone number he'd given me.

"No, and I don't care. You promised to get me Carol when we found her. She's dead, but I have someone else I need you to get in her place."

"What? This person... She touched your woman?"

"That's what I aim to find out."

My footsteps echoed on the concrete floor of my dilapidated building. As soon as Sansone called with the information he'd delivered my quarry, per my request, I gave Madison an excuse for leaving. I hated the needy glance she hid from me after hearing my reason, and I vowed to myself I would fix what I'd broken.

And I had broken something. Despite her reassuring smile that she was okay, I knew she wasn't. I'd become an expert in Madison's smile-ology and physiognomy, able to distinguish the difference in her smiles down to the lumen per watt. And she was no longer giving the full intensity that held me captive and solidified my purpose as her man.

But once I got my answers, I intended to run straight home and dedicate as many hours, days, weeks, even years, to bringing the brightness back to Madison's heart and smile.

"Whoever you are, you've made a huge fucking mistake. My name means something in this city," the voice of the woman I was here to meet screeched through the empty halls, gaining in volume the closer I got to her.

"Does your name carry more weight than mine, Paulina?" I asked as I walked through what remained of the crumbling doorway.

"Kent? Wh-what's the meaning of this?" She shook her shoulders from side to side, her mobility hindered by the ropes binding her to her chair.

I prowled around her, seething while keeping my face neutral. "Is something wrong with your accommodations?"

She swiveled her head, never letting me out of her sight. "You're joking, but this isn't funny. Untie me, now!"

"You're pretty demanding for someone who attempted a coup of my company."

She froze for a millisecond before flipping her bob away from her face and scoffing. "I don't know what you mean."

"Oh, aren't you confident? You think I wouldn't link you to all those anonymous LLCs and trusts you used to hide your identity as a shareholder?" I ran down a list of five to prove she couldn't hide from me. "I bet there's an ethics violation somewhere about you not disclosing what companies you own shares in, but that's neither here nor there. I want to discuss some of our mutuals." I ended my saunter in front of her again.

She watched me warily. "I'm sure we have many mutuals. Douglas society isn't that large."

I grinned at her deflection, although it didn't meet my eyes and lacked warmth. "True, but only two have tried to harm me and the women in my life."

"Women?" she sneered. "None of those pieces of trash could ever be called women, especially your new Oyingugu replacement."

"What did you say?" Shock choked the words through a tiny hole from my mouth.

"You heard me." She stretched her neck until a crack broke the stunned silence, and she dropped her mask. "Oh, my God! You have no idea how long I've held that in. After all these years, you haven't changed and neither has your shitty taste in women."

The woman before me bore none of the characteristics I'd seen over our many years of interacting with each other. Even as she sat tied to the chair, devoid of her earlier rage or fear, she sneered her disgust at me.

"What does my love life have to do with you?"

"Do you even remember we attended the same high school?" From her tone, the question was more rhetorical than curious. However, no memory of her came to my mind.

"Why is that important?" I asked, unable to connect any logic with her line of questioning.

"Because I saw you first. On the first day of ninth grade, I told my friends I would marry you. Had our meet-cute all set up. I'd already amassed a following and they were happy to spread the word about how great I was so you'd hear it before we physically met. Everything was going to plan, then fucking Oyingugu passed by you in the hall and ruined everything. You didn't notice anyone, even though I crashed into you and we almost fell to the ground. That bitch didn't say a word to you and you couldn't keep your eyes off her then, even while I stood in front of you. Me, the most gorgeous girl the school had ever seen. Winner of Miss Teen Douglas."

"You're telling me you've held a grudge since high school? You're sick."

She threw her head back and laughed. The sound was healthy, lacking the crazed touch I expected of someone who'd confessed to an unhealthy fixation. "You're mistaken. You confuse an illness with dedication. I follow through on my goals, and when you never broke up with that woman after senior year, and I had to see the two of you lost in each other at college, I vowed to take everything you loved and destroy you." She shook her head ruefully. "It's taken me a long time to get traction, but every time I'd get close to destroying you, you bounced back. But the joke's on me. I keep relying on failures. First Trent, then my cousin, Carol, and lastly, Hal. What will it take to cut you down to your knees?"

"Did you say, Trent? As in Duncan Trent?" My heart pounded as memories from Lola's bloody confession and the painful years after she died replayed themselves.

"Ooh, you didn't know I had a hand in that, too, huh? How much did you find out? Did you discover the affair?"

I froze at the mention of the plan Duncan had for Lola.

"Mmm, the look on your face right now is so delicious." She

inhaled as if she could smell a mouth-watering aroma and sucking it in nourished her.

"They didn't have an affair. That motherfucker raped my wife, and you're admitting you sent him to do it."

"Rape? Are you sure Oyingugu—"

"Her name is Oyinlola!" I stepped away, trying to cool my temper. Although I hated everything coming out of her mouth, the darkness inside me compelled me to know every vile thing this woman master-minded while I lived my life in ignorance.

"Whatever. Are you sure she didn't lie to cover up the truth? She was a whore who begged Duncan for sex. He gave her what you failed to provide. It was only natural for her to seek what she lacked at home."

"I don't need to defend my wife to the likes of you. Even on her worst day, she was more beautiful and worthy than you on your best."

"Is that why it took you so long to get over her? Because she was so good? Or because she destroyed your trust?" Paulina raised her chin to look down at me from her position.

She failed. I would never be beneath a woman like her.

"For those first few months, while you walked around with the most pitiful, heartbroken expression on your face because your poor wife was no more, I was on cloud nine. Then you buried yourself in your work and tripled your success. Success I as your rightful wife should have shared. I should have been beside you, lording my status over Douglas society, but you never saw me. No, you started your fuckboy phase with all those empty-headed bimbos."

"Was your cousin, Carol, a bimbo?"

"That girl." Paulina snorted. "Her family couldn't handle her. She was always going off her meds and causing problems. Well, I don't have to tell you about the trouble she brings."

"What did you promise her to damage my reputation?"

"That's the beauty of my gullible cousin. I promised her nothing. I just had to show her a picture of you after she'd been off her meds for a month. Had her singing *Nothing Compares 2 U* on repeat. She was so far gone that I only had to mention those other women to convince her to work with Hal. Carol terrorized those women until Hal ended their suffering. They were such a good team." Paulina eyed me up and down with a sneer marring her mouth. "At least they were before your new plaything entered the picture."

"Do you even care Hal killed Carol?"

"He did what was necessary. Carol wasn't made to live life on the run. It was only time before someone connected her with her real identity and then to me. I couldn't have that."

"And my daughter? She's innocent in all this. Why did Hal have a folder in his murder files with her name on it?"

Paulina rolled her eyes. "No one around you is innocent, least of all the spawn of that whore. You know, Hal and I discussed when and how to end her life to maximize the blow to you. My vote was while you were out on bail, but you know what happened with that. Then the asshole had to go and get caught. Regardless, there's always someone willing to do anything for the right price."

"I still don't understand. Hal worked for me for years. What did you promise him to turn on me?"

"Your company. There is a sweet irony in enthroning the person who hated you as much as I do as the successor to everything you built, knowing he would run your company into the ground while you sat behind bars unable to do shit about it. All because that man has an unchecked ego without the skill to back it up."

"But your plans didn't stop with my company and my daughter. You put a target on Madison."

"She was the prize I didn't know I needed." At my confused frown, she laughed. "You shouldn't have brought her to that charity gala, Kent. God, the look on your face. I hadn't seen that expression since Oyingugu."

My phone dinged, stopping me from unleashing all my rage and choking her to death. Although I could ignore the message, I needed the distraction. I left her and walked out while dialing the number in the text.

"What happened?"

"Mr. Luxe, while Ms. Montgomery was out today, I thwarted an assailant." The man was the undercover guard I kept from Madison.

I continued walking until I got to my car. "Does Madison know about him?"

"Not yet. Should I inform her?"

Madison's face from the night she admitted her terror while inside Hal's home rose in my mind. "No. Madison doesn't know about you, and the knowledge will only scare her. Where is the man now?"

"I have him out of sight. He said someone hired him to abduct her."

"Bring him to me. I have a few questions I'd like to ask him in person." I took padlocks and steel chains from my trunk and re-entered the run-down building.

The time away did me good. Now I could return to Paulina with some semblance of calm to deal with her.

Paulina whistled a carefree tune that riled my blood. She peered at me when I entered the room and she smiled. Then she noticed my calm expression and the chain wrapped around my arm. The grin fell from her face.

"Why do you have a chain?"

Instead of answering her question, I said, "I'm curious. You've been very forthcoming. I didn't have to threaten you. Why is that?"

"Because you won't do anything to me. I'm untouchable."

"Pray tell, how?" I unwound the chains from my arm.

"I guess you'll find out soon enough. Remember, I told you there's always someone willing to do anything for a price? Well, I found one willing to keep your little bitch on ice for as long as I need. So, why should I be afraid of what you're going to do when I can do way worse?"

"Ahh, all this time you had leverage. That's why you had no problem admitting your crimes against me. It all makes sense now."

"Mr. Luxe?" My man's voice came from down the hall.

"I'm in here," I yelled, allowing him to find me.

The guard entered, dragging the man who attempted to take Madison. When he appeared, for the first time, genuine fear entered Paulina's eyes. The man holding Paulina's attention had a bruised face, held his ribs, and had a bloody wound on his thigh, causing him to limp.

"Thank you, you may leave."

My man nodded and backed out with my new captive, purposely keeping his eyes on the ground.

"He stays," I said, regarding the beaten man.

Without another word, my guard abandoned Madison's would-be assailant.

"Listen, I was only doing a job, man. Whatever this is, I don't want no part of it." The man stared at Paulina's bound body.

"You know what I find funny, Paulina?" I punched the man in the face, knocked him unconscious, then dragged him toward a pillar and roped a chain around him before closing the padlock and fixing him to the building. "You speak on others' illness and ego, never recognizing the same issues in yourself. You're as sick as your cousin was and should be institutionalized, but you obviously hid it better. Because what else other than sickness would make you think you could compare to my Lola or my Madison? Both women far surpass you in beauty, grace, intelligence, talent, sexiness... pretty much every metric that matters, they blow you out of the water. Oh, I forgot to mention, sanity."

"I am all those things and more, asshole."

"Then why did I never see you? You never registered when we were in the same class in high school, barely when we were in college. It took you getting a government position that directly affected my company before I acknowledged you, and you forced that bit of exposure by demanding a monthly lunch. You were and will always be a desperate nobody in my world."

"No, I am somebody. You need me."

"Paulina, no one needs you. When you disappear, no one will care." I dragged her chair to the one intact concrete wall in the room where a set of eyebolt screw wall anchors protruded from the wall.

I fed another chain through the holes. The last chain I'd brought from my car, I wrapped around Paulina, winding it around her torso, over her shoulders, and under the seat of her chair while she protested. Every curse she piled onto my head satisfied my banked rage. I lifted her chair and locked the chain connected to the wall with the chain wrapped around her body. Now, even if she freed herself of the rope, she wouldn't escape the chains.

"You can't leave me like this!" She twisted and banged against the wall while I turned my back on her. Her legs dangled feet above the ground.

I leaned against the pillar with the unconscious man. "You know, when I connected you to Madison's attempted murder, I considered so many ways to make you pay. I never thought your intentions began years ago or were more diabolical than I could have ever imagined. But after listening to you, the best revenge is leaving you alone." I glanced down at the unconscious man. "Well, he doesn't count. When he regains consciousness, he won't be able to help you. You'll both suffer from dehydration and starvation. Only the two of you will hear each other's desperate cries for help. After a couple weeks, you'll have no more moisture to cry. Your organs will shut down, which I've heard is very painful."

"If I meant nothing to you, why would you want to watch me waste away that way?"

"Watch you? Paulina, once I leave I won't return. I'll forget about you as quickly as I've done every other day of my life. You're a nonentity. And when this place gets demolished, the only evidence you existed will be your dried-out skeleton. And even then, no one will report your remains. You'll become commercial waste."

"You're forgetting. I hold an important office. People will look for me."

"For a few days, they will. But then they'll replace you at your job and call off the search when there are no leads. Hell, they might think Hal had gotten to you first since he also had a folder with your name on it."

She gasped.

"Didn't know he also had plans for you? You worked with a serial killer who murdered women and thought you were safe? Well, at least I saved you from Hal. Too bad there's no one who will save you from me."

CHAPTER 36

 adison

I'd dropped my mask and had been trying for days to put it back on. Ever since the night I told Kent about finding the evidence that cleared him of murder, he'd changed. As if he continued to blame himself when the dam I'd built to hide from my dismay broke. As if he didn't believe me when I forgave him for forcing my confession.

A part of me understood I was at fault for his continued misunderstanding. Because I still lived with dread hanging over my head, but not the kind Kent assumed. The spankings provided an outlet for me to release the emotions I bottled inside myself. However, that night, neither of us expected everything I'd withheld from him to gush out of me so violently. Since then, I hadn't addressed his misread of the situation for fear he would discover my other concern. Regardless of my intention, after tonight I'll exchange my worries for something far more depressing.

"I can't believe you convinced me to have this party." Kent strode out of the walk-in closet as he tied his bowtie.

I stared in awe, drinking in everything about him. His freshly trimmed beard, the rueful grin on his pink lips, his gelled hair begging for me to rumple a few strands. So many things I would miss.

I placed my hands over his. "Let me."

As I retied his tie, an excuse to feel his heat and be close to him, he stared at me. Warmth, love, and concern shone from his gaze.

"After this party, we're going to have a serious discussion about our future. We need to plan around your company in D.C. If you commute, what that'll look like, or if your company moves to Douglas." Kent stroked the side of my face. "It'll be less of an issue once I open a Luxe Locations office there. Then we'll commute together. Maybe even move there permanently."

"I didn't know you planned to expand into D.C."

"Other than the hotel already there, I didn't."

"Then, why?"

"Little bunny, I understand your major client base is in D.C. I would never ask you to sacrifice your success especially as you're still growing your brand and reputation. So, if that means I meet you where you need to be, as your man and partner, I will. Plus, how long do you think I can survive nights away from you?"

"Why do I think your last point outweighed all the others?" I patted his beautifully tied neckwear, trying not to tear up at his thoughtfulness.

"Because you know I need my little bunny more than air itself." Kent leaned forward and pressed his lips against my forehead.

I closed my eyes, relishing the softness of the kiss and his body heat. With a sigh, I stepped away. "If you don't leave soon, you'll be late," I said.

"You aren't even dressed yet." He studied my robe, then peered at the dress I picked to wear tonight laying on the bed beside a curled-up Tyger.

Kent's silent acceptance of the gown meant it met with his approval. Otherwise, he would have voiced his opinion while shredding it into unwearable strips. Although I enjoyed teasing Kent with certain outfits, tonight, my mood was too somber to torment him.

I patted his chest, needing to feel him beneath my touch for reassurance. "I'm not driving with you. I have something I need to pick up on my way to the venue." I was doing the right thing, even if he wouldn't agree once he discovered my plan.

Kent clasped my hips, bringing me closer. "I can have someone pick it up in your place. I think I'm going to be thirsty on the ride to the party, and only you can quench my need."

A shiver of desire zinged through my blood, calling to my pussy. "You know how to tempt me." I pulled his hands from my sides. "But I need to inspect the surprise to make sure it's perfect."

Kent stared at me and I opened my eyes wide, praying I showed him the love I felt for him and not the other emotions I hid underneath. Finally, he nodded and kissed me.

"I'll miss you every second we're apart," he whispered, his lips inches from mine.

This time, I lurched forward and kissed him, deeper than our first. I memorized the contour of his mouth, the texture of his tongue, and the hard planes of his teeth. I didn't want to let go, but I did.

His blue eyes blazed with passion, probably equal to the fever in my gaze. When he leaned forward again, I pressed my finger to his mouth.

"You'll never leave if I let you do what you're thinking."

"So?"

"I spent a lot of time planning this party. You don't want to disappoint me, do you?"

He hung his head and sighed. "Only for you, little bunny." He straightened. "Don't keep me waiting."

"I won't," I said.

As soon as he left. I threw off my robe and enacted my plan. Frantic, I ran around collecting my things and throwing them in a suitcase.

"So you do intend to keep your promise."

I lurched with my heart thundering in my chest. "You scared me, Ife. Why are you here?"

She shrugged and fully entered the bedroom while looking around at my half-packed bags. Tyger had moved from beside my dress to make a bed inside a bag.

"So many days have passed since Hal's arrest, I thought you forgot and wanted to renege on our deal."

I sat and stared at her. "You won't change your mind about wanting me to leave? Despite knowing what your father and I mean to each other?"

Ife hugged herself. "Why don't you understand? Every time I look at the two of you it's like a knife stabbing me in my heart. Do you think it's easy to cut you out of my life? Do you think I want to hurt my father? You were the sister I never had, and you destroyed my trust. We can't rebuild while you're around my father. Especially if you want me and my dad to repair our bond. You must understand that if nothing else."

I swallowed the distasteful truth. She was right. If I stayed, Kent would push for us to deepen our relationship until I said I do to vows I could only imagine ever saying to him. I stood, feeling ancient, defeated, and bruised. "I don't have much time before Kent becomes suspicious. You should leave and keep him distracted. Buy me time to disappear."

Ife eyed me, then glanced at Tyger peacefully purring inside my luggage. "Are you taking the animals with you?"

I stared with longing at my first and only cat. I stroked his soft fur and shook my head. "I'm already taking so much from him. Kent will need them when he's alone."

"Alright. You have maybe forty-five minutes before my dad suspects anything. You need to be long gone by then."

I nodded and shoved more clothes into my bag. "Ife, please know, I love you so much. I'll run to you whenever you call."

She sniffed and turned her back. "I don't know how soon that will be. My pain runs deep." She left without another word.

When I had everything I intended to carry, I left an envelope on my pillow. I recognized the cowardly act for what it was. I lacked the courage to end things to his face, but I needed him to understand why

I had to leave. Being with me would only bring him lifelong regrets. He'd already proven to anyone out to get him I was his weakness.

One day, he would make one sacrifice too many on my behalf, and I couldn't allow him to do that.

I bid farewell to Benson, Stabler, and Tyger, telling them to be good to their daddy, and I walked away from the best future I could ever have hoped for.

CHAPTER 37

ent

Mal pounded my back. "You must be on top of the world right now. Exonerated for crimes you didn't commit, your reputation on the mend, and your position as CEO and president secured. This calls for a toast." He raised his tumbler to me, his grin a match for his ostentatious purple tux.

I stopped scanning the room for Madison and clinked our glasses together. "It is a relief. And I'd like to thank you."

"For?"

"You helped me keep control of Luxe Locations." I scanned the party-goers, friends, and industry professionals with connections I'd established years ago as well as others on my wish list.

Madison's knowledge and strategic abilities always awed me. How did she even know about half these people?

"Look, I'm young and adaptable, but I prefer not to get used to a new boss. I was doing myself a favor more than you." Mal emptied his glass.

"Sure. I also have to thank you for Ife. I can rest assured she has someone in her corner until she's ready to work on our relationship."

Pink tinged Mal's cheeks and he stared into his glass. "No problem. Hey, looks like we need refills. I'll be back." He took my glass and walked away.

I ignored the awkwardness of the moment to check my watch. Where was Madison?

Unease slithered down my spine. I wanted to dismiss the sense I'd overlooked something. Was it from tonight or earlier the feeling first plagued me?

"Dad?" Ife broke into my thoughts.

"Hey sweetheart, you came."

"Where else would I be on a night celebrating you?" She hugged me.

"Does this mean you won't run the second Madison arrives?"

My daughter stiffened in my arms. "Don't ruin the moment, Dad."

"Ife—"

She pulled away with a bright smile that didn't meet her eyes. "Why don't we try some of the hors d'oeuvres on offer?" She pulled me toward one with a smoked salmon and caviar-topped blini.

I took one, still glancing around. Every time my distraction showed, Ife hailed an acquaintance. After an hour, there was no sign of Madison and my unease turned into panic. I shrugged Ife's hand off my arm.

"Dad?"

"I need to leave."

"But there are people you haven't greeted yet."

"Make my excuses for me." I patted her shoulder and rushed out.

Had something happened to Madison? I checked my phone but there was no message from any of her guards. I was so sure I'd handled all threats directed at her, but what if I missed something? Had Paulina hired another person in the event the first mercenary failed to abduct Madison?

My thoughts ran wild as I rushed home. All the cars were in their spots in the garage. If she hadn't left yet, something bad must have happened. I ran into the elevator and punched the button for our floor over and over while praying for it to move faster.

The doors opened, and her guards were in the foyer. Standing. Chatting.

"Where's Madison?" I stormed inside.

The closest man to me averted his gaze. Guilty expressions abounded.

"Answer me!" I yelled.

My scream caught Benson and Stabler's attention. They came wagging their tails, but their welcome did nothing to calm me.

Finally, one stepped forward. "Ms. Montgomery told us not to follow her."

I closed my eyes. "What did you say to me?" I strangled the words as they came out of my throat.

"Ms. Montgomery ordered us to stay here. Since she never gave us an order like that before, we thought she meant to return."

"And when she didn't, why didn't you call me?"

They shared a look that spoke volumes of their fear of retribution without uttering a word. "She said not to."

I stepped back, my breathing erratic. No, I had one other safety measure in place. I retrieved my phone and called the undercover bodyguard.

"Mr. Luxe?"

"Where is she?"

Silence met my question.

"Where is Madison?" I yelled into the phone, barely holding my shit together.

Benson and Stabler whimpered.

"I don't know. I followed her to the airport, but lost her in the TSA line."

I disconnected, unable to accept what I'd heard. My men were full of bullshit. Madison had to be here. She had no reason to be at an airport. The first room I checked was the bedroom.

My blood froze at the thick envelope sitting on her pillow. My hand shook as I reached for the item. A sense of foreboding swirled in my gut as I ripped through the seal and extracted ten water-splotched pages.

Words, useless words stared at me. Apologies. Excuses. And sharp, stabbing pain. Each sentence inserted an icicle into my heart, closing off my arteries and atrophying the muscle in my chest.

She'd really left me and told me not to follow.

She'd lost her goddamn mind.

I crushed the pages in my hand. Despite her warning that I wouldn't find her, I knew where she would go. She had nowhere else. And I would be right behind her. Madison belonged with me. I'd cautioned her before that she didn't get to walk away. Apparently, my little bunny needed a reminder.

I called my man at the airport. "How many flights are scheduled to depart for Ronald Reagan Washington National Airport?"

"One left maybe an hour ago. There's another expected departure in two hours."

"Meet me at my airstrip." I disconnected and called my pilots as I stomped out of the penthouse.

My little bunny was going to get a taste of the wolf she would never forget.

Warring emotions fought a pitched-fork battle inside my chest. Anger at her for daring to leave in the most cowardly way imaginable. Worry because she was alone and without her bodyguards to keep her safe. And uppermost, was sadness. The stained letter I couldn't leave behind told a story of the tears she cried as she wrote her farewell. I choked back everything because once I saw her again, nothing else would matter.

After a three-hour flight, I disembarked in Washington D.C. Golden rays from the sun peaked over the horizon, and I boarded the helicopter I'd arranged in transit. I was in no mood to face D.C. traffic when I was on a mission to save my future.

As I flew over the urban skyline, I barely noticed the growing congestion below. My thoughts were on what I would do once I saw Madison. She had a lot to answer for after leaving me with a ten-page break-up letter.

We landed on the helipad above her building, and I made my way to her apartment.

I nodded toward my guard. "Open the door."

Once inside, I dismissed him. While I waited, I wandered through the rooms. Despite the length of time Madison had been in Douglas, her apartment maintained a memory of her scent. I breathed in deep gulps, but nothing soothed me. I'd once likened her place to a blank space, and I wished I was wrong. Her sparse furniture, blank walls, down to the few pictures she displayed on random surfaces felt like a tease. As if Madison had been here but not when. Only the lack of staleness in the air supported my need to feel her surrounding me, which made her obvious absence even more painful.

I found a seat to wait for her. Hours passed without me moving. The sun rose and sank, welcoming the night, and still, I sat waiting for her to walk through the door. Another sunrise and sunset passed, and still, I sat waiting. She had to be on her way. She would show up.

My phone rang nonstop. Omar wanted to know when I would be in again because I hadn't shown up for meetings; my pilots called to find out how long they needed to be on standby; and Ife… Seeing her name on my caller ID affected me the most. Although Madison's letter didn't name her as the reason for her leaving, she didn't have to. Ife was the only person who could convince Madison to leave me, and from everything I'd seen, she'd succeeded.

By day five, the truth began to sink in. Madison had no intention of returning. She'd truly left me.

CHAPTER 38

 *adison*

"Madison, sleep. You've been going nonstop since you landed five days ago," Emily said.

I'd barely left her guest room, I was so busy trying not to leave a trail for Kent to follow. Now, I was exhausted. I hadn't slept, my appetite was nonexistent, and I battled myself every day. From one second to the next, I convinced myself Ife would forgive me if I succumbed to my heart's desire before recalling her steadfast refusal to absolve me for betraying her trust.

I lived in hell.

I shook my head and concentrated on Emily, eager for the distraction from my thoughts. "Has your contact gotten the documents I need to disappear?" Although I began the process of transferring my company to Emily and set myself up to escape to a country Kent wouldn't find me, I had a few loose ends I needed to tie up.

Once I decided my destination, I'd call my parents and explain what I could. Leaving Kent felt like I'd ripped my heart from my chest.

I had nothing left inside me to tell my parents I was leaving and I wouldn't return to Douglas. The next time I saw them, they would have to come to me.

Emily bounced on my bed. "I don't get why you have to go so far." She stiffened, then grabbed me, concern wrinkling her brow. "Did this guy abuse you? Are all these preparations because—"

"Stop, Kent would never hurt me. If anything, I've hurt him by leaving." I sniffed and blinked away the tears that refused to stay behind my eyeballs.

"Then why are you looking for countries where he doesn't own real estate?"

I swiped under my eyes and cleared my throat. "Because if he owns property there, he has political influence he can use to find me. Not to mention he's rich as King Midas and has no problem using his wealth to get what he wants."

Emily ran out of the room and returned a few moments later with single-serve wine bottles and cheese crackers. "Then I have a proposal. My contact can get you the documents you need, but if your man is as influential as you say, he can compel organizations to use facial recognition to hunt for you." She handed me a bottle and a snack.

"What do you suggest?" I set the food aside while I plucked at the bottle cap. I hadn't had much of an appetite, given my circumstances.

"I know a makeup artist who's worked on some big Hollywood movies. She can give you a new face to get through any airport. Once you get to your final destination, you can revert to your normal face."

"How soon can your guy deliver what I need?"

"A week after we deliver your photos to him."

"Good. The only thing I have remaining is my apartment."

"Which I will pack up and put on the market for you."

"Emily, you are a godsend."

"Am I really? You're giving up everything you've worked your ass off to avoid this man."

"No, I'm keeping a promise to someone who means the world to me. If not for abiding by my word, I'd be in his arms as we speak." And with those words, I keenly felt the loss of Kent's embrace. I hugged myself, but my arms were a poor substitute for what I needed.

"Aw, Madison. I wish—" The doorbell's ring interrupted Emily. She arched her brow at me in question.

I shrugged. "You aren't expecting someone?"

"At this time? No." She stood to leave but I grabbed her arm.

"It might be Kent."

"Don't be paranoid. It could be my neighbor." She patted my hand and walked away.

I whispered at her back, "If it's Kent, I'm not here."

"Duh, give me more credit, please."

Emily lived in a detached condo unit with a front and rear entrance. However, if Kent was at her front door, he didn't come alone. I had no way of sneaking out and had to hide here. But only if the person at the front door was Kent.

I swung the bedroom door until a sliver of space remained and stood to the side to observe who Emily's guest was.

"Whose there?" she asked.

"Kent Luxe. I'm looking for Madison." His voice sounded gruff and tired, even muffled by distance and two doors.

My heart did a sad jig from the pain he couldn't hide and the excitement of hearing his voice again. It was the oddest sensation, experiencing joy and sadness at the same time. The emotions struck so sharply I clutched my chest and found it difficult to catch my breath.

"Madison's not here."

"Emily, is it? You have a choice here. You can let me in, or I'll force my way inside."

At his warning, I spun around and saw all the signs I had in the room that would betray my presence. As quietly as possible, I ran around the room collecting everything. Because one thing I knew for certain was Emily had no chance of keeping Kent out of her condo. I hid everything in the closet and smoothed the covers on the bed.

When Kent's voice increased in volume, my heartbeat skipped. I'd hidden the signs I was staying here, but my efforts would be futile if I didn't hide in the event he decided to search every room. I glanced toward the window, but my name wasn't Lara Croft and jumping from two stories up was not a skill I'd ever had any interest in pursuing.

Sweat slicked down my back as he neared my room, while he ignored Emily's protests. At times like these, I wished I were more slender and able to fit in a suitcase. Hiding under the bed would be too obvious. As would the closet. That was when I spied the panel in the ceiling.

Emily had an attic.

Hopefully, Kent would pass over the panel and leave once he didn't find me. I rushed up the foldable steps, making sure to remain quiet. I managed to close the panel as the bedroom door swung open. Unlike the guest room, the attic housed many hiding spots, but to get there I needed to move, however, any motion might alert Kent, and I couldn't risk it.

I stuffed my hand into my mouth and lay paralyzed while Kent and Emily searched the room below me. I thought sneaking away from him while he attended the party I threw for him was hard, but being so close and pretending I wasn't close enough to touch him was a new kind of torture I wouldn't wish on my enemy.

"I told you she wasn't here." Emily's angry statement filtered up to me. "Please, leave."

"I was so sure... You were the last of—I'll go, but if you hear from her—"

"I'll let her decide if she wants to speak to you. However, if she listens to me, you won't hear from her ever again." A door slammed after Emily cut Kent's plea short.

A few minutes passed when she whispered, "Madison? If you're still here, you can come out now."

I pushed the attic door and descended into the room.

"I am so happy you hid up there and didn't jump out the window." Emily clutched her chest.

"I thought about it, but Kent probably has people watching outside. Thank God you live in a place with an attic."

"So that is Kent. Girl, you sure know how to pick them. Are you sure you don't want to go back to him? That specimen is a national treasure."

"Emily, please. I'm weak as it is. Don't tempt me when you know I can't." I sat on the bed, deflated and feeling Kent's loss anew.

Emily picked up her phone.

"What are you doing?"

"Calling my friend, the make-up artist. The sooner we get your new face, the sooner you get out of the country."

Two days after we photographed my face full of prosthetics for one set of passport pictures, Emily barged into her condo frantic and out of breath.

"What's wrong?" I pulled her toward the couch and went to the kitchen to pour her a glass of water.

She took the cup with shaky hands. "Thanks."

I sat and waited while she drained the glass.

"I have bad news. I went to your place to start labeling things per the moving company's instructions."

"And?" I asked after she lapsed into silence.

"Either someone robbed you or Kent took everything."

I shook my head because I must have misheard her. "I'm sorry. What did you say?"

"The place was so empty, not even a dust bunny had the nerve to make that place its home. Well, except for this." Emily handed me an envelope.

I ripped it open. The message inside was terse.

If you want your belongings, you know where to find them.

"What does it say?" Emily asked.

"He isn't giving up." I handed her the note and dropped my head onto her lap while she read the letter.

"Now I understand why you insisted on going where he doesn't have reach. You're about to turn him into a stalker. Actually, he kind of already is. You know, he showed up at everyone's house looking for you? The entire office was abuzz about it. Are you sure he isn't dangerous?"

"Not to me, he isn't." I covered my eyes with my arm, but couldn't prevent tears from leaking out of the corner of my eyes. "I miss him so much, Emily. Every second of every day. All I think about is being in his arms."

She stroked my hair. "Madison, is sacrificing him worth keeping your promise?"

"I don't know. I hope so? I need it to be." I curled onto my side and stifled my sob.

For hours, Emily comforted me although I was inconsolable. My eyes swelled until I couldn't keep them open any longer. At some point, I fell asleep.

The next morning, I woke up drained and listless, counting the days until I put more distance between me, Kent, and all the memories I wasn't able to relive yet without gut-wrenching sorrow.

Thanks to Emily's friends, I landed in Santa Marta, Colombia within a week. I was still getting used to my new identity, but I expected it would take months. I found a modest home and set up a VPN. My first message was to my parents. The second and most nerve wracking was to Ife. I had little hope she would respond, but if she ever did, I wouldn't think twice before going to her.

My new home was colorful with comfortable furnishings. The climate here was always warm, but I rarely felt the heat. A chill took up residence inside me and nothing I did thawed the frost. My only comfort was the picture of Kent I kept on the pillow beside me at night. Without it, I slept fitfully and woke without feeling rested.

A month dragged by, but I had no desire to do anything but watch the sea on my balcony. I had plenty of funds to last me years and no ambition to find alternative employment. Maybe one day when I could get through the hours without crying myself to sleep.

The worst part was I only had myself to blame. I made the choice, now I had to live with the consequences. My only regret was Kent was somewhere also living with the repercussions of my decision.

One day, maybe he would forgive me, even if I didn't deserve his absolution.

ent

"Dad?" The worry in Ife's voice failed to move me today. As it had failed yesterday and the day before and every day for the past month.

She wasn't alone in her ineffectiveness. Nothing, unless it dealt with Madison's whereabouts, moved me.

Ife appeared at the threshold of my living room, concern dominating the features so much like her mother's.

Looking at her hurt. Not because she reminded me of losing my Lola. That would have been an easy reminder to live with. At this moment, seeing my daughter only reminded me why Madison chose to sneak away like a criminal on the run. I avoided her gaze, preferring the amber liquid in my hand. I gulped mouthfuls, welcoming the burn as it slid down my throat.

"How long are you going to be like this?"

I stared into the bottle I held in my hand. Last time it took two and a half bottles before Madison visited me in my dreams. However, I'd passed that one bottle ago and was still conscious. Why wouldn't drunken sleep overtake me and allow me the few moments of sweet torment that made waking up to another day bearable?

Why did I still want to wake to a new dawn when dreams of my sweet Madison were better than my reality? Because with every sunrise came the hope I'd hear news of Madison's location.

"When's the last time you walked Benson and Stabler?" Ife switched the topic since I refused to discuss the company.

I glanced toward where the boys had taken up vigil. Like me, they barely moved from their spot in front of the elevator.

"A dog walker takes them out," I said, dragging my eyes away from them.

Her mouth turned down in a frown. "Why is it they don't move from that spot whenever I visit?"

"They're waiting for their mother to come home. They seldom move from there, and when they do, it's for food or water. Then they return to their vigil." I guzzled from the bottle until only an inch or two remained.

Ife huffed, then snatched the liquor from my hands. "Dad, I could really use your help. I've been trying to keep the company afloat without you. Since you stopped showing up, the board voted me in as the interim CEO but I'm so out of my depth."

Although she changed the subject, I was no more interested in the topic. "Who cares? You can sell the business if it's too much to handle. You have my proxy. It was probably what put you in the CEO seat. Use it to liquidate or whatever you want to do."

"You don't mean that. Not after we fought so hard for you to maintain your control."

"Ife." I sighed, mentally and emotionally exhausted. "Be honest with me. Was Madison the price for my company?"

She stepped back. "W-w-why would you ask me that?"

I pulled the letter I kept over my heart. "Good question. Maybe because I've read and reread this letter countless times, but it makes little sense. Despite loving me, Madison still left." I turned and captured Ife's watery gaze. "You're the only person she would abandon everything she loved for. But then I think about the days I was in jail. You two almost seemed close again. So how did your rapport disappear as if I'd never seen it? As if you'd struck a deal." I met Ife's eyes.

Now she avoided my gaze. "I don't get it. When Mom died, you weren't like this. You buried yourself in work, making Luxe Locations a titan in the industry. If it worked once, it can work again to help you get over her."

"Ife, I don't want to get over her. And even if I did, I couldn't."

"Why? Are you saying you love her more than you loved Mom?"

"Ife, your mother died! It's not about who I love more. I had no hope of ever seeing Lola again, so yes, I used work as a crutch. I still love Lola, but she isn't here and I've found love again, one I never thought to experience again. With Madison, not only is she alive, but she's alone somewhere and she's suffering." I stretched my hands out, noting their emptiness. "So I'm suffering. Her pain, your pain, their pain"—I pointed toward the animals—" And my pain. With all that, why should I care about a company that cost me my heart?"

Ife kneeled before me, placed the liquor bottle on the ground, and held my hands. She kissed my knuckles one hand at a time.

I brushed Ife's hair over her ear. "Tell me something. Did you at least promise Madison you would support her, even from a distance?"

She sobbed. "D-do you hate me for separating you?"

"No, sweetheart. However, I am deeply disappointed."

My daughter wiped the tears from her face. With a last sniffle, she said, "I don't understand how you could think only of her at a time like this. Doesn't our relationship mean anything to you?"

"Ife, you're my daughter. My love for you will never change, and I'll never accept you cutting yourself out of my life. That's not the kind of man I am."

"And that applies to Madison, too?"

I firmed my lips. "I will find her. When I do, I'm spending my life with her as her husband. Until then, there's nothing important enough to move me from this spot."

"Okay, I give. I can't keep watching you waste away like this." Ife sat on her feet, her shoulders sloped downward. "Although I don't see a future where I'll ever approve of my father and best friend being together, I love you. And I once loved Madison. I'll stop punishing you and step aside. Despite my actions, I want you to be happy, and if Madison is the solution, so be it."

For a moment, my heart skipped with joy, until I remembered Madison was in hiding somewhere I couldn't find her.

"Thanks, Ife. It might take a while. She's done a great job of covering her tracks. I'm almost certain she left the country, although no airport has flagged her passport."

"Maybe this will help." She stood and retrieved her purse from the foyer. While she rifled through the contents, she said, "Madison promised she'd come running if I needed her. Here." Ife fiddled with her phone.

My cell dinged with an alert.

"If you email that address, she'll come to you."

My hands shook as I reached for my phone. I stared at the address, skeptical my happiness was an email away.

"Once you retrieve her, will you come back to the office? I wasn't lying when I said I was struggling."

I blinked my eyes free of the sheen covering them. "I can't promise anything, but I'll give you some advice. Mal is a good man. Rely on him to guide you as you learn the ropes. And Omar is very knowledgeable. Trust your instincts. I'm certain you'll succeed."

"I wish I were as confident as you."

I nodded absentmindedly, my mind still on Ife's email. "I have some planning to do." I stood and headed toward my bedroom, but hesitated as a thought sprang in my head. "Ife, I understand your stance, but I'll still give you the option to refuse. Whenever I return with Madison, she'll be coming as Madison Luxe. You're more than welcome to attend the wedd—"

She sadly shook her head. "I won't stand as witness to that, I'm sorry, Dad. I just...can't."

"I understand. And thank you." I left her to show herself out, while multiple schemes ran through my head.

My first call was to the Montgomerys.

CHAPTER 40

$\mathcal{M}$adison

I need you.

The message and an address came sooner than I expected. I thought it would take Ife a year at least before her feelings turned neutral. Another year before she reached out.

Without thinking twice, I booked the next flight to Saint Ginelle, an archipelagic island nation in the Pacific Ocean. There were no direct flights. The first leg of the first flight left two days later, and I made sure my butt was the first one on the plane.

After a full day in transit and passing the international dateline, I disembarked two days after leaving Colombia and walked toward the exit. A professional driver held a sign with my name written in large, bold letters.

I hefted my travel duffel over my shoulder. "I'm Madison Montgomery."

The man smiled. "What a relief. I showed up for the past three days to wait for you." He took my bag from my shoulder. "By the way, I'm Pierre. I'll be your driver while you're on the island."

"Three days? Don't you have other things you need to do?" I followed him because he had my bag. Boy, did I hope he was legit.

"Oh, not really. This is the best paid gig I've ever had. My employer makes sure I'm paid for every hour I'm working." Pierre opened the door of a Porsche Cayenne SUV and my doubts softened to a whisper.

Now Ife was generous, but this level seemed more excessive than usual. Plus, with the uncertainty surrounding our relationship, this level of luxury seemed out of place. We drove past Saint Ginelle's capital and into the mountains. Despite the island's small size, we drove for an hour over steep, well-maintained roads. During the ride, Pierre pointed out sights of interest and little history lessons he'd learned as a child.

I hummed my interest, but my unease grew. Despite Pierre's jovial manner, the more remote our surroundings became, the more life and volume the whispers I had before getting in the car gained.

Had I taken one look at this man's fancy vehicle and convinced myself he was safe? Now, like a fool, I'll never be seen or heard from again?

Please, Lord, don't make this be the end of me.

"We're here." Paul directed the car through a dense copse and my panic almost deafened me. Then we broke from the thicket and my breath left me.

A concrete mansion of one, two, three, no, four stories stood at the end of the drive. Lush palm trees of various species, hibiscus flower bushes, birds of paradise, and ginger flowers proliferated the front yard.

Pierre opened my door, startling me. I hadn't realized we'd stopped. I exited the car to walk up the two stairs to the wooden front door.

A woman opened the door as soon as I stood before the glass inlays. "You must be Ms. Montgomery. Call me Marion. We've been expecting you." She took my bag from Pierre and looked me over. "You must be real tired. Follow me and I'll show you to your room."

Was it my wrinkled clothes? I pulled my shirt down and brushed at the folds.

Or was it my face? I touched my cheeks and under my eyes, wondering what she'd seen for her to draw her conclusion. Even if I was exhausted, she didn't have to exaggerate how pronounced my condition was. I shrugged away my annoyance, understanding my sensitive reaction was a symptom of my weariness. "Where is Ife?" I asked, fighting a yawn out of sheer stubbornness. I refused to give more reason for Marion to remark on my current state.

"Ife? Oh, well, everyone went to town. They should be back shortly."

Marion led me to an enormous suite on the first floor. The room opened to a private porch with an infinity pool and patio furniture.

"If you need anything, there's an intercom by the door. I'll return with some refreshments. I'm sure the food on the plane was not the best."

Feeling icky after Marion's comment about my appearance, I jumped into the shower as soon as she left. As water pounded my muscles, I tried to revive myself with a second wind, but I'd used my second, third, and fourth winds while flying. I almost fell asleep with the washcloth in my hand and almost slipped on the wet tile.

It would be just like me to sprain or even break something in the shower because I was so tired my body wanted to shut down on me. I rushed through the rest of my shower and barely donned a sleep shirt before crashing on the bed. Of course, I didn't forget the sleep aid I'd depended on since leaving Douglas. My muscles locked into position with Kent's portrait pressed against my chest and everything else on strike. Not even the delectable scent of freshly baked bread roused me, despite my stomach growling its need.

After I fell asleep, a furnace warmed my spine, and a heavy weight covered my arms. My body relaxed into the comforting heat. My sleepy brain told my mouth to say, "Kent." But I'd gotten used to uttering his name at random in the state between waking and sleeping, so hearing his name on my lips didn't jar me to full awareness.

The bed bounced and more weight landed on my legs, heating

another part of my body. The action jolted me awake, however, my heavy, dry eyes refused to open and I was on my way to falling asleep again. Moments later, soft fur brushed against my skin, burrowing under the small space between my arms and the bed. When the bundle began to vibrate and emit a soothing purr, my eyes popped open and I almost jumped out of bed, all signs of my prior exhaustion dissipating after the sudden adrenaline injection.

My heart pounded in my ear as I stretched toward the night table and fumbled around for the lamp. I clicked the light on and gasped. The portrait of Kent I fell asleep with stared at me. Benson and Stabler raised their heads while their tails pounded against the mattress, taking my attention off the photo I should still have clutched to my chest. Tyger, who I'd displaced by rising, rose and pressed his forepaws on my chest so he could close the distance to my chin. He rubbed his face against mine, over and over, making up for the weeks he'd missed.

Even as joy filled me for being reunited with my animals, their presence meant one thing. I shifted my vision without moving another part of my body. From the corner of my eye, the very sexy torso that had dominated my sexier dreams lay in real life. An internal tug of war began. Joy pulled from one end while Sadness and Fear teamed up to destroy any progress Joy made.

I reached for the edge of the sheet to flip it over and make a hasty escape when a shiny glimmer halted me. On my fourth finger was the most obscene diamond ring I'd ever seen. I couldn't take my eyes off the glittering canary yellow color or the size that spanned past my knuckle.

"What the fuck..." I said without moving my lips.

"Good, you're awake." Kent sat upright and scooched until his spine met the headboard.

I spun on him and ignored his sexy, rumpled hair and sleepy eyes. "H-h-how are you he—Why is this on my f-f-finger?" I shoved my hand under his nose and wiggled my finger.

He took my hand and kissed the ring then my knuckles. "Ask me something else. Like why, even though I want to pick a fight with you for leaving us the way you did, I can't because I'm so damn happy to know you're safe? Or why a man you ruined would track you down so he could spend the rest of his life ensuring you kept ruining him?"

"What about, how did you find me?" I tried to get out of bed, but Benson and Stabler took turns jumping on me and keeping me hostage.

"They sat by the door every day waiting for you to come home. The same way I did. And it wasn't comfortable. I wish I'd had your picture at night to make my dreams less chaotic, but I had the letter you left. It smelled of you, and although I hated seeing it, the paper held the memory of your tears."

I stretched my neck to avoid the puppy kisses the dogs directed at my face. It was a ploy to ignore the most heartfelt of his confessions. I wasn't ready to hear about his suffering, because I would have to confront I'm the reason behind it.

"How is that possible? You're the CEO. You love Luxe Locations so much you fought hard to maintain your title." I avoided watching him. I had to. If not, he would see the chink in my armor and exploit my weakness.

Kent pulled Benson then Stabler off me and commanded them to stay. While they settled, Kent cocked his head to study me. "Funny how losing someone will put things into perspective. For me, being available if you chose to return home was more important than budgets, market strategies, or the next development."

"You can't say things like that when being with me is a liability." Courage failed me and I peered into my lap. "You say you're fine with neglecting your company now, but one day you'll resent me for it. I explained this to you in my letter."

"Little bunny, how do you think I got your email address?" Kent pinched my chin and forced my head up. "You only gave it to Ife."

"She... she gave you the address? But that would mean—"

"We had a productive talk. Ife still doesn't approve of us, but she wants me to be happy and knows you're the key to my happiness."

"Oh." The tiny flicker of hope Kent sparked with Ife's name fizzled out as quickly as it had sparked to life. "But then this ring. Isn't it premature to put it on my finger? If she won't accept us, then—"

"Little bunny, make no mistake. Our future is ours to determine. I gave her the opportunity to show up for us. Ife refused."

"Oh." I twisted the ring around my finger. Maybe it was time to accept my friendship with Ife was over and I would always have a hole in my life where she belonged.

"But your parents are here. Your mother even agreed to officiate our wedding."

I couldn't have heard him right. Too much was happening at once and my brain couldn't process the truth before me. "My mother agreed to marry us? My mother? Nikita Montgomery?"

"Well, a conditional agreement. She needs to hear you want to marry me as much as I want to be your husband." Kent glowered as if recalling an unpleasant memory. "She also threatened to end me if I try to coerce you."

I glanced at Tyger who hugged my shin with a death grip, then Benson and Stabler who hadn't stopped staring at me. If not for Kent's command, they would be all over me, inundating me with sloppy kisses. "You're brave to test my mother this way because if them being here isn't coercion, I don't know what is."

Kent snaked his arm around my waist and pulled me to his side, displacing Tyger who growled and repositioned himself to hold onto my leg. The stiffness in my spine melted upon contact. "Be honest, little bunny. Do you want me?"

"So much it hurts."

"Enough to be my wife?"

I peered into his blurry face. Kent was a man who demanded to share my burdens rather than watch me struggle alone. Even through his pain, he put my safety above the damage I'd inflicted on him. If he'd approached me with anger, bruised pride, and accusations, I might have had a defense against him. However, he discarded his righteous fury for openness and vulnerability.

I was done warring with my heart. Once I landed on my decision, I broke out into a teary grin.

"Little bunny?"

I cupped both sides of his face. "I have conditions."

"You wouldn't be Nikita's daughter if you didn't. But I'm telling you my non-negotiable right now. We aren't leaving this island until your name is Madison Luxe. Your parents only have a week to spend, and I will take advantage of every second of that time. So, let's hear your terms."

I narrowed my eyes at him. "You won't budge on this?"

"Nope," he said, exaggerating the p with a pop.

"So if my heart is set on a big wedding?"

"We can have it. As a second wedding. The biggest, most obscene ceremony and reception that will keep Douglas society pages full for months after. However—"

"I'll already be Mrs. Kent Luxe," I finished for him.

Kent pressed his lips against my forehead. "Glad you understand." His lips traveled over my cheek and lower, with no intention of stopping.

"Well, here's something I want that has to happen before we exchange any kind of vow." I pushed his face from my neck, knowing where this would lead. "I want a proper proposal."

"Doable." He tried to lower his head again, but I resisted him when he was so close his beard brushed against my chin.

"And an engagement party. One with good food and music."

"Done." Kent closed the distance between us and kissed me.

He started sweet, brushing his lips against mine, re-familiarizing himself with the contours of my mouth. In doing so, he reminded me what I'd been missing. I gasped as remembered sensations sparked to life in my body, and he took advantage of the opening. Kent plunged his tongue inside. Our passions swiftly rose to unimaginable heights, frying my brain from the inside.

My grip on his face transferred to his ear and I pulled him closer to me. No amount of skin on skin was close enough. Kent rolled over to kneel above my body without breaking our embrace. Our kisses deepened until I couldn't tell who was the giver and who the receiver was.

I dragged my legs up and crossed my ankles at his back. I was ready for him. More than. When I'd changed into my sleep shirt, I was too tired to bend down and put on panties. I was open, slick, and ready to properly reunite with Kent.

"Oomph." Kent fell forward, pressing his weight on me. "Dammit, Tyger, read the room."

Our cat peered over Kent's shoulder as if checking on me. The absurdity of the situation got the better of me and I giggled.

Kent glared at me, though there was no heat in his glower. "That's it. Reunion over. Mom and Dad need their time alone." He rose with an aggrieved breath.

Tyger, losing purchase, clung to him. When the cat was about to fall, he made a last-ditch effort to climb the rest of the way up to Kent's head then to leap on me.

"I don't think so," Kent said as he plucked the cat off my body. "You and your brothers sleep outside." He put all the animals out, then turned to me. "Now, where were we?"

"I need you to accept my apology for leaving you the way I did."

"Apology accepted."

"But I didn't explain that—"

"You did it for Ife? I know all that. And I know it must have hurt a lot to make the choice."

"But…"

"Tell me one thing. When you left, did you take my most cherished gift with you?"

I clutched my chest, recalling the words I'd spoken during his homecoming. "No, my heart is still in your safekeeping."

"As I thought." Kent sighed and shook his head. "Little bunny, do you think I don't understand how difficult it was for you to walk away, knowing you left a piece of yourself behind? Or that you loved my daughter enough to sacrifice a love unlike any other? Or that I wouldn't love you more for not wanting to be the source of friction between us? The apology you owe me is for deciding without me. You once said we needed to be partners. Where was our partnership when you didn't include my wishes?"

I nodded, humbled by his reasoning. "You're right, and I am sorry for excluding you. I promise I'll include you from now on."

"Now that that's out of the way—"

"I also want to pick out my wedding dress," I blurted.

The gleam in his eyes as he sauntered towards me was a sign I wouldn't have another opportunity to voice my wants before he over-whelmed me with passion.

Kent stumbled and a flush rose to his face. "Would you be willing to accept a dress your mother chose?"

My heart skipped. "That depends. Was it a dress she wore when she exchanged her vows?"

"She mentioned something along those lines. With updates to make it a little more modern, of course. If you don't like it, take up your issues with your mother."

I'd loved my mother's wedding dress from the time I could crawl. "I want to see it now." I flew out of the bed, but Kent wrapped his arm around my waist and swung me back toward the bed.

"You will wait until morning. Any other demands?" He kneeled before me and spread my legs open. He hissed at the sight of my wet, naked pussy peeking from between my thighs. "Little bunny…"

"Yeah, I have one more." I moaned with a devilish smile. "Put your mouth where—"

EPILOGUE

ent

Hope and new life whispered in the winds as they caressed my face. The sun's warm rays added to my excitement, a sentiment I'd built up over the last six months.

Once Madison agreed to the wedding and convinced her mother I hadn't coerced her into accepting my proposal, we honeymooned for four months with a random trip home. Ife continued to run Luxe Locations as the interim CEO while Madison and I strengthened our bond.

I planned to return in another month or so because Valentino's recently appointed Director of Boards and Commissions approved a new Luxe construction project. The company would have to demolish a dilapidated property we had on the books for a while, and I intended to oversee it while establishing a beneficial working relationship with the new director.

Apparently, the previous director went missing and hadn't been found. I didn't follow the case since all my focus was on finding Madison. Afterward, I was too busy rediscovering the world with Madison. I'd promised to build a life together and my first step in making good on my vow was to build memories unique to us. As much as I would have loved to continue, I married an ambitious woman who thrived on challenges.

Now that we'd returned to Douglas, she insisted on starting a new business. Of course, I offered her space in my office where she could work. She declined, ruining my hope of using the frosted glass feature during our private lunches.

"I can't believe today is finally here." Madison suppressed a girlish squeal. I couldn't help but find her reaction amusing, although I too had anticipated this day for months.

"Are you ready to go inside?" Thrilled, I stared at the landscape while Madison vibrated with energy beside me.

When tasked with designing the home of our dreams, I'd told Madison money was not an option. If she wanted a mansion that rivaled Buckingham Palace, she only had to dream it for me to fulfill it. Instead, she chose a more modest two-story home.

"Am I ever! No more penthouse. We have a yard for Benson and Stabler. And—"

"We'll be as on top of each other as we were at the penthouse. This place is only marginally larger."

"I thought you were happy with the size of the house." She pouted.

Little did she know how many sexy fantasies she inspired when she set her mouth like that. She only encouraged me to find creative ways to get a smile back on her face.

"Your reasons convinced me this is the perfect fit for us."

And it was. This was the home for a family. I peeked at Madison. I was more than twice her age, but she wouldn't have to convince me if she ever shared a desire to have children.

"Damn right. Although those big houses make beautiful pictures in Architectural Digest, I don't want to go on a treasure hunt to find my husband. This is much more preferable." She sighed as she took in the house again.

"Then let's see if the decorators got everything right." I led her inside.

As we went room by room, I barely registered the furnishings, the artwork, or anything really. My eyes were glued to Madison's joyful smile and giggles as she toured our new home.

As her husband, I prided myself on giving her the life of her dreams. I'd only failed in one aspect, but there were some positive signs on that front. Madison and Ife agreed to put their histories in the past and try afresh to learn about each other and possibly become friends again if not besties. They were in the bumpy early stages, and though I wanted to intervene, this wasn't an area I could magically repair. Especially considering my relationship with Ife was still in a restoration phase.

At least my daughter no longer rejected my and Madison's joint invitations.

"Mom will love this kitchen. I can't wait for her to visit." Madison trailed her fingers across the granite countertop as she circled the room.

"Give us some time before you invite anyone."

She stopped to frown at me. "What about our housewarming party?"

I stepped in front of her, caging her between my body and the counter. "Before we host a party, we need to christen every room. Make sure they're up to par." I grabbed her hips and hoisted her onto the counter.

She locked her legs behind my back and pulled me into her body. "I guess we need to start here." She lowered her dress strap over her shoulder.

"Little bunny, did you wear this to toy with me?" I distractedly fingered her exposed shoulder.

Smooth brown and pink skin gleamed at me, tempting me to taste.

"If I did, I must have miscalculated. I mean, you had the entire car ride here and you didn't feel me up once." She peeked up at me through her lashes, another sexy pout on her lips. "If you had, you would have discovered the surprise I had waiting for you."

I lowered my face until our foreheads met. "Are you telling me you were like this when we collected the keys from the builders?"

"Yup."

"When the wind blew so hard you fought to keep your skirt in place?"

"I had to protect my modesty. After all"—Madison flicked her tongue on my lips—"We agreed my pussy is for your eyes only."

"I hope you're not attached to this dress."

"I a—"

Riiip.

"Kent!"

"You spoke too late." I shrugged and threw the outfit over my shoulder.

"What will I wear back to the penthouse?" Despite her protest, she laid down on the counter and disentangled her legs from my waist to rest her feet at the edge of the raised surface.

Her nipples puckered in the cool air, a desperate cry for attention.

I plucked the swollen nubs. "Funny you think you're leaving here before we fuck our way through every room."

"You can't expect me to walk around naked for days." She arched her spine, shoving her breast against my hand.

"You had no problem doing just that on our honeymoon." I slid my hand down her soft belly. Unable to resist the temptation any longer, I buried my face in her waist to kiss, lick, and suck on her supple flesh.

Madison combed her fingers through my hair and gripped the strands until I felt a delicious sting on my scalp.

I nipped beside her belly button in retaliation.

"Lower, Kent." She pushed, guiding me to the treasure between her thighs.

"Don't rush me, little bunny. We have hours before the first moving van arrives."

"Moving van?" Madison sat upright and dragged my head away from my feast. "What moving van?"

"The one with all our clothes and keepsakes. And of course, the kids won't be far behind. They'll need to explore their new home. I'm sure Tyger will lay claim anywhere you are." I pulled her hands away and journeyed below again.

Madison shoved me away after I caught a whiff of her desire. "How do you expect me to greet them when you've destroyed my dress?"

At my limit, I grabbed behind her knees and pulled until she fell back on the counter. "I came prepared. There are at least three changes of clothes in the car trunk because you always like to pull a stunt on me with your clothes. The dress lasted as long as it did because it was more modest than your usual teases." I rubbed her clit in slow circles while watching her desire rise. "Now will you let me get to work?"

Before she protested, I pressed the back of her thighs until her knees were even with her shoulders and I dove in.

Madison writhed against my tongue. For hours, I kept her at my mercy. By the time the movers called to warn me of their impending arrival, we hadn't moved from the kitchen. I rushed to retrieve Madison's change of clothes as she was limp and unable to move after her sixth orgasm.

While we oversaw the unpacking, Madison leaned toward my ear. "I forgot to mention, we'll have to contact the decorator again for the room next to ours."

"Why's that?"

"Because it doesn't have a crib."

SNEAK PEEK

Thank you so much for reading Ruin Me. Don't forget to sign up for my newsletter to get a bonus scene.

Please consider leaving a review to let me know how you enjoyed Kent and Madison's story. Continue reading to discover your Mal and Ife's chemistry in an unedited excerpt from my next Savage Boss novel Spoil Me.

Spoil Me

Chapter 1

I was about to do something stupid. I knew it. A random stranger on the street would know it, too. Damn near everyone would advise me not to follow my impulses, but I would argue being in my car and driving to the blinking dot on my GPS wasn't following a whim.

I'd thought about what I should do. Agonized about my options. So, of course what I was about to do wasn't hastily decided.

Still stupid.

I hated intrusive thoughts. At least the ones that weren't helpful and only argued with me once I made a decision. Especially after they planted the idea in my head.

All I did was mention Ekele often disappeared around this time of year like it was a special anniversary or something.

"Please, shut up." I closed my eyes to shut out the doubts that came rising to the surface with the reminder.

Ekele was my man and had been for almost four years. We loved each other, and I trusted him.

So why are we tracking his phone?

I turned on the radio to stream music from my phone and increased the volume to drown out my thoughts. Marvin Gaye's smooth voice belted out the lyrics from *I Heard It Through The Grapevine*.

I blindly switched to a new playlist before he finished mentioning his lover's plans to make him blue while silently cursing myself out for leaving my phone on my classic Motown playlist. *Heartbreak Hotel* came on next, inspiring the same action.

Then Glorilla's *TGIF* song came on. I would usually bump to the popular tune, but there were too many similarities to my current situation. My clock read 7 PM. Tonight was Friday night. I hoped the parallels ended there. However, she questioned how was Ekele my man when he was there with her. Hell no! Bumping over. Glorilla was now on my do *not* play list.

Girl, you trippin' cause what song are you listening to? She never said nothing about no Ekele. Mm-mm you're projecting so hard you could be a drive-thru movie theater.

"I didn't ask you." I banged my steering wheel.

A slew of cheating songs, one after the other, followed no matter how many times I skipped or noped out of the playlist or station. My final straw was Cardi B's Be Careful. Avoidance was the only thing keeping me driving without swerving all over the place.

However, no matter how hard I tried to ignore the radio waves, another truth damn near shouted at me. My streaming service had it out for me.

Dammit! I didn't need an outside influence to feed the paranoia inside my head when I was on my way to Ekele's destination.

That trust thing is really working out for you, huh?

"Bitch, if you don't leave me the fuck alone—I trust Ekele."

And why wouldn't I? An untrustworthy man wouldn't give me the kind of free rein he did with his devices. He permitted me to answer and scroll through his phone without hesitation. Even going so far as to share his location with me. I never took him up on his offer.

Until tonight.

"I needed his location tonight because he left something important at the house. Now shut up and let me think."

Yeah, you're going to need to think up a good excuse for showing up wherever he is with that bracelet he said he'd never take off and yet he did.

"I truly detest you."

Redirect that energy where it needs to be.

I gritted my teeth, determined to ignore...myself? Did other people argue with themselves this way? My best friend, Madison didn't, but she was normal. What would she say if I hadn't hidden so much about the inner workings of my relationship with Ekele? Considering she never dated anyone seriously or long enough to make future plans, she probably thought Ekele and I were an anomaly.

We planned a future together. He'd met my mother's side of the family in Nigeria, and I'd met his family while we were there. Any day now, he would propose and I would introduce him to my father. Although Dad knew about Ekele, I would never present a man who hadn't proven he was serious about me to *the* Kent Luxe.

My father was too protective of me to watch my relationships fall apart and not teach my exes a lesson. Kent was the perfect example of what a man was supposed to be, and his marriage with my mother exceeded couple's goals. Unfortunately my dad broke the mold. Thankfully, Ekele came close and was the only man who checked most of my boxes.

I switched the radio on again, this time playing my favorite podcast to ease my mind. The hosts rarely talked about relationships, and tonight I was in luck. Now if this good fortune would follow me to my destination and after I talked to Ekele, all would be right in my world.

Thirty minutes later, I rolled up to a residential address in Silver Spring where the dot I tracked hadn't moved. I parked in front of a two-story neo-classical house sitting on a quarter acre of land. The front lawn was well-maintained with floral bushes past their flowering season. Ivy crept up a side column of the home but hadn't yet reached the second floor.

My heart sank and my stomach churned when I saw the familiar LUV2BME license plate on Ekele's Mercedes AMG GT 53 coupe. I'd bought him that car for his birthday earlier this year.

Wait, I was getting ahead of myself. Yes, Ekele said he had to leave for a business trip. He worked for a large political action group with international ties and frequently travelled. Maybe he had time before his flight left and had an errand to run. Me and my intrusive thoughts—

Don't bring me into this. This is all you.

The fact was, there were any number of legitimate reasons for Ekele to be at a suburban single-family home at 7:45 in the evening that had nothing to do with him seeing someone behind my back. This place was made for a family. I doubted bachelors lived here, so whoever was here had a family.

Are we standing out here all night or are you going to drop off the all-important bracelet and bounce?

If I had a body to glare at, I would do so now. Instead, I breathed in and out until my stomach settled before ringing the doorbell.

The door opened to the laughing face of a gorgeous Black woman around my age.

"Hello?" She looked me up and down, the joyous light in her eyes dimming as the seconds passed.

"Babe, I'm going to bathe and put Junior to bed, then I'll come back for you." The voice coming from behind her shattered everything inside me. Not because it belonged to my Ekele, but because I'd never been on the receiving end of that level of unfiltered desire.

"Ekele?"

"Yes, that's him. Is there something I can do for you?" The woman blocked the door.

I tried to swallow the painful lump in my throat. I got it down on my fourth attempt. "I'm sorry." I shook my head. "Would it be possible to ask Ekele to come to the door? There's something important I need to say to him." The words came out as clear as my surprisingly dry eyes.

"Who should I say is asking for him?" Only curiosity stared at me while I stood on this woman's front porch.

"Tell him it's Ife."

She backed into her house. "Would you like to come in and wait?"

"Thank you." I followed her inside.

She led me to a family room filled with pictures. The last string of veins holding the broken fragments of my heart together split, allowing the pieces to scatter and disappear.

Photographs of the woman spanned years. Images of her and Ekele holding her baby bump, celebrating 'Junior's' first and second birthdays, and the two of them kissing. Cards commemorating their love in shadowboxes decorated the walls. Greeting cards saying Happy Father's Day and Happy Birthday Dad stabbed me but nothing as deeply as the photos of the three of them dressed in matching outfits as Ekele held the smiling child whose face was identical to the photos his family shared with me on our trip to Nigeria.

Everywhere I looked, proof of their relationship mocked me.

I took the bracelet Ekele told me meant the world to him from my pocket and placed it on the fireplace mantle in front of a family photo and walked out without waiting for Ekele. In my car, I drove aimlessly, surrounded by silence.

Funny how the cure for intrusive thoughts was getting one's heart broken. Nothing penetrated the fog I was in while I steered my car on auto-pilot. The opening of my Georgetown townhouse's garage door brought me out of my self-absorption and to finally hear my phone's ringtone.

My hand shook as I reached for the device.

"Are you fucking stalking me?" Ekele's voice sounded like a bomb detonating in my car. "How dare you show up unannounced after I told you I would be out of town?"

All the questions I had amassed blocked my airways, one on top of the other, worse and heavier than a 70 car-pile-up.

Ekele waited all of one second before he laid into me. "You rushed your ass over here to talk, but now you got nothing to say? You upset Danielle for no fucking reason. And what was the point of leaving that bracelet behind? You wanted to stir up drama? Damn, you must think because of your daddy and his money I have to be at your beck and call. That's not how things work, Ife. Now, forget this address. And don't expect me to return next week. I have to see about Danielle and little Eke." He disconnected the phone without waiting to hear anything from me.

At this moment, I wished rage would wash over me like it did for Bernadine Harris. However, I lacked the energy to run through my house searching for everything Ekele owned. That and he still had the car. There would be no setting his things on fire.

A chill started inside me as I stared at my home. My safe haven until tonight. With a deep breath, I backed out of my driveway, unable to confront the emptiness inside my home and my body at once. Instead, I drove to the Capitol Hill Luxe Continental.

As soon as I entered, the staff greeted me. Here, like at every Luxe Continental location, I was treated better than royalty—not an exaggeration. My favorite royal couple, Emir Javed ibn Al-Kamran and his rockstar wife Khadijah from the band Liquid Obsession stayed here while the prince was visiting the White House. The staff redecorated their suites to look like home. They researched the couple to find their favorite foods, scents, and entertainment, going so far as to import everything in readiness for their arrival.

As the owner's daughter, the hotel hospitality doubled their efforts despite me never making a request. I put them out enough by dropping by without a reservation like I did tonight. Despite the flurry of activity happening behind the scenes, I saw none of it.

Once I entered the suite always available for me and my father whenever he visited, I spied the butler and told him I didn't want to be disturbed for at least twenty-four hours. Finally alone, I poured a glass of red wine and stared out at the D.C. night sky.

I was numb, I realized. The chill hadn't melted. The pain I expected after the initial discovery of Ekele's unfaithfulness had yet to visit me in full melodramatic fashion. It would come, but as I checked for signs of its impending arrival, I felt nothing.

Girl... I'm here for you. You can curse, scream, and cry about that no-good piece of shit two-timing never good enough posing ass wannabe. You can do whatever, except this silent shit. It ain't healthy.

I allowed my thoughts to be without opposition. Not pushing back put my intrusive thoughts into overdrive, but I'd learned my lesson. One thought sent me on the road to pop the happiness bubble I'd lived in all these years, oblivious to reality. I was no longer giving her the time of day to worsen my despair.

I was here for an escape and escape I would. There were no knickknacks, souvenirs, clothes, pictures, or the smallest thing to remind me of Ekele, and I needed that more than I needed to vent and despair. Tomorrow... who the fuck knew what I would do tomorrow?

Ife got dealt a painful hand. No wonder she wasn't having anything to do with Madison's betrayal. Thank goodness there's a man waiting in the wings to help her heal. Preorder your copy of Ife and Mal's story now.

https://www.amazon.com/dp/B0DLK6JGQ3

OTHER TITLES BY MELVERNA MCFARLANE

Jessie & Giorgio: Inescapable (Oliveri Mafia Book One)

René & Nico: Inevitable (Oliveri Mafia Book Two)

Onika & Lorenzo: Indomitable (Oliveri Mafia Book Three)

Fayth & Keoni: A Test of Fayth: A Single Dad Romance
(Heart of a Wounded Hero)

Celia & Everett: Everett: A Sweet and Steamy Café L'amour Duet

Yomaris & Lochlann: Caught Red Handed

Sloane, Valentino & Tácito: Valentino DeLuca: Savage Bloodline

Zakiya & Sansone: Sansone DeLuca: Savage Bloodline

Kenya & Cameron: Snaring Her Man

Zaïre & Lucien: Ruthless Protector

Aniyah & Aris: Stolen Bride

Portia & Katsuo: Maid for the Yakuza

Kori & Masanori: Catering to the Yakuza

Ife & Mal: Spoil Me: Savage Bosses

Cantrelle & An Bao: Ruthless Enforcer
(newsletter exclusive prequel to Ruthless Protector)

ABOUT THE AUTHOR

Melverna McFarlane loves love stories with Happily Ever Afters. After years of characters taunting her imagination with their potential, she decided it was time to write her own scorching hot romances. She moved to America from Jamaica at a young age, and has lived up and down the east coast most of her life. The bitterly cold winter of 2013 was the last straw, driving her back to island life—this time to Hawaii. When not writing, she is reading romance, YA, and Fantasy, country hopping, or vicariously obsessing over other people's cats, because she can't have one.

You can find Melverna on Twitter, Instagram, Facebook, Patreon, and on her website www.MelvernaMcFarlane.com. Drop her a line, or tease her with pics and stories of your cat's antics. She might feature them in her next book.